Paige Toon

ALL ABOUT THE HYPE

SIMON & SCHUSTER

First published in Great Britain in 2016 by Simon & Schuster UK Ltd
A CBS COMPANY

1 3 5 7 9 10 8 6 4 2

Simon & Schuster UK Ltd
1st Floor, 222 Gray's Inn Road
London WC1X 8HB

www.simonandschuster.co.uk

Simon & Schuster Australia, Sydney
Simon & Schuster India, New Delhi

A CIP catalogue record for this book
is available from the British Library.

PB ISBN 978-1-4711-4610-7
eBook ISBN 978-1-4711-4611-4

Typeset in Goudy by M Rules
Printed and bound by CPI Group (UK) Ltd, Croydon, CR0 4YY

For Pernille Meldgaard Pedersen
I thought it was about time your name made it into
one of my books... Hope it makes you smile x

Chapter 1

I lie on the sofa in front of the television with my head on her lap. Her fingers are cool as they brush across my temple and trail down the length of my light-blonde hair, getting caught up in a knot. She abandons her soothing stroking and fixates on unpicking the knot instead.

'Ow, that hurts!' I complain.

'Your hair is not getting the better of me, Jessie Pickerill,' she warns, and I know that she won't be defeated until I'm tangle free.

So I endure the pain because I love her and I know that she loves me.

That's right, I remember. Her hands were always cold.

I squeeze my eyes shut and sob quietly, muffling the sound with my pillow.

Today is my sixteenth birthday and I woke up with the sickest feeling in the pit of my stomach. For the last hour, I've been racking my brain for the tiniest details, the seemingly unimportant ones, the ones that I'm most likely to forget.

1

But I *don't want* to forget her burning our dinner because she was distracted playing air guitar to Starship on the radio. I can't bear to lose the memory of her jumping on my bed and throwing shapes to my music while I resignedly got ready for school. I'm even clinging to the vision of her discarding another outfit on her bedroom floor and mischievously turning her attention to my wardrobe.

She always woke me up gently, quietly calling my name and stroking my arm.

Unless it was my birthday and then she'd bound into my room, shouting 'WAKEY-WAKEY!' like a lunatic.

She clambers onto my bed and straddles me, squeezing the air out of my lungs and making me groan.

'Happy birthday!' She shakes me. 'I got you PRESENTS!' she exclaims, and I stare at her blearily as she beams down at me, her light-brown eyes shining with excitement. 'I got you this.' She places one wrapped package on my chest. 'And this.' Another. 'And this, and this, and this!' She piles them up all over my face. I laugh and try to sit up, but she's still on top of me.

'Get off!' I grumble good-naturedly, shoving at her knees. She giggles and complies, then thrusts a present in my face.

'I swear you get more enjoyment out of my birthdays than I do,' I say wryly, taking it from her.

'Open it!' she urges.

That was a year ago. A year ago to the day. And, hours later, my mum was taken from me, never to be returned. My chest shakes violently as I sob.

I have no idea how much time passes, but a sense of

responsibility begins to mingle with my grief at the realisation that my little brothers will be up soon. The thought of them seeing me like this is enough to stem the flow of my tears. I push the damp pillow away from my face and reach for my phone. The digital display reads 06:30, so, if they're not awake now, they will be soon. I need to pull myself together.

My body feels like lead as I drag myself from bed and stumble through to the bathroom. I flick on the light switch, flinching at the brightness and then recoiling at the state of my reflection in the mirror. I turn on the tap and reach for a flannel, hoping to cool down my splotchy, puffy face.

I can hardly believe how much my life has changed in the last twelve months. I thought my mum had taken the secret of my biological father's identity with her to her grave and, after my initial shock and grief had passed, I became angry. I hit out at the only parental figure left in my life: my stepdad, Stu.

But last summer he came clean. He'd known the truth all along, that my real dad is Johnny Jefferson, the legendary, infamous rock star. Suddenly I had a new dad and a stepmum, Meg, and the cutest little half-brothers you could ever imagine in Barney and Phoenix. They're British like me, but they live here in Los Angeles and last summer I came to stay with them, to meet them for the first time. Since then I've been back and forth between America and the UK, but now I'm here to stay.

At least I think I am. I start a new school on Tuesday, and for a few moments nerves battle it out with despair to take control of my stomach.

I sigh as I press the cold flannel to my face. It's probably just as well Jack and Agnes are away. They've been in Washington State for the last couple of days, visiting their grandparents, and

3

initially I was disappointed that they weren't going to be around for my birthday, but the last thing I feel like doing right now is celebrating.

Agnes is a friend I made last summer, and her older brother Jack is... Well, I don't know what he is, actually. Is he my boyfriend? Are we official? Agnes is the only one of my friends here who knows about us, and the reason for this is complicated.

Butterflies swarm into my stomach at the thought of Jack's blue-grey eyes staring down at me, moments before the last time we kissed. It was in the very early hours of January 1st, a few days ago, and the memory of his lips against mine is spine-tinglingly fresh.

I fell pretty hard for him when we met last summer, but things went sour. So, when I returned to start the new school year in England, I tried to forget about him.

But I failed. Even when I started going out with Tom, the universally acknowledged hottest boy in school, I failed.

Anyway, within the space of about two months, certain uncontrollable events at home tore me away from my lovely new boyfriend and brought me back to LA.

Jack plays the lead guitar in an indie rock band called All Hype, and I soon discovered that Eve – the lead singer and Jack's ex – had quit. When Jack overheard me singing with my dad, I found myself being drafted in as Eve's replacement. I had my first gig three weeks ago in San Francisco – a *horrendously* nerve-wracking, but ultimately incredible experience – and afterwards I kind of lost my head. Jack and I have always had chemistry. I'd been fighting it, but the chemistry won out and I ended up kissing him and, in doing so, cheating on Tom, my gorgeous, kind, devoted boyfriend. When I went home for

4

Christmas, I confessed to Tom what I'd done, but it was the end of our relationship.

I hurt him so much and I still feel sick to my stomach about it. I emailed him the day before yesterday, asking for his forgiveness, but he hasn't replied. I said that I hoped we could still be friends, though I think I'm kidding myself. You don't let someone down that badly and get away with it.

I sigh and dry off my face, returning to the comfort of my warm, snuggly bed, but, as soon as I rest my cheek on my tear-sodden pillow, I'm reminded of what today is: the anniversary of my mother's death. And it will be for every single birthday for the rest of my life.

My throat swells up and tears prick at my eyes, but, before my sorrow takes hold again, I'm diverted by a commotion outside my door.

'Shh!' I hear someone warn. Meg? Johnny?

'I want to go inside!' That was Barney. No doubt about it.

'No!' Meg replies in a loud whisper. 'Let's give her until at least seven o'clock.'

'But I'm going to drop her presents!' he whines at top volume, completely neglecting to keep his voice down.

'Oh, buddy,' I hear Johnny chide gruffly and my automatic reaction is to smile.

'I'm awake!' I call, propping myself up.

The door bursts open and in they spill: the four people I can now call my family, all still dressed head-to-toe in their pyjamas.

Barney, aged four and a half, comes first, tearing into the room and clambering onto my bed, his arms full of brightly-coloured packages and his grin threatening to explode his face.

Then comes Meg with a babbling one-and-a-half-year-old

Phoenix attached to her hip. 'DEZZIE!' he calls, mispronouncing my name and flashing me a mostly toothless smile.

And finally in follows Johnny in a white T-shirt and crumpled grey PJ bottoms, still looking half asleep.

Meg once told me that Johnny rarely used to roll out of bed before midday, but having children has changed all that. She used to work as his personal assistant, but they fell in love and the rest is history.

'Happy birthday!' Barney yells, piling presents up on my chest and scrambling back across the bed to retrieve a few more from his parents. They hand them over with amusement and he returns to place some more on top of me. My heart pinches as I think of Mum doing the same thing last year, but I try not to let my pain show.

'Hey,' Johnny says in a deep voice still thick with sleep, as he wanders over to sit on the bed beside me. He reaches across with one tanned, tattooed arm to ruffle my hair. It's several shades lighter than his and quite a bit longer – his comes to his chin and always looks just-slept-in – but our green eyes are practically identical. His are fixed on me now and they're full of concern. He hasn't missed the fact that I've been crying. He squeezes my shoulder consolingly, but stays silent. I'm glad. Sympathy will only make it worse.

'Hey, you,' Meg says gently, regarding me with her warm brown eyes. She and Phee look so alike, but Barney is the spitting image of Johnny – and me.

Meg doesn't wish me a happy birthday because she knows that it's not a totally happy thing, and she also knows better than to mention my appearance.

Barney has no such qualms. 'Why does your face look funny?'

Before Meg or Johnny can speak, Phoenix distracts everyone by squawking and wriggling to get down from his mother's arms. Meg puts him on the bed and he crawls up the length of my body, pushing presents out of the way until he's pressing his little face to my neck. My arms wrap round his solid, onesie-encased body and suddenly I'm fighting off another very strong urge to cry.

'Phoenix, move!' Barney yells. 'Jessie wants to open her presents!'

I can't help giggling at the rude interruption. Phee sits up perkily and reaches for a rectangular-shaped package in lime-green wrapping paper with a yellow ribbon.

'Yes, you can open it,' I say, passing Barney a bright pink box tied with a purple ribbon. 'Come on, you guys can help me.' We all get stuck in.

Ten minutes later, my eyes are popping out of my head.

I have a new laptop ('for school'), a new iPad ('for fun'), a pampering voucher for two at a posh spa, a black Burberry lambskin biker jacket that I swear I've seen modelled by Cara Delevingne, plus other items like photo frames and fairy lights to cheer up my room.

Now I'm left with one last present.

Barney has unwrapped it to reveal a small velvet box, but Johnny swipes it at this point and hands it to me.

I lift up the lid to see a delicate-looking silver charm bracelet resting inside.

'Whoa.' I take it out of the box. 'It's beautiful!'

There are a few charms attached and I pause at the sight of a tiny, diamanté-studded guitar.

'They're real diamonds,' Meg whispers with a smile.

I gasp. 'I'll be *so* careful not to lose it,' I vow seriously.

'We thought you could collect charms that mean something to you,' Johnny says, as I turn the bracelet around in my fingers and spy the number sixteen dangling there. A lump springs up in my throat.

'But that's not the last present,' he adds quickly, taking the bracelet from me and placing it back in the box.

'Disneyland!' Barney interrupts with a gleeful shout.

'BARNEY!' Meg and Johnny bellow at him simultaneously.

He freezes and then stares at them contritely.

'That was supposed to be a surprise!' Meg scolds.

'Disneyland?' I manage to ask, as Johnny tickles Barney's ribs and makes him squeal with hysteria.

'Where are we going?' Johnny asks his tiny son as he falls back on the bed, narrowly missing my head.

'Disneyland!' Barney barks between giggles. Phoenix waddles over to join the fun and Johnny grabs him and tickles him, too.

'VIP access,' Meg says to me knowingly, amid the mayhem.

'What, today?' I ask weakly.

'Yeah! Today!' Barney shouts, scrambling to his feet and proceeding to bounce on my bed.

Oh.

That's the last thing I feel like doing.

I don't mean to seem ungrateful. I'd love to go to Disneyland sometime, but I'd planned on staying here and having a quiet one today. I can't imagine having fun.

Johnny is completely oblivious to my internal dilemma. 'Who are we seeing today?' he asks Barney.

'Mickey Mouse!' Barney obligingly replies at high volume.

I glance up at my half-brother's beaming face and know that my plans to wallow are shot. How can I possibly disappoint him?

'What time are we leaving?' I ask.

'NOW!' Barney yells.

'No, not now,' Meg says brusquely, making a grab for him. 'We've got to eat breakfast first, and get ready.'

'And we still have to give Jessie her last present,' Johnny interjects.

'What, my last present isn't Disneyland?' I ask with confusion.

'Nope,' he replies, throwing me a key.

A car key.

A *Fiat* car key?!

I have a sudden vision of the crummy old white Fiat that Stu used to have, but I don't care! It's a car! A *car*! I'm sixteen and in America that means I can get my driving licence!

I leap out of bed and all five of us race down the stairs in our PJs to the front door. I wrench it open and my jaw drops.

'It's a Fiat 500 Abarth,' Johnny says proudly.

The model means nothing to me. All I know is that what sits before me is one of the coolest little cars I have ever seen: matt-black with red wing mirrors and a red racing stripe down the side – *nothing*, absolutely nothing, like Stu's former old banger.

'I thought it looked kind of cheeky. Like you,' my dad adds with a shrug.

I squeal, running out of the house, unlocking the car doors with a button on the key as I go. Meg laughs and Johnny chuckles as he follows me, both of us hopping gingerly over the sharp gravel beneath our bare feet. I almost go to the right-hand side of the car, but remember that the driver's seat is on the left in America. I climb in and Johnny gets in the passenger seat beside me.

'Like it?' he asks, grinning across at me.

'Are you kidding me?' I gape at him. 'How soon can I drive it?'

'Aah, well,' he replies ominously. 'I'm afraid you have to jump through a few hoops first. You need a learner's permit before you can drive on the road, under adult supervision until you do your actual test, of course. But to get your learner's permit you have to do a Driver's Education course – six hours of driving lessons with a qualified instructor and a written test. Annie's told me how it all works over here.' Annie is his PA.

'No problem,' I reply with a grin, glancing to my right to see Meg taking the boys back inside. Johnny spies them, too.

'Breakfast,' he notes. 'Eddie has made you a crazy big stack of pancakes.'

'Aw,' I say. I adore their cook. He doesn't work on weekends so he must've prepared them yesterday.

'You OK?' Johnny asks quietly, all amusement vanished from his expression.

I nod quickly, tears automatically springing to my eyes. 'It's probably best if I don't talk about it,' I say in a small voice. I don't want to lose it again.

'OK.' He jerks his head towards the house and reaches for the door handle. 'Come on. Food first and then we'd better go and see frickin' Mickey, before Barney spontaneously combusts.'

Chapter 2

To my surprise, I had an appetite once I sat down at the table, and now we're on our way to Disneyland in Johnny's black Mercedes limousine. The Jeffersons' long-term driver, Davey, is chauffeuring us. When I got in the car, I found a present from him between the children's car seats: a gift bag full of bath goodies. I was so touched at his thoughtfulness.

Johnny may be an A-lister, but he doesn't have loads of staff. Meg once explained that he likes his team to feel like family, so I'm on first-name terms with everyone from Sharon and Carly the maids to Santiago the gardener/pool guy and Lewis, Samuel, Wyatt and Austin, the bodyguards. Samuel and Lewis are currently following behind us in another car and I know them best of all, especially Sam, because he looked after me in the UK, when the press found out who I was.

We tried to keep my identity under wraps at first so I wouldn't be hounded, but my secret didn't stay hidden for long. Now everyone knows that I'm Johnny's daughter and I'm kind of

11

glad it's out in the open, even though it means that my life has changed dramatically. I'm not sure I'll ever get used to having a bodyguard following me around.

The closer we get to Disneyland, the more excited Barney becomes. I'm still being assaulted by memories of Mum, and I feel like I could burst into tears at any given moment, but one look at Barney and Phee has me smiling again.

I can't imagine being happy today, though. Not properly. Perhaps it won't be as awful as I was expecting, and that's a good thing. Mum wouldn't want me to be inconsolable.

And then I see her twisting her long, dark, wavy hair into a messy bun and securing it with the biro I was using to do my English homework.

'Oi! Give that back!' I shout, as she laughs and runs from the room.

I quickly train my sight on my little brothers.

I'm a bit hurt that Stu hasn't called me yet, but I know he'll be finding today difficult, too. Perhaps he's just taking a while to get his act together so he doesn't cry down the phone. I'm sure we'll talk later.

As soon as we walk through the gates to Disneyland, the air is filled with the sweet scent of popcorn and candyfloss. Barney's enthusiasm is pretty infectious because my excitement is growing by the minute. He can barely contain himself as our effervescent VIP Disney guide, dressed in blue-and-red tartan, leads us down Main Street between the pastel-coloured shops and eateries. Sam and Lewis flank us, and people stop to gawp at Johnny as we pass. Wherever he goes, heads turn, women scream and people want his autograph, but I hope he doesn't get constantly harassed today.

We soon come to a stop in front of a bronze statue of Walt and Mickey. Behind them is Sleeping Beauty's castle, its towers spearing the sunny sky in all its pink, blue and gleaming gold splendour.

'Where first?' I ask Johnny, smiling at three little girls dressed in princess costumes, passing by with their parents.

'It's up to you,' he replies with a shrug.

'Peter Pan!' Barney shouts, jumping up and down on the spot.

'Are you sure about that?' I ask my dad with amusement. I think we all know who the boss is here. 'Can we go straight to Peter Pan, please?' I ask our guide with a smile.

'Sure.' She doesn't move, though, her smile frozen on her face as she looks from Mickey and Walt to Johnny and Meg and back again.

I wonder what she's waiting for. Are we supposed to show the statue more respect or something?

And then Johnny's and Meg's faces light up at the sight of something behind me. I turn round to see a cart being drawn by a real horse, and then, from behind it, Libby, Natalie, Lou and Em emerge! I almost die on the spot as my British friends run, laughing, towards me. And the boys follow: Dougie, Aaron, Chris and – no way – is that *Tom*? I stare at him in shock, and then I spy Stu with who I *think* are Libby's and Tom's mums, but my eyes are so full of tears, it's hard to tell.

My friends engulf me and there is so much screaming going on that it almost bursts my eardrums. Eventually I make it to Stu and I'm pretty sure he's crying as we hug. I can't believe almost everyone I care about is here. And was I dreaming? Did I really see Tom?

I break away from my stepdad and look around for him and,

13

sure enough, my recently ex-boyfriend is standing awkwardly beside his mate, Chris.

He meets my eyes and gives me a small smile and then Natalie is accosting me.

Natalie is a relatively new friend, as are Em, Dougie and Aaron. I started to hang out with them earlier last year when I went through a particularly rough patch. They're older than me – they all go to college now – and Stu wrote them off as a bad influence with their drinking, smoking and late-night partying. I think he now understands that they helped me in their own way, even if he didn't approve of their methods.

'Get a look at Em, would you?' Natalie whispers in my ear.

Em's eyes are bulging out of her head as she stares at my dad. Johnny pretends not to notice. Em's his biggest fan. I watch Johnny greet my geeky stepdad with a backslap-mini-hug, but Stu can't quite carry the gesture off with the same swag, bless him.

'How did you all get here?' I ask.

'Your dad flew us over,' Libby tells me. My oldest friend's grin is nearly splitting her face in half.

'Business Class!' Dougie interjects, pumping the air with his fist.

'He's paying for this whole trip,' Libby adds. 'My mum and Tom's mum came as chaperones.'

I lock eyes with Tom. I want to pull him aside for a proper talk, but it's too hard with everyone around.

'Hi,' I say.

'Hey,' he replies quietly.

This is so awkward...

Chris comes to our rescue, wrapping his arm round Tom's neck. 'So where are we going first?'

'Barney wants to go on the Peter Pan ride,' I tell them.

'It's your day, Jessie,' Meg says firmly. 'You choose.'

'Let's go on Peter Pan,' I decide, smiling with affection at my little bro.

'We can always split up later,' Johnny chips in. 'He won't be able to go on Space Mountain, but *I* can't wait!'

He looks even more like Barney than usual.

I soon find out that my dad got in touch with Stu to arrange this whole thing. They weren't sure my friends would be able to make it at such short notice, but apparently every single one of them jumped at the chance. Everyone except Tom, who Lou tells me took some persuading.

'We knew you'd want him here,' she says, as she, Libby, Natalie and I board the log ride at Splash Mountain. Em is in the log ahead, staring manically at the back of my dad's head. 'I hope I was right?' Lou checks worriedly.

'Absolutely. I emailed him a couple of days ago asking if we could stay friends. I'm so glad he's here, even if he doesn't look too happy about it.'

'You should talk to him, reassure him,' Lou says. She was the new girl at school last term and she goes out with Chris, so I'm sure she knows the inside scoop about his best mate.

'I will as soon as I get a chance,' I vow.

My opportunity comes not long afterwards, inside the creepy Haunted Mansion. Tom and I find ourselves standing beside each other in the foyer. Suddenly the floor starts to move downwards and I press my palm to his chest with alarm.

'You're wet,' I notice, patting his T-shirt.

'Log ride,' he replies stiffly. I quickly drop my hand and edge away a little.

15

'Nat got the worst of it in ours,' I tell him.

'Muggins here sat in the front,' he reveals with a small smile.

Both of us fall silent, but I force myself to speak.

'I'm glad you're here,' I whisper.

'Your email persuaded me,' he replies in a low voice, glancing down at me, his brown eyes glinting in the darkness.

The doors open to let us out of the foyer, but we stay side by side as we walk along the spooky corridors towards the ride.

The prevailing memory I have of Tom right now is of the last time we saw each other, when he was on his knees on my bedroom floor, bleakly staring up at me. He was so gutted that I'd cheated on him. His last girlfriend, Isla, did the same, and I'd always thought she was completely mad.

Tom had told me that he 'never goes back', so once it's over with him, it's over, period. I didn't think he'd forgive me, even if I begged him to, but I'll never know for sure because I didn't even try to stop him from breaking up with me. In my heart, I'd chosen Jack.

Now that Tom's beside me, though, I feel a sharp sense of loss.

'How are you?' he asks as we wait in line for the Doom Buggies.

'Fine.' It's not an honest answer to describe how I'm feeling on the anniversary of my mother's death, but I don't know what to say to him. It occurs to me that if we're going to be friends, like I want us to be, I need to try harder.

We're next in line so when we climb into the buggy together – just the two of us – I turn to him and force a small smile.

'Actually, I'm not fine,' I admit, swallowing. 'Today was always going to be hard, but it helps having you all here.'

'I figured you'd need friends around you,' he says, as our car

16

takes off. His tone is unmistakeably gentle, even over the noise of the spooky voices and old-fashioned music.

'You're right.' I lean into him instinctively, resting my cheek against his shoulder. He feels achingly familiar and I don't want to move away, but I do as soon as he asks his next question.

'How's it going with Jack?' He sounds tense.

'OK,' I reply edgily.

'I didn't know if he'd be here today.'

Oh my *God*, can you imagine? I'm suddenly incredibly relieved that Jack and Agnes had family commitments.

'No, he's visiting his grandparents.' I pause and then turn to Tom with a frown. 'But you still came, anyway?'

He shrugs. 'Some things are more important.'

The ride whooshes round the corner and I clutch his arm, but force myself to let go and steady myself on the rail in front instead. See-through ghosts are dancing the waltz before us, but it's hard to concentrate on the ride.

'How's your mum?' I ask.

She's been nothing but kind to me today, though I still feel uncomfortable that she's here. I dread to imagine what she thinks of me, considering I broke her son's heart.

'Not great,' Tom replies. 'I'm going to see my dad tomorrow so she's a bit upset.'

'You're going to see your dad?' I ask with surprise.

'Yeah. I thought, well, I thought I might as well, seeing as I've come all this way.' He sounds self-conscious.

Tom's dad left his mum a year and a half ago and moved to San Francisco to be with another woman. Tom was devastated. He hasn't seen his dad since, but they spoke to each other recently.

17

It hurts to lose a parent, even when they're still living and breathing.

'How long are you going to stay with him?' I ask, trying not to get sidetracked by thoughts of Mum.

'A week. I'm taking a few days off school.'

'I hope it goes well,' I say.

'Thanks.'

I don't like this. We're right next to each other, but we're so far apart. I used to be able to console him, but now I can't even touch him without thinking twice about it. I have no idea how we're going to be able to stay friends.

I realise with dismay that our buggy has almost returned to its starting point. This ride has been way too brief.

'I'm sorry,' I blurt, knowing we're out of time.

He glances at me, taken aback.

'I'm sorry. I hope you can forgive me,' I say urgently.

'No,' he states, his eyes even darker than usual as he gazes back at me. My heart sinks, but he hasn't finished. 'Not yet. But I will one day. And yeah, we can try to be friends.'

I'm so thankful I could cry.

'Don't,' he implores, noticing my eyes well up. The safety rail lifts and he touches my cheek before turning to climb out of the car. He offers his hand to help me out after him.

His kindness does nothing to help the rapidly growing lump in my throat, but, as soon as our friends surround us once more, my grief recedes into the shadows.

There's so much going on in the next few hours that I barely think about Mum at all. Sometimes it occurs to me to feel guilty, like I should be honouring her memory today, rather than enjoying myself, but it's hard to be glum at the sight of all of my friends having so much fun.

Eventually my dad rounds us up and tells us that it's time to go.

'But what about Buzz Lightyear?!' Barney whines.

'We can come back another time, buddy,' Johnny tells him.

'YAY!' comes his son's ear-splitting reply.

It's only late afternoon when we walk out of the park and we're going to miss the Disney firework show, but I know my friends are shattered. They only flew in last night – Johnny is putting them up at a hotel in downtown LA. The time is eight hours ahead in the UK so technically they should be going to bed right now, but there's no chance of that. They're desperate to see my new pad.

Pizza, popcorn and a chilled-out evening in my dad's private cinema would be pretty much perfect.

'I'm assuming you want to travel with your friends,' Johnny says, as they excitedly pile on to a sleek black bus.

'Definitely.' I'm about to start after them, but I halt in my tracks and turn round. 'Thank you so much for today,' I say sincerely.

'You're welcome,' he replies gruffly. 'See you back at the house in about an hour. Your driver's going to take you on a mini tour of Hollywood first.'

'Cool!'

The bus was lent to Johnny by his record company and there's a huge bench seat at the back, wrapped round a shiny black table. There are crisps, sweets and cans of soft drink already laid out.

Stu, Caroline, Tom's mum, and Marilyn, Libby's mum, sit in seats further down the bus, leaving us to it.

'Is it wrong that I'm actually craving a salad right now?' Libby asks, tucking her ginger hair behind her ears. 'I've had so much sugar I think I'm going to take off.'

Libby was my best friend for most of my life, but she and I drifted apart after Mum's death when I grew close to Natalie and co. Last term at school, Libby made a new BFF who turned out to be a total nightmare in more ways than I care to mention. I'm so glad she and I have come full circle and are friends again.

'Have you guys had fun today?' I ask, looking round the table at everyone.

'Are you kidding? It's been the best day of my life!' Em squeals, making us laugh.

Natalie cracks open a can of Coke. 'It's not over yet,' she says, her blue eyes sparkling mischievously at me.

An hour or so later, we're winding our way up through the hills of Bel Air, home to loads of the rich and famous. My friends try to catch glimpses of the mansions behind the high garden walls and neatly trimmed hedges.

'That's where Charlotte Tremway lives,' I point out.

'Oh, wow!' Libby exclaims, whipping round to look at me. 'Don't you know her?'

I nod. 'We've hung out a few times,' I reply.

Charlotte Tremway – or Lottie, as her friends call her – is the star of one of our favourite TV shows: *Little Miss Mulholland*. Lottie's dad is the executive producer and he's mega wealthy. It was at his fortieth birthday party that I met Jack.

As I gaze out of the window, I let my thoughts drift to the guy who may or may not be my boyfriend. He's eighteen, with black hair and blue-grey eyes, and he's tall and fit and so damn sexy that he makes my blood sing. I can't wait to kiss him again.

The memory of his fingers in my hair and his body pressed against mine brings on a hot flush, and then I'm jolting with shock as I realise that this same memory is the moment I cheated on Tom. I flash Tom a guilty look and try to push Jack from my mind.

I'm so relieved he's not here. The thought of him and Tom meeting is too awful to contemplate.

As we drive through the gates of the Jefferson mansion, everyone sits up straighter and stares out of the windows. It's getting dark now so there's not much to be seen, but lights from the house are glowing through the leafless trees situated outside my bedroom window.

'What's that?' I hear Natalie ask and I look to my left to see a huge white structure in the garden.

'I have absolutely no idea,' I murmur, confused.

'It looks like a giant igloo,' Dougie comments.

Indeed it does. *What the hell?* And then I see a group of people I don't recognise lurking in among the trees and suddenly other things register – *bam, bam, bam* – one after the other: the festoon lights glowing in the branches; music coming from unseen speakers; and Jack, Agnes and my All Hype bandmates, Brandon and Miles, standing on the drive as the bus pulls to a stop. My mouth drops open, aghast, and then I'm looking at Tom.

Oh, shit.

Chapter 3

'Surprise!' Agnes shouts, as I warily step off the bus. She runs forward and, as she embraces me, I gaze over her shoulder at Jack.

'Hey,' he says, sounding amused as he tugs me out of his sister's arms. He gives me a hug and releases me so that I can say hi to our bandmates, but, as he withdraws, his lips brush against my ear. That small contact alone makes my heart flutter and we haven't even kissed. We *can't* kiss. Not here, not now.

The reason Agnes is the only one of our American friends who knows about our relationship is because Brandon and Miles would hit the roof if Jack got it on with another All Hype singer. Eve, their last lead singer, quit because it didn't work out between her and Jack, causing all manner of grief. Back in the autumn, when I returned to LA, they were auditioning for a guy so history would have no chance of repeating itself – but their attempts failed and they widened the net.

Jack is known for being... *tactile*. But he swore to Brandon and

Miles that he wouldn't jeopardise the band by mixing business with pleasure again.

Whoops.

We figured it might be a good idea to keep our relationship under wraps for a bit.

'What the hell is going on?' I gasp, extracting myself from Brandon to look towards the giant white structure in the back garden. 'And what is *that*?'

'It's an inflatable igloo,' Agnes states nonchalantly. 'An igloo disco. You're having a party.'

'But I don't know enough people to fill that thing!' I exclaim.

'Agnes has invited half of your class,' Miles tells me.

'Actually, I've invited *all* of your class and all of the year above, too,' Agnes corrects him. 'You don't want to leave anyone out when you're starting a new school. They'd hate you for it.'

At this point, Johnny joins us. 'Did you know about this?' I ask him, probably resembling a goldfish.

He raises one eyebrow at me. Stupid question. As if anyone could have got it past him.

'He masterminded it,' Agnes chips in with a grin. 'He gave me permission to invite everyone.'

'She's been on her phone for the last two days solid,' Jack says.

'But I thought you were in Washington?'

'We were,' Jack replies. 'She's been organising your social calendar from there.'

They came back early for this? For *me*? Jack gives me a sexy, lazy smile and my heart skips a beat. *Must not kiss him. Must not kiss him.*

'Meg's taken Phoenix and Barney to stay at a friend's tonight,' Johnny tells me.

'Speaking of which, introduce us to *your* friends!' Agnes cries.

I come down to earth with a bump. Anxiety racks my stomach as I turn to see that everyone is now off the bus. I point at each of them, saying their names. I feel Jack tense as I get to Tom, and Tom has seen pictures of him, so he knows *exactly* who Jack is. *Gulp.* If looks could kill...

I'd give anything for a bolt of lightning to strike a hole in the ground so I could jump into it. Damn LA for being so storm-free.

'Right, ladies!' Agnes barks. 'Come with me!'

'Where are we going?' I hiss, as she drags me away, hoping that Jack will make himself scarce and won't attempt to speak to Tom.

'You're not wearing *that* to your sixteenth birthday party,' Agnes states, glancing at my jeans and T-shirt. 'I've brought some stuff. For your friends, too.'

This should come as no great surprise. Agnes wants to be a fashion designer and styled me for my recent All Hype gig. She's always telling me what to wear. Not that I mind. She's brilliant at what she does.

Sam, my favourite security man, is waiting inside the house. I say hi to him as we head up the stairs to get ready. I assume he's in charge of making sure the majority of guests stay outside tonight.

'I've set everything up in your room,' Agnes tells me.

I belatedly realise that my friends are not immediately behind us. Coming to a stop on the landing, I turn to see them walking in a daze up the wide staircase, looking around at the house that I now call home. The architecture is modern and open-plan and the furniture is designer and minimal. Enormous floor-to-ceiling windows offer a view over our infinity pool to the City of Angels in the valley below. I smile at the expressions on my friends' faces.

24

'My room is this way,' I say, turning right at the top of the stairs.

Agnes has set up two clothes rails in my bedroom and they're bursting with colourful, shimmering party dresses. 'Choose anything you like,' she directs my friends. 'You,' she says to me, 'are wearing this.'

She passes me a long emerald-green dress. It has an asymmetrical strap going diagonally across one shoulder and it's cut square under the opposing arm, with a thigh-length slit up the side.

'I love this colour on you,' she says, and I'm reminded of the first time I wore a green dress belonging to her. She took me to Lottie Tremway's house to hang out. 'Try it on.'

All around me, my friends eagerly strip off and do just that with the glittering array of dresses hanging on the rails. I don't hesitate to join them. The green dress fits like a dream.

'Oh, wow!' Lou says suddenly. She's staring straight at me.

'You look amazing!' Libby exclaims.

Agnes, appearing pretty pleased with herself, pushes me in front of the floor-length mirror.

'Oh, Agnes!' I squeak. 'I love this dress!'

My American friend is a couple of inches taller than me, at about five foot eight, and her very dark hair has been cut into a blunt bob. Her trademark eyeliner is perfectly applied in its usual feline flick. Her reflection briefly smiles back at me, but a moment later she's serious and businesslike again. 'Strappy heels,' she decides abruptly, going to my wardrobe and hunting some out.

Natalie flashes me a knowing smile. I've told her Agnes is a force to be reckoned with.

'Did you know about tonight?' I ask Natalie, remembering

25

her earlier mischievous look and her comment about the night not being over.

'I knew something was happening,' she admits. 'I heard Johnny talking to Stu.'

'I didn't have a clue,' Libby interjects.

'I bet your dad didn't trust us not to blab,' Lou points out with a smirk.

'On that note,' I say, growing serious, 'Brandon and Miles don't have a clue about Jack and me getting together, so please be careful what you say.' I turn to Natalie. 'Can you warn Aaron and Dougie?'

'Sure.' She nods decisively.

'I'll tell Chris and Tom,' Lou chips in.

'Thanks.' I flash her a grateful smile.

Lou and I hit it off straight away when she joined our school last term, but, after I left England, she and Libby became friends. It bothered me initially, the thought of them growing closer without me, but hopefully I'll feel better when I make new friends of my own.

A flurry of nerves goes through me at the thought of starting school in a couple of days.

I refocus on the here and now and realise with a jolt that everyone is dressed.

Lou has chosen a metallic silver slip dress, Libby has gone for a long black dress with beaded detailing and Natalie has opted for a midnight-blue fringe dress. They all look totally stunning, and I tell them so.

'Do you really like your dress?' Agnes asks.

'I love it,' I reply with awe.

'Good, because it's your birthday present. I made it for you,' she adds with a sheepish smile.

'You *made* this?'

'Uh-huh.'

'Bloody hell, Agnes! You are *so* talented, it's not even funny!' She blushes as I throw my arms round her.

'You're not done yet,' she says with a giggle, pulling away. 'I have to do your hair and make-up.'

She's halfway through when the door flies open and Lottie bursts in.

'There you are!' she shouts, spying me. 'Your man downstairs told me that no one without an English accent was allowed inside. It's just as well I can act.'

'Hello, you,' I say, laughing, certain that Sam knew *exactly* who she was. She must've been on his list of friends allowed inside. 'Everyone, this is Lottie,' I say after I've given her a hug. Only then do I realise that the room has fallen silent. They're all completely star-struck by the A-lister in their midst. I laugh as I introduce her to everyone.

'Are you guys nearly done?' Lottie asks, flicking her long dark hair back. She's wearing a red dress and looks unbelievable as usual, with bright red lipstick to match, her perfectly curved eyebrows framing her oval face.

'Pretty much,' Agnes answers her question, dusting some blusher onto my cheeks with a fat brush.

'Good, because I really need a drink.'

I hate to disappoint her, but I doubt there'll be booze. Johnny is teetotal. Although he has let me have the odd drink in the past, so maybe we'll be allowed one or two…

'Why are you so desperate for a drink?' I ask Lottie, as she and I lead the way back downstairs.

'I need a distraction.'

'From what?' I frown at her.

'Brandon,' she mutters.

I soon discover what her problem is. Maisie, Brandon's girlfriend, is here. Brandon usually keeps her all to himself – I didn't even know he had a girlfriend at first because he always flirts with Lottie and it's hard to imagine how any girl could ever compete with her. But I met Maisie at the All Hype gig and she's lovely, with big dark eyes and a shy sweetness about her. She and Brandon have been going out for a long time.

I didn't actually know that Lottie cared this much, so I'm kind of flattered she shared her feelings with me.

As soon as I get outside, I'm hit by another attack of anxiety. Earlier I managed to convince myself that Jack and Tom will have kept their distance from each other, but now I'm not so sure. We head straight for the igloo, where 'Reptilia' by The Strokes is blaring from the speakers.

'I take it your dad's responsible for the playlist,' Jack says drily, materialising at my side. My heartbeat spikes. There are dozens of people around us, but my attention is now entirely on him. He looks hot in grey jeans and a fitted black shirt. His rolled-up sleeves reveal his comic-book-style POW! tattoo on his right forearm.

'What's wrong with the playlist?' I ask, trying to act cool when all I really want to do is pounce on him. 'I love this song.'

'So do I, but Isaac over there tells me he's only allowed to play stuff from the 2000s for the first coupla hours.' He glances in the DJ's direction. 'So far we've had The White Stripes, Arctic Monkeys, Gorillaz, The Libertines, The Streets and Yeah Yeah Yeahs.'

'What are you complaining about?' I smirk. 'You love those guys.'

'Yeah, but do we really need to hear *only* stuff from your dad's decade? He'll be playing Fence next.'

Fence is the name of Johnny's band from before he went solo.

'I was born in the 2000s,' I point out. 'I'm sure it's more about that than my dad's ego.'

'If you say so.'

I grin at him because I know he's teasing. 'I'm sure you can get on the decks later,' I say.

He cocks one eyebrow at me. 'You think?' He sounds sardonic. 'I'm sure Isaac would love that.'

'Who *is* Isaac?' I ask with a frown.

'Isaac Paulson.'

'Oh, wow.' No further introduction needed. He's, like, an *incredibly* famous DJ. 'My dad really went for it.'

A couple of seconds later, the smile on Jack's face fades.

'So.'

Even from this one word, I know that's the end of our light-hearted conversation.

'Tom, hey?'

'I had no idea he was coming,' I reply fervently, hating the change of subject. 'But I'm glad he did,' I add, prompting Jack's eyes to widen fractionally. 'I mean, I emailed him,' I quickly explain. 'I wanted us to stay friends. I'm glad he's willing to try.'

Jack stares at me humourlessly for a long few seconds. 'You want to stay friends,' he repeats slowly.

'Surely you don't mind?' I say irritably. 'If you avoided every girl *you'd* ever hooked up with, you wouldn't have any female friends at all.'

He averts his gaze and I feel a little bad, but unfortunately what I've just said is pretty damn accurate. Agnes told me that

29

Jack has messed around with loads of her friends – even Lottie – and I have no idea how many girls he's gone all the way with. I'm sure he had sex with Eve, my All Hype predecessor.

As my thought process plays out, I feel increasingly nauseated. And here I am thinking that we might actually have a shot at being boyfriend and girlfriend.

'How many girls have you slept with?' I find myself asking.

His eyebrows jump up. 'Are we really having this conversation now?'

'No.' I shake my head and look away, slightly mortified that that just came out. 'No, we're not. I've changed my mind. I don't want to know.'

We stand there in stony silence. 'Hey,' he says eventually, rubbing his thumb across my hipbone. I jump at the contact, then glare up at him. 'People are gonna think we're having an argument,' he says.

'Aren't we?' I challenge him.

'No,' he says reasonably. 'We're having a conversation. But this subject is not going down too well so how 'bout we change it?'

'Great idea,' I reply sarcastically.

I stiffen as he slides his hand round my back and draws me closer, leaning in to speak in my ear. 'You look hot, by the way.'

My body softens towards him and then Brandon sticks his face between ours, making us both jerk away from each other. 'Hands off my bandmate,' he jokes, pointing one finger mock accusingly at Jack.

Brandon is tall, slim and very good-looking with light-blond hair styled in a quiff. He has a tattoo of a seagull on his right shoulder, and you can just see the bird's feet poking out from beneath the short sleeves of the tropical Hawaiian shirt he's wearing. A little bit of irony in the middle of winter. Not that it's particularly cold here. This is LA we're talking about.

'Jessie, Maisie, you've met,' Brandon says, bringing his girlfriend into our huddle.

'Hi.' I give her a warm smile.

'Happy birthday,' she replies timidly.

Suddenly Natalie grabs my hand and yanks me away.

'Why didn't you tell me that you knew Margarita Ramirez!' she demands to know.

'I *don't* know Margarita Ramirez,' I reply hopelessly.

Margarita Ramirez is an all-singing, all-dancing child star turned sexy popstar.

'There she is, over there!' Natalie squawks.

I follow the line of her extended digit to see that Margarita Ramirez does indeed appear to be on the other side of the igloo. She's petite and curvy with olive-toned skin and glossy black hair that curls in waves to halfway down her back. She's absolutely stunning.

'Wait, is she talking to Gina Miranda?' I ask in astonishment, looking at the tiny, ringlet-haired redhead standing next to her.

Gina plays the teenage daughter of a drug lord in an edgy crime drama series that got some of the best TV ratings of last year.

Natalie swears under her breath. 'Holy shit, she is! And Oh. My. God. Who is *that*?'

I follow her gaze and my eyes light on an absolutely drop-dead gorgeous guy. He's got to be a male model. I can't think of any other explanation for someone who looks as smoking as he does.

'Rafael Rios,' Agnes says, joining our conversation with a grin.

'He's just won the new CiaoCiao campaign.' CiaoCiao is a major fashion house.

'Excuse us while we have a mini meltdown,' I say. 'Do all of these people go to my new school?'

'Yep. And they're all *dying* to meet you, so come with me.'

I mouth an apology to Natalie as Agnes whisks me away and, for the next hour, my head spins as I'm introduced to stars and starlets and the offspring of famous actors, musicians, models and sportspeople. Everyone is affable, some to the point of being completely OTT, but I decide I'd rather they were fake than unfriendly or bitchy.

Speaking of bitchy, where's Lissa? Agnes told me she'd invited *everyone* from school, but I haven't seen the tall, skinny blonde girl who last summer tried to out me to the press. She didn't succeed at the time, but she made life much more difficult for me and I wouldn't mind never setting eyes on her again.

'She moved to New York!' Agnes tells me, laughing at my delighted expression. 'Her dad took a job out there. I can't believe I didn't tell you!'

'Oh my God, you have *made* my night,' I say with a laugh.

School is becoming less scary by the second.

Isaac is mixing up his own beats now and loads of people have taken to the dance floor, so it's getting harder to talk in the igloo. There are caterers circulating with Mexican canapés and after a while I spy Lou.

'Is Tom OK?' I shout over the music.

She looks uneasy. 'I think so. He and Chris are outside. I was just getting us some drinks. Want to join us?'

I have a flashback to the way it used to be when we were a foursome. It hurts to know that those days are gone.

I'm saved from answering her by Jenna Kelly, one half of famous blond-haired, blue-eyed, brother-and-sister twins. They present a Saturday morning tweenie music show together. 'Jessie, can we get a selfie?' she asks.

'I'll catch you later,' I say to Lou, watching with regret as she walks away.

Jenna and Justin press their beaming, tanned faces to mine as Justin holds his phone aloft. Their teeth are practically glowing, they're so white.

'Thanks!' Jenna exclaims. 'We've just got one with your dad, too.'

'I bet he loved that,' I reply with a grin.

'Your accent is so cute, I just *cannot* get over it!' Justin gushes. He's so much camper than he comes across on the telly.

'You'll have to come to *our* birthday party next week!' Jenna chips in.

'I'd love to,' I reply with a smile.

It's a while before I can extract myself. All of these introductions are quite overwhelming, and the small talk is wearing me out. I'm desperate to be with my real friends. I haven't seen Jack for a while, but I find my British posse outside the igloo, sitting on the grass in a circle. I sigh with relief as I plonk myself down beside them.

'I swear I just saw Ellie Tomlinson,' Lou is saying.

'You did,' I reply, finally giving myself permission to yawn. I've been stifling them for ages.

Ellie is the daughter of Jessica River, a famous actress, and the younger sister of Jake Tomlinson, who's just been cast in a superhero franchise.

I'm so past caring right now.

'Courtney Victor's daughter is here, too,' Dougie says, nudging Aaron's arm. 'What's her name again?' he asks anyone who's listening.

'Sienna,' I reply wearily. Courtney is a supermodel and Sienna is following in her mother's footsteps.

They continue batting names around and I want to ask if we can talk about something else, but I don't want to sound uptight. I catch Tom's eye across from me and give him a tired smile. His corresponding look is laced with concern.

'*You* OK?' he mouths.

I nod. A feeling of intimacy passes between us and I have to force myself to avert my gaze. Where *is* Jack? I turn and scan the crowds of people hanging out under the festoon lights and spot him having a cigarette and talking to Lottie in her bright red dress. His arm is round her shoulders and he's saying something that makes her throw her head back and laugh. He's cheering her up – I guess that's a good thing.

I return my attention to the group and find Tom still watching me. I'm guessing from his expression that he's noticed Jack, too. I wish I could explain to him that Jack has always been tactile, that this is nothing new or anything to be alarmed about.

At that moment, one of the caterers comes along and asks us to go inside the igloo. I unenthusiastically get to my feet and dust myself off, looking over my shoulder in time to see Miles pulling Jack away from Lottie.

'He's very touchy-feely, isn't he?' Tom says drily, joining me. I watch as Jack and Miles disappear from view behind the igloo.

'Yep,' I say curtly. 'He's always like that.'

'Doesn't it bother you?'

34

'Please don't,' I reply, shooting him a rueful glance. 'I'm too tired to argue.'

'I know you are,' he says quietly. For some reason, we both hang back from the crowds moving inside. 'How are you feeling?' he asks.

'Surreal. I feel like I've stepped onto the pages of a glossy magazine.'

'Tell me about it.'

'Are *you* OK?' I ask him worriedly. 'I'm sorry he's here, that you had to meet him.'

'It is what it is.' He winces. 'Anyway, it's only for one night.'

'I wish you guys could stay longer,' I mumble, hating that they're all leaving tomorrow.

'Do you?'

I glance at him. 'Yes. You've all helped take my mind off things today, but it doesn't change anything. It's going to be even harder when you leave. I won't be able to stop thinking about her.'

A memory assaults me from out of nowhere.

She cups my face and beams at me as her light-brown eyes shine with excitement. She's just given me tickets to see Noel Fielding, one of my favourite comedians.

'I thought we could go together!' she blurts out.

I realise with a start that the gig has come and gone and I missed it without even thinking about Mum.

My bottom lip starts to tremble.

'Hey!' Tom says with dismay, running his hand down the length of my bare arm. But it's not enough. I really want a hug right now. Before I can think about what I'm doing, I step forward into the arms of the boy who was there for me when I needed him. And he's still here for me now. His arms close round me and I squeeze my eyes shut, but tears still escape.

'It's alright,' he murmurs, holding me tight.

'I still can't believe she's gone,' I cry, my chin resting on his shoulder.

'It's alright,' he says again, and I'm so thankful to him in that moment for having agreed to try to be my friend.

But then it dawns on me that what I'm doing isn't fair. I may have hurt him, but that doesn't mean the feelings he had for me are gone.

And I realise at that moment that my feelings for him haven't left me, either, even though I've chosen to be with someone else.

I blink and try to pull myself together, but, as I step back from Tom, I see Jack about twenty metres away, staring straight at us. And he does not look happy.

'Jessie!' Natalie shouts from the entrance to the igloo. Her eyes dart between Tom and me as she hurriedly beckons for me to go inside. When I look towards Jack again, he's gone. I brush away my tears and move in a daze towards her.

'*Where is she?*' I hear Johnny's voice come over the sound system as I walk inside. The music is no longer playing.

'She's here!' someone shouts and, as the crowd parts to let me through, I see Johnny standing on a small stage near the DJ decks, holding a microphone. 'There she is,' my dad says in his familiar, deep drawl. 'I thought I was going to have to send out a search party. Come through, Jessie.'

I do as he says, my cheeks flaming as a hundred pairs of eyes turn to look at me. When I get closer, I notice that the drum kit from Johnny's music studio has been brought out here, and there's an amp hooked up to what looks like... *Jack's guitar?*

'Now I know that you should really be up here instead of me,' Johnny says as my All Hype bandmates come through the igloo's rear entrance and take to the stage. Brandon and Miles grin at me as the former picks up his bass guitar and the latter sits down behind the drum kit and twirls his drumsticks in his fingers.

Jack is stony-faced as he slips his guitar strap over his head.

Johnny continues. 'But do your old man's ego a favour and let me sing you a song for your birthday.'

There are a few 'aahs' from the audience and then all noise is drowned out as Miles starts to hammer out a beat and Brandon comes in on the bass and I know exactly where they're going with this, because it's one of my favourite All Hype songs. It's called 'Birthday Girl' and it's an ironic punk-rock number that's guaranteed to get people jumping.

Johnny launches into the lyrics and, even though I hate that Jack is angry with me, I can't help but clap my hand over my mouth and laugh at the sight of my famous dad singing an All Hype track. At that moment, Jack lifts his eyes to meet mine, and the corners of his lips tilt up at the sight of me smiling. I beam back at him, relieved that he's not glaring at me, and he steps forward to his mic to sing backing vocals, never taking his eyes from mine.

Christ, he is so sexy.

'I can see why you fancy him!' Natalie shouts in my ear. I didn't realise she'd come up to the front with me and I'm so happy to see her. I grab her arm and squeeze it.

'Seriously! Hot!' she yells, as I flash her a grin and remind her to '*Shh!*'

It's then that I notice the sea of smartphones and the rapt faces around us.

When the song ends, everyone bursts into applause and starts cheering, me included.

'Get up here,' Johnny says to me, jerking his head towards the stage. I hope he doesn't want me to sing. There is no way in hell I'm singing.

But then from out of the back door comes Eddie, our cook, carrying an enormous three-tiered chocolate birthday cake, its top tier alight with large candles. The band strikes up again and Johnny reaches for my hand to pull me up on the stage while he sings 'Happy Birthday' straight to my face and everyone else joins in. I am so embarrassed, but he's really ramping up the 'aw' factor so it's kind of cute, too.

Eddie comes towards me with the cake, and as I step forward to blow out the candles – all sixteen of them – I remember Mum looking harassed as she tore out of the house to buy my birthday cake a year ago without so much as a 'see you later'. She was running late and I was annoyed at her because I'd wanted her to help me curl my hair before my friends started to arrive.

I suddenly realise that I'm about to lose it in front of all these people.

My breath comes out in short bursts. I try to focus and inhale enough air to blow out the candles. I manage it in two torturous attempts, and then everyone's clapping and all I want is to get down from the stage and disappear.

But Johnny has other ideas.

'Your turn,' he says, handing me the mic.

I shake my head, staring at him pleadingly. *Don't do this to me…*

'Come on, chick,' he urges, his eyebrows knitting together. 'Your friends should get to see how awesome you are.'

He's always encouraging me to sing in public, to get over my fears, but can't he see that now is a terrible, *terrible* time?

38

All Hype launch into 'Disco Creep' and I feel like I'm on a very fast train that I can't get off. I reluctantly take the mic as Johnny jumps down from the stage. He stands right at the front, next to Natalie, and grins up at me.

It's bizarre how, when it comes down to it, singing the song is easy. From the moment my mouth opens, instinct takes over and suddenly I'm just the fourth member of a really cool band, and I couldn't care less who's watching or judging me. I scan the crowd, seeking out my friends and smiling inwardly at their blown-away expressions. Then I see Stu, ten people deep and off to one side, and suddenly I'm being assaulted by more memories. Memories of how, when they found her, she had an M&S bag with my birthday cake inside. We couldn't afford to shop there usually, but that day she splashed out. And, for all her trying, the cake she bought still paled into insignificance in comparison to the one Eddie has made.

I have no idea how I make it through the song, but, when I do, I am well and truly done. I push past Johnny as he proudly claps me on my back, I push past all of the people who I can't yet call friends, and maybe never will, and then I'm in Stu's arms and I'm begging him to please, please get me out of there.

Chapter 4

Johnny finds us in the kitchen, nursing mugs of tea with a mound of tissues piled up on the table between us.

'Hey,' he says, looking absolutely gutted. 'Sam said you were in here.'

'Sorry I ran out,' I mumble.

'No, I'm sorry I pushed you. I'm *really* sorry,' he says, stressing the word.

'Does everyone think I've lost the plot?' I ask miserably.

'Nah.' He shakes his head. 'I don't think anyone even noticed you were upset. They just thought you were making a dramatic exit.'

I stare at the wall in a daze.

'Your song went down really well,' he says sincerely, before his expression morphs back into one of guilt. 'Not that I imagine that's foremost in your mind right now.'

'No, but thanks.'

'Your friends are wondering where you are,' he says gently.

'I bet they're knackered with the time difference.' It's the early hours of Sunday morning in the UK so they've effectively been up all night.

'We should be going to the hotel soon,' Stu concedes, as it dawns on me that if I were in England, the anniversary of Mum's death would have already passed.

'Can I come with you?' I ask Stu in a small voice, looking at him first and then at Johnny.

Stu looks at Johnny, too. I dry my fresh tears with another tissue and notice my poor rock-star dad is looking decidedly jaded.

'You can if you want, chick,' he says heavily. 'I'll get Annie to make you a reservation.'

'No, don't bother her this late,' I say. It must be after eleven. 'I'll crash with Libby or Nat. I'm sure they have a sofa or something.'

Johnny nods, staring morosely at the table.

'You don't mind, do you?' I ask him, getting to my feet unsteadily.

'Of course not,' he says gruffly, standing up also. He seems a bit awkward, like he wants to give me a hug, but doesn't really know how. After all, my stepdad was the one I turned to when I needed support. I cringe as I realise this – it was automatic, because I was thinking about Mum.

'I'll go and get everyone together,' I say quietly.

'I'll do that,' Johnny says.

'I'll help,' Stu adds, standing up.

'OK.' I squeeze Johnny's arm as I leave the room. I still call him Johnny most of the time – 'Dad' doesn't come naturally to me. We've still got a long way to go before we feel like a proper father and daughter. The thought of this makes me pine for Stu and I'm crushed at the thought of him leaving tomorrow. I hurry away before my emotions can take over again.

A knock on one of the floor-to-ceiling windows catches my attention as I walk back through the open-plan living room. I turn to see Jack standing outside on the terrace.

'It's just Jack,' I tell Sam, who's already on his way to the glass door. 'I want to talk to him.' I move past Sam and slide the door open, stepping into the cool night. Jack has moved away from the window and is now a silhouette outlined by the lights of LA in the distance.

'Hey,' he says, lifting his right hand to his mouth. He takes a drag from the cigarette he's holding and, for a couple of seconds, his face is bathed in amber light. 'I was worried about you,' he says, exhaling.

'Were you?'

'You sound surprised.'

'I am a bit,' I admit. 'I thought you were mad at me.'

He leaves a long pause before answering. 'I'm not mad.' He walks over to one of the ashtrays and stubs out his cigarette. 'But I'd really like to take you somewhere private so I can remind you why you chose me over him.'

Butterflies crowd my stomach and I'm rooted to the spot as he slowly walks towards me.

'I don't need reminding,' I murmur, as his hands slide round my waist. My head tingles as he bends down and presses his lips to my neck.

'Are you sure?' he asks in a low voice, thick with meaning.

'I'm sure,' I whisper, as he kisses my jaw. A little sigh escapes me and then his mouth is on mine.

He kisses me passionately, his fingers tangling in my hair at

42

the nape of my neck as his tongue invades my mouth. I grab his shoulders for support as my knees turn to jelly.

'JACK! ARE YOU THERE?'

He breaks away immediately and puts some distance between us as Brandon emerges from the side of the house.

'I knew I'd find you out back with a girl,' he teases, rolling his eyes at me.

I realise he wouldn't be reacting this jovially if he'd caught us kissing. Wait, he *expected* to find Jack making out with someone else? Great.

'Maisie wants to leave,' Brandon tells us. 'Why didn't you stick around for your encore?' he asks me.

'She was a bit upset, dude. Let it go,' Jack says.

'Upset?' Brandon looks confused.

He probably doesn't even know the significance of today – we may be bandmates, but we're not properly friends yet.

He shrugs. 'It's your party, I guess.'

'Yep, and I can cry if I want to.' I force light-heartedness into my tone and turn back to Jack. 'Listen, I'm going to go and stay with my friends at the hotel tonight.'

He looks instantly alarmed, but he can't get into a conversation about it in front of Brandon.

'Do you know where Agnes is?' My eyes dart between the two boys. 'I want to say goodbye.'

'She's with Brett,' Brandon reveals.

'Brett?' I say with surprise. I didn't realise he was even here tonight. Brett is the Aussie guy Agnes almost lost her virginity to when we were in San Francisco. She's known him since she was ten, but he went back to Australia a couple of years ago and is only in California on holiday.

'Yeah, she invited him along. She didn't think you'd mind,' Jack explains.

'Of course I don't.' She's probably been pining for him since she's been in Washington. 'Do you guys think you could track her down for me, though? I want to thank her again for tonight before I leave, but I don't really want to face anyone else.'

'Sure,' Brandon says.

'See you soon,' I say, stepping in to give him a hug.

'Band practice this week,' he reminds me.

'I'm looking forward to it.' I turn back to Jack. 'I'm going to go and pack my overnight stuff.'

I can tell he's frustrated at not being able to talk openly.

'Let me drive you to the hotel,' he says, giving me a meaningful look.

'No, it's OK. I'll go on the bus with the others.'

He stares at me for a long moment, then turns to his bandmate. 'Dude, can you go make a start on finding Agnes?'

Brandon gives him a weird look, then shrugs and sets off back round the side of the house. As soon as he's out of earshot, Jack turns to me again.

'Let me drive you,' he says firmly.

'Fine,' I reply, relenting. I was kind of looking forward to getting back on the warm, safe bus with my friends, but I don't want to piss him off any more tonight.

Jack is parked on the road outside, so we agree to meet by the bus so we can walk up the super-long drive together.

My friends are already waiting by the time I make it outside with my overnight things. The party is still in full swing in the igloo and I feel a pang of guilt that I'm leaving Johnny to deal with everyone.

'Are you sure you don't mind me going?' I ask him when I find him talking to Stu. He doesn't even have Meg here for company because she took the boys to stay at a friend's house so they wouldn't be disturbed by the noise.

'Of course not,' he replies gruffly. 'I'll see you in the morning, yeah?'

'Not too early. I might have breakfast with my friends.'

'You're all welcome back here afterwards. They're not flying out until the afternoon.'

'I wish they didn't have to go at all.'

He looks disheartened as his shoulders slump. 'Sorry, chick, the weekend was the best I could do. They've got to be back for school.'

'I know. And I really do appreciate it,' I tell him sincerely, squeezing his arm.

He gives me a small smile as he pulls me in for a hug.

'Jack's giving me a lift to the hotel, by the way.' I throw that casually in there as we step back from each other.

His eyes widen. 'What? Why aren't you catching the bus?'

'Please don't make a fuss,' I beg. 'He wants to drive me.'

'Follow directly behind the bus, then,' he commands, and I get the feeling I could get away with pretty much anything tonight if I asked. 'No detours.'

'I promise,' I declare.

'The bus driver will drop you at Jack's car,' Johnny adds, getting onto the bus to tell the driver before I can object.

'Are you OK?' Agnes asks cautiously, appearing with Jack. 'Jack said you've been upset.'

'It's been a strange day, but I'll talk to you later. We've got a lot to catch up on!'

'On that note, Tuesday, after school,' she states. 'You, me, Jack, Brett, let's go for a coffee to celebrate your first day.'

I smile at her. 'That's a perfect idea.'

We give each other a hug and I thank her again for the dress, the make-overs and all of the organising she did, not to mention how she took me under her wing earlier and introduced me to everyone under the sun. School is going to be far less frightening, thanks to her.

Finally I turn to Jack.

He doesn't look enthralled with the small change in our plans, especially as a hush falls over my friends when we board the bus.

'Jack's giving me a lift to my hotel,' I explain. 'The driver's dropping us at his car.'

Natalie edges over to make room for us, but you could cut the tension in the air with a knife as we sit down. Tom stares at Jack blackly from the other side of the table. Jack looks away, seemingly nonplussed, though I'm guessing he's anything but.

'Are you cool with me crashing on your floor?' I ask, looking at Libby, Lou, Natalie and Em in turn. I don't care whose room I sleep in, I'm just trying to break this awkward silence.

They all gush that of course it's absolutely fine, and there are two double beds in Libby and Lou's room, and I can have one of them, and I'm barely even listening because Tom's jaw is twitching and his hands have flexed into fists on the table.

Jack abruptly gets to his feet and walks down the length of the bus to talk to the driver. A few moments later, the bus slows to a stop.

'See you guys in a bit,' I say apprehensively. The doors whoosh open and I follow Jack off.

He looks livid as he points his key at his dark-grey Audi A3.

46

The lights flash as the doors unlock and he opens the door for me, standing back to let me climb inside. He slams the door behind me and I flinch as he goes round to his door. The bus hasn't set off yet, and I'm all too aware that my friends may be watching.

Jack keeps his eyes forward as he starts up the ignition and pulls away from the kerb.

'That was fun,' he mutters sarcastically.

'You should've let me go with them, then,' I state with annoyance.

'Just tell me one thing,' he says forcefully, glancing at me. 'Should I be worried about Tom?'

'No!' I exclaim, shocked. How could someone as cool and confident as Jack feel threatened?

'Because if I was going out with someone who screwed me over, I sure as hell wouldn't fly across the Atlantic at her beck and call.'

'Well, that's just it, isn't it?' I snap. 'You've never had a proper relationship with anyone, so how the hell would you know what lengths you'd go to for someone you really cared about? And he *does* care for me, Jack! We were friends first, and he knows how hard today was going to be for me. My mum died a year, a year—' My voice breaks and my throat swells and suddenly I can't finish my sentence.

He roughly shoves his hair back from his face in frustration as he senses where this is going. 'I'm sorry,' he mutters, but it's too late. I let out a sob. 'Oh, God,' he murmurs, his anger evaporating as he places his hand on my knee and I proceed to cry my heart out. He pulls over to the side of the road and wrenches his handbrake on, then turns and takes me in his arms, stroking my hair as I snot all over his black shirt.

A little voice inside me wonders if this is putting him off, if this is too heavy for him, but another voice shouts over it that if it is, so be it.

This is me. This is part of who I am.

'My dad's going to go ape-shit if you don't follow the bus,' I mumble eventually, my voice muffled against his shoulder.

He reluctantly lets me go and starts the car.

I dry my eyes and blow my nose on a tissue from my overnight bag and then cast him a long look as he takes off down the winding hill. He still seems very apprehensive, but he's no longer mad.

'Do you wanna talk about it?' he asks carefully after a while.

'What, my mum?'

'Yeah.' He swallows. 'You've never really talked about her. How did she…'

'Die?'

He nods, his expression tense.

'She went out to buy my birthday cake and the glass from a fourth-storey window fell onto the pavement where she was walking.'

'Jesus.' He exhales heavily.

I want to tell him about the cake, that Mum had saved up to get it from a more expensive shop than we could usually afford, but Jack comes from a wealthy rock-star family himself, so I doubt he'd understand what it meant to me. His dad, Billy Mitchell, was the lead singer of Casino Girl, so Jack has more in common with Jessie Jefferson, my new self, than with Jessie Pickerill and my past.

Jack takes my hand and brings it to rest on his thigh as he drives, giving it a squeeze before reaching for his iPhone in the centre console. He turns it on and starts searching for something.

'You shouldn't be messing with that while you're driving,' I scold.

'It's OK, I got it,' he replies. 'Something to cheer you up,' he adds, as The Wombats' 'Greek Tragedy' starts to play.

I smile across at him as he taps out the drumbeat on the steering wheel. The Wombats are one of my favourite bands and they always take me to a happy place.

I swivel to face him, feeling a bit better as I lean my cheek against the cool leather of the seat.

'Can you play the drums?' I ask, watching him.

He nods, but doesn't stop singing along.

'That's cool.'

'Miles can play guitar, too. Did you know that?' He gives me a sideways look.

'I didn't. But none of you play the keyboard?'

'Not well. You still wanna learn?' he asks.

'If you guys think it'd be a good idea,' I say. It was Johnny who'd suggested it.

He flashes me a grin. 'Definitely.'

I stay there like that, watching him with a flutter in my stomach as he sings along to the rest of the song, and then another track comes on, and another, and my eyelids begin to feel heavy. The next thing I know, he's unclicking my seatbelt.

'Where are we?' I ask, jolting awake.

'Hotel.'

I look out of the window to see the upside-down, red-and-white sign of The Standard, the super-cool hotel where my friends are staying.

Jack brushes his thumb along the side of my face. 'You OK?' he asks softly, staring into my eyes.

I nod sleepily. 'Tired.' I jolt again. 'Where's the bus?'

'Right in front of us,' he says. 'I caught it up.'

'Top marks.'

He gives me a small smile. I gather my things together and turn back to him before exiting the car. 'I'll call you tomorrow.'

He glowers as he looks past me to the bus, and Tom, I presume.

I lean forward to give him a quick peck, but, as I'm about to draw away, he takes my face in his hands and deepens the kiss.

'I told you I don't need reminding,' I murmur against his mouth as my insides turn into a mushy mess.

'Not worth the risk,' he replies, letting me go with a smirk.

I get out of the car to find Stu frowning at me, and my friends looking tactfully away. So they all saw that. My face burns and I feel slightly sick as I walk towards them.

I was trying not to rub Jack in Tom's face, and I've just failed miserably.

'Straight to bed, guys,' Stu says slightly sternly, as we all walk into the hotel lobby together.

Half of my friends have moved on to college so they really must be knackered if they're following their ex-teacher's orders without so much as a roll of their eyes. I cast an apologetic look in Tom's direction, my heart clenching as I realise he's angry and upset. He doesn't meet my eyes as I call out goodnight and we file into our respective bedrooms.

I'm sharing with Libby, and Lou, who uses the bathroom first, while I kick off my shoes and flop down on the bed. Libby comes to lie beside me, offering me a small smile.

'You did it,' she says quietly. 'It's after midnight.'

I smile at her, and then suddenly everything goes blurry and all I can see of my oldest friend is a cloud of ginger hair framing her kind face.

'Oh, Jessie,' she says, taking my hand and cuddling me to her as I burst into tears again.

We lie with our heads on one pillow, our foreheads pressed together, and it occurs to me with painful clarity that the last time we did this was on the night of my mum's funeral. Libby is my dearest friend in the whole world, and she and her entire family had been at the church that day, but Marilyn and Libby had sat up at the very front with Stu and me. I'd begged for Libby to be allowed to come and stay at my house that night. She'd slept in my bed and held me, just like she's doing now. I don't know how I ever grew apart from her, how I could ever have pushed her away, but I did. I'm so glad she's here now, because no one else knows what I've been through as well as she does.

'I love you, Libby,' I say in a small voice.

'I love you, too, Jessie,' she whispers, and I can hear from her tone that she's also crying. 'Now try to get some sleep.'

Chapter 5

Tom is leaving to catch a bus to San Francisco after breakfast, and I'm gutted at how quickly my time with him has slipped away. I ask if we can talk in private before he goes.

He nods reluctantly and we head upstairs to the rooftop. There's a swimming pool up here and a bar, too, plus several big, red, pod-like things with mattresses inside them.

'Shall we sit in there?' I point at one of the pods and lead the way, gasping with surprise when I climb in and the mattress wobbles beneath me.

'A waterbed!' Tom exclaims, as he enters the pod through another entrance. We both try to crawl across the bed to the edges, but we give up and collapse onto our stomachs, laughing.

Somehow we manage to turn onto our backs. We continue to chuckle and it breaks the ice. Eventually we fall silent and lie side by side, looking out at the view of downtown's nearby skyscrapers piercing the dreary morning sky. The sun is hidden behind thick grey cloud today.

Now that we're here, I don't know what to say, other than that I'm sorry, and I've already said that a hundred times.

I reach over and take his hand, giving it a squeeze. A moment later, he squeezes it back.

'Are you sure about him?' he asks quietly.

'No,' I reply honestly.

He turns his head to look at me. I try to roll onto my side to face him, but the movement makes me feel queasy.

'Urgh,' I say, pulling a face.

He looks momentarily amused, but his expression soon grows sombre.

'Why?' he asks, and I think he means: why Jack? 'I know he's good-looking and everything, but I get the feeling he'd go for anything in a skirt.'

I shake my head, my stomach lurching, now for reasons other than the heaving surface we're lying on. 'That's not true.' Although it might be – sort of. 'He's not like that with me.'

'Isn't he?' Tom challenges.

'I don't think so…' I reply. 'He's different when we're alone.'

'It shouldn't matter if you're alone or not,' he says. 'I barely even saw him speak to you last night, apart from when you were in his car.'

He looks thoroughly sickened at the reminder. My heart twists because I really regret kissing Jack like that in full view of everyone. It just sort of happened. Jack does that to me – he makes me act without thinking. OK, so *he* kissed *me*, but I could have stopped it from turning into a full-blown snog.

'He couldn't cosy up to me at the party because no one else knows that we're together.'

'So Lou said. To me it just sounds like he doesn't give enough

53

of a shit about you to rock the boat with his mates.' He rakes his fingers through his brown hair and rests his head on his hand, staring dismally up at the roof of the pod.

'That's not true,' I try to convince him. 'He *does* care about me. You don't know him. You should have seen how he was with me in the car last night.'

'I *saw* how he was with you in the car last night,' he reminds me with disgust.

'I meant before that, when I was crying,' I say quickly. 'He does care about me, Tom. I know you don't believe it but he does.'

'So that's it, then? Is he your boyfriend now? I mean, have you well and truly moved on?'

I swallow. 'Yes,' I tell him truthfully, although I'm still not sure about the boyfriend part. 'And you should move on, too.'

He sighs heavily.

'I still hope we can be friends,' I say quietly.

'I said I'd try,' he states flatly.

'I'm glad you came,' I reiterate gently, wishing I could touch him, but knowing I should keep my distance.

'I'm glad, too,' he says eventually. 'Despite having to see that total dick in person.'

I decide not to annoy him further by jumping to Jack's defence.

'Good luck with your dad today,' I say.

'Thanks,' he mumbles, sitting up and causing the mattress to wobble violently. 'Christ,' he says, clutching his hand to his stomach. 'This thing is making me want to hurl.'

I laugh and sit up, too. 'I guess we'd better join the others for breakfast. Can I call you next week? Find out how it all went?'

He pauses for a moment before nodding. 'Yeah, OK.'

We go through the rigmarole of climbing out of the pod again,

54

but, once we're standing in front of each other, the smiles slip from our faces.

'I still care about you,' I blurt, my eyes welling up with tears.

'I care about you, too,' he mumbles. And then he pulls me in for a hug, crushing the air out of my lungs as he squeezes me once – hard – before letting me go.

Later that afternoon, I find myself sitting outside on the bench on our terrace, resting my elbows on the stone table in front of me as I gaze down at the city. My friends have all left now, and Stu, too, and there's still a deep sadness in the pit of my stomach – a knot that I haven't been able to unravel all weekend.

Meg came home a couple of hours ago and now she and the boys are inside with Johnny.

I walked in on her hugging my dad earlier. She looked like she was comforting him. I presume he's told her that I bailed out of my own birthday party, the one that he so painstakingly arranged.

I take a deep breath and let it out loudly. I feel so drained, I can't believe I have any tears left in me, but suddenly my eyes are stinging with a fresh onslaught. I tense at the sound of the living-room doors sliding open and hurriedly dry my eyes with the sleeve of my jumper before Barney or Phoenix can see me. But, when I cast a look over my shoulder, I see that it's only Johnny.

'Hey,' he says heavily, as he approaches. He slides onto the bench beside me. 'You OK?'

I take another deep, shaky breath.

'Stupid question,' he answers before I can respond. To my surprise, he reaches over and places his hand on top of mine. 'I know I fucked up,' he says in a low voice, and I note with alarm that his hand is shaking. 'And I'm sorry.'

'You didn't,' I begin to protest.

'I did, and I'm sorry,' he says again.

'But I *loved* having my friends here,' I insist.

'I know. And I should have stuck to that. I don't know what I was thinking when I planned that party last night.' He sniffs. 'I guess I was trying to take your mind off everything, but that wasn't what you needed. I should've known better.' He brushes at his eyes and I'm astonished when it dawns on me that he's actually crying. 'I've been there myself,' he adds. 'I know what it's like.'

Johnny lost his own mum to cancer when he was just thirteen. 'The firsts are the worst, the seconds are bad, but it does get easier,' he promises, in a choked voice.

A river of tears trek down my face as he takes his hand away from mine and wraps his arm round my shoulders, pulling me close to his side.

'I'm so sorry, Jess,' he whispers against the top of my head. 'I'm sorry I didn't know better.'

I want to tell him that it's OK, but I'm crying too hard.

This weekend I've turned to Stu, to Jack, to Libby and to Tom when I've sought comfort, but this time it's my real dad who comes through for me. He's warm, strong and solid and I feel a lot better once my tears begin to dry up. He still holds me, though, rocking me, for a long time afterwards.

'I don't know how you feel about this,' he says, still close to tears. 'But could we look at your photo albums together? I'm guessing you brought them back with you after Christmas?'

The knot inside my stomach pulls tighter.

Johnny asked once before if he could see some pictures of my mum – Candy, the one-time rock chick who fell for him when he was in Fence. He confided that he'd started to fall for her, too, but he pushed her away and she ran for the hills. Neither of them knew that she was already pregnant with me.

I don't know how different my life would be right now if she'd told him about me at the time, instead of keeping her secret from everyone, bar Stu, her then best friend and ex-boyfriend. She was terrified that if she did come clean, she might lose me.

I nod, knowing that, however painful it's going to be, I need to immerse myself in my memories – at least for today.

Barney and Phoenix are nowhere to be seen when we go inside, and I'm grateful to Meg for keeping them occupied. Knowing her, she counselled Johnny to come outside to speak to me. I shouldn't blame him for being a bit hopeless. There's still a lot we're getting used to – both of us. This is a journey we're on together.

In my bedroom I go to my wardrobe and pull out the albums I brought back to LA with me, and return to my bed where Johnny is waiting. We sit side by side, turning the pages.

'This is in the park near our home,' I say, tracing my fingers across the first two photos of Mum. It's the middle of winter and she's wearing a thick coat, her dark hair partly covered up with a chunky purple hat. The rest of her hair flows down across her shoulders. She's smiling straight at the camera in one photograph and looking off to her right in another.

Johnny stares at the pictures with a strange expression on his face, a mixture of fascination and sadness.

I turn the page, trying to swallow the lump in my throat and giving up as more tears stream down my face.

'And this is us in Windsor.' We're standing arm in arm with Windsor Castle behind us, smiling at Stu, who's taking the shot. We'd gone there for a day trip – I was only about twelve.

A couple of pages later, I gulp back a sob at the sight of my thirteen-year-old self lying across Mum's lap on the sofa. I'm fast asleep, but she's smiling up at Stu with shining eyes, her hand resting gently on my face.

She always had cold hands…

Johnny wraps his arm round me as we both break down. 'She loved you so much,' he says, between sobs.

'I know,' I gasp.

'I'm so sorry you lost her. So, so sorry.'

He gathers me against his chest and holds me tight while I cry.

Somehow we make it through both of the photo albums and afterwards I feel oddly free, lighter, like the knot in my stomach is starting to unravel.

What's more, I feel closer to Johnny than I ever have.

'Are you hungry?' he asks gently. 'I think Eddie's left pizza in the fridge.'

The mention of Eddie makes me remember something else.

'Chocolate cake!' I exclaim. 'Is there any left?'

'Are you kidding?' he asks with a wry grin. 'There's a mountain of it. We'll be eating it for weeks.'

'Thank you for asking him to make it,' I finally think to say. 'It looked amazing.'

'I'm glad you liked it,' he replies downheartedly.

I feel a surge of pity for him. He may not have got everything spot on, but his heart was in the right place.

'OK, that's it,' I say, getting down from the bed and adopting a no-nonsense tone. 'I've had enough of feeling sorry for myself for one weekend. Let's go and get the boys and Meg together for a cup of tea and a piece of cake.'

'Good plan.' We walk together to the door and he opens it. 'At least this weekend has taken your mind off one thing,' he says as he stands back to let me walk out first.

'What?' I ask, looking back at him.

'Your first day of school,' he says with a wink.

Gulp.

Chapter 6

The intention was for Davey or Sam to drive me to and from school every day, but on Tuesday morning Johnny comes to me with my Burberry biker jacket and a brand-new plan.

'Seriously?' I say with a grin as he hands me my helmet. 'You want me to go into school with helmet hair?'

He raises one eyebrow. 'You care about that?'

'No,' I reply with a grin, sliding my hands into the cool material of my jacket. It warms up almost immediately against my skin.

Turning up for my first day at a new school on the back of my legendary rock-star dad's motorbike? Why the hell not?

Barney doesn't start back at nursery until next week so he, Meg and Phee come outside to wave us off.

Johnny stands in front of me as I pull my helmet over my head and tuck my loose hair into my jacket. He fastens my helmet for me and checks the fit, his green eyes especially piercing because he's wearing a helmet himself and they're all I can see of his face. Satisfied, he climbs onto his shiny black Ducati and pats the seat behind him. I know what I'm doing now, so I stand on the footrest with my right foot, swing my left leg over the back of the bike, and sit down.

'You look like a proper biker chick,' Meg says with a grin.

My corresponding laugh is drowned out by the sound of the engine firing up.

'Have a good first day!' she shouts.

'BYE!' Barney waves manically and Phoenix copies him.

I wave and smile at them both and then Johnny and I flip down our visors at exactly the same time. I see Meg laugh and shake her head with amusement before we drive out of the garage and down the long, winding drive.

Lewis opens the gates as we approach, and then we're on the road and tearing round the hills.

My new school is about a twenty-minute drive away in Coldwater Canyon, so I relax into the ride, the thrill temporarily replacing the nerves in my stomach. But, as soon as we pull up outside, they're back in force. I climb down from the bike and Johnny takes off his helmet, raking his hand through his dark-blond hair and gazing at me with a grin.

'Want me to walk you up?' he asks, a twinkle in his eye.

I shake my head. 'No, it's alright.'

'Sam will be back for you at three,' he tells me.

'Jack's driving Agnes and me to the coffee shop,' I remind him with a frown.

'Then Sam will follow you.'

My heart sinks at the note of finality in his tone. I nod. My safety is not up for negotiation. I suppose that's a good thing.

His shoulders relax. I think he was expecting an argument. He grins at me. 'Good luck, then.'

'Thanks.'

He leans down, offering his cheek. 'Humour your old man with a kiss.'

I plant a swift kiss on his cheek and he steps away, grinning. He nods behind me as he puts his helmet back on.

I glance over my shoulder to see groups of people dotted around, most of them looking our way.

'*Embarrassing...*' I mutter under my breath.

Johnny chuckles and flicks his visor down, revving the engine. He screeches away from the kerb.

'That's one way to make an exit,' I hear a girl say, as I watch him ride away. I turn to see Margarita Ramirez, the child star turned sexy pop starlet, standing nearby. Is she talking to me? I have a quick look around, just to be sure.

She smiles. 'Hey, Jessie. First day at school today, right?'

'That's right.' I nod, trying to unfreeze my rabbit-caught-in-the-headlights expression.

'I can show you to the office, if you like?' she says.

Margarita Ramirez is offering to show me around? Natalie would have a fit.

'Thanks,' I reply, trying to be cool.

'Hey, Jessie!' I hear someone else call, as we walk towards the school buildings.

'Hi, Jenna!' I call back, spying the tiny blonde TV star standing with her brother Justin and a few others I vaguely recognise.

'Hey, little Miss Jefferson,' Justin says.

My chest contracts at the sound of Johnny's surname as I return his wave. I'm still officially Jessie Pickerill, but I'm going to have to accept that being a Jefferson will make things a whole lot less complicated.

'She'll be starring in her *own* show next,' I hear a familiar voice drawl, looking over my shoulder at Lottie, who's tutting good-naturedly at Justin's reference to her show, *Little Miss Mulholland*.

I grin and embrace her. It's good to see someone I've met more than just the once.

Lottie is a junior and in Eleventh Grade which, confusingly, is the year above me, even though I'm in Year Eleven back home. Unfortunately we won't share any lessons, but Agnes, who was one of the youngest in Lottie's year, got held back and is still a sophomore like me. She had a tough time when her parents split. Her dad used to mess around a lot – much like my dad did – and he and her mum finally got a divorce. Her mum remarried, but that marriage broke down, too, and her parents ended up getting back together. Sadly, her dad soon went back to his old ways and they split up again, with her mum marrying Stepdad Number Two. Jack told me all about it. They're his parents, too, of course.

What Tom said about him isn't true: Jack wouldn't have opened his heart to me about his family situation if he didn't care about me.

I guess only time will tell how much.

The day flies by. I'm increasingly grateful to Johnny for throwing me that party because, even though it went a bit pear-shaped at the time, it has given me a big advantage. Most people seem to know me or know of me, and I find myself being welcomed by everyone with open arms. Even Gina Miranda, the edgy drama series actress, shows me her photos from Saturday night, and Jenna Kelly tells me that the video she took of Johnny singing the All Hype song already has over a million hits on YouTube. My nerves are a distant memory by the time the final bell rings.

63

Agnes hooks her arm through mine as we walk out of the wide school halls to the front door.

'Job done,' she says. 'First day of school complete.'

Jack is already waiting and so, I see, is Sam. I wave at Jack, but go to say hello to the big bear of a man sitting in our slick black Mercedes.

'Are you coming with me?' Sam asks in his deep, gravelly voice.

'No, with Jack.'

He stares at the sky and I smirk at him.

'Johnny said you'd follow behind.'

'I will,' he confirms. 'Where are you going?'

'Somewhere called Intelligentsia Coffee in—'

'Silver Lake, West Sunset Boulevard,' he finishes my sentence for me. 'Hanging with the cool kids,' he muses. 'You're getting to know your way around. I'll be right behind you.'

I walk over to Jack's car. He has his window open with his elbow hanging out and he watches me with a lazy grin as I approach. Brett, I see, is in the front passenger seat, so I climb into the car behind Jack.

'Hey,' I say to them both. I nearly kiss Jack hello, but don't in case one of my classmates sees and it gets back to Brandon or Miles. They used to go to school here, so they're still connected. At least Brett knows about us – Agnes told him – so we won't have to worry once we're at the coffee shop.

Jack's bluey-grey eyes fix on me in the rear-view mirror. 'Good first day?'

'Yeah, great,' I reply with a grin as he starts up the car.

Agnes chats away animatedly as we drive, filling the boys in about the day we've just had and the buzz around my birthday party.

'Johnny singing your song has got, like, a million hits on YouTube or something,' she tells them.

'No shit?' Jack looks stunned. 'Jess, can you text that to Brandon and Miles?' He grabs his phone from the centre console and passes it back to me.

'What's your passcode?' I ask, as I switch on his iPhone. He tells me without hesitation and it occurs to me that he wouldn't let me have access to his phone if he had anything to hide. The thought makes me smile, but I wish I wasn't being so paranoid. Tom has shaken me up.

The journey to Silver Lake only takes about fifteen minutes and soon we're walking into Intelligentsia. Sam, I notice with relief, stays in the car, presumably content to keep an eye on things from out there.

The terrace is buzzing with LA archetypes: hipsters, models, actors, plus a few wacky-looking individuals. We pass a table of four beautiful young women, all wearing big dark sunglasses. I hear a yap and look down to see tiny pooches in two of their handbags.

Inside, the floor and bar areas are covered with beautiful blue-and-white mosaic tiles. There's not a lot of seating in here – so there are just a couple of people on their laptops – but Agnes spies a table outside so she and Brett grab it while I wait with Jack in the queue.

He puts his arm round my waist and hooks his thumb into my jeans pocket. 'This is cool,' he says, fingering the collar of my biker jacket.

'Thanks,' I reply. 'Birthday present.'

'I still haven't given you mine.'

'Have you got one for me?' I ask with surprise.

'Yeah, it's in the trunk of my car.'

I try not to show how pleased I am as the guy behind the counter asks for our order.

The prices are crazy, but Jack insists on paying, even though I want to get one for Sam, too. 'It's the best coffee, trust me,' he says, as I carry three lattes atop with foam flowers to our table.

'Thanks,' Agnes says when I pass one to her. She and Brett are cosying up to each other on the bench seat, so Jack sits opposite them while I walk out to the pavement to hand over Sam's coffee.

He looks a little taken aback, but seems to appreciate the gesture.

'Are you OK out here?' I ask.

'Happy as Larry,' he replies, and it sounds funny, him saying such a British phrase in his American accent. I laugh and return to our table, sitting beside Jack.

He turns round to face me, resting his elbows on his knees. I turn to face him, too, butterflies taking flight in my stomach as he smiles his sexy grin at me and reaches forward to pull my chair closer to his. My legs are now resting between his and he places his hands on my thighs and stares at me directly. Seconds tick by and the jittery feeling inside my stomach increases as I stare back at him with amusement.

We haven't done much of this: hanging out like an actual couple. Apart from band practice, we've barely seen each other during the day. The first time we kissed was on the night of Agnes's sixteenth birthday party back in the summer. The next time was in San Francisco when I cheated on Tom. There's always been a spark between us, but it wasn't until New Year's Eve last week that I felt I could kiss him without guilt, and without worrying that I'd be leaving to return to England.

We kissed on Saturday night, of course, but again that was different to what's happening here and now. We're out in the open and there's nothing to hide behind, no cover of darkness. He looks at my mouth and I want to scream at him to do it, so I'm delighted when he actually does. It's just a brief kiss, and I'd prefer to snog his brains out, but it's kind of sweet that he leaves it at that.

'Aw,' Agnes says, smiling at us.

I blush and reach for my coffee and Jack does the same, but keeps his left hand on my thigh.

We sit and talk about anything and everything for the next half an hour, and it is so incredibly nice. I'm used to Jack being tactile, but this is on another level entirely and I'm scared how much I like it. At one point, a black feeling comes over me as a little voice inside my head warns me not to fall too hard, but I push it away.

I just want to enjoy this while it lasts.

That thought sends another flurry of unease swirling round my stomach. How long *will* it last?

He's never had a long-term girlfriend. What makes me think that I'll be any different?

I push that thought away also.

After a while, Agnes and Brett go inside to get the next round of coffees and some pistachio tea cake which is apparently amazing. Jack stands abruptly and nods at the bench seat where Agnes and Brett were sitting. I grin and get up, going round to the other side of the table.

'I'm pretty sure there aren't any paps here today,' he says with a smirk, as he drapes his arm round me and pulls me close, kissing my temple.

He's right: we wouldn't want to be photographed like this. I'm happy to trust his instincts, though, and, frankly, I'm done with waiting to kiss him. I tilt my face towards him and this time he deepens the contact. Shivers rocket up and down my spine.

'Mmm,' he murmurs. 'I wish we were in my room right now.'

Nerves pulse through me at the thought. He is *way* more experienced than I am.

'So, are you going to give me my birthday present or what?' I ask cheekily, changing the subject.

He looks at me with amusement and then slides out from his seat, striding across the terrace to his car. He returns a moment later with a huge rectangular package. I stare in astonishment as he approaches and then come to my senses and clear our empty mugs from the table to make room for it. He watches me as I tear off the wrapping paper. My mouth drops open.

'You got me a keyboard?' It's a Yamaha and it looks expensive.

'You wanted to learn.'

I'm shocked. 'Yes, but this is too much,' I say, shaking my head.

He arm-bumps me. 'Get over it. It's for the good of the band, right?'

I stare at him sideways and he grins at me. 'I don't know what to say,' I murmur.

'Actions speak louder than words,' he replies, cocking an eyebrow at me. I smile and lean in to kiss him, but what was meant to be a peck somehow transforms into another full-blown snog.

'Get a room,' Agnes interrupts. She and Brett smilingly pull up the chairs across from us.

'When are you flying home?' I ask Brett, fighting off a blush.

'Next Friday,' he replies.

Agnes stares at the table, disheartened. I feel a surge of pity for her. She's going to be devastated once he's gone.

'Damn,' Jack says suddenly, taking his arm out from behind my shoulders. I follow the line of his sight to see Brandon getting out of a car.

I edge away from him, disappointed. Brandon asked what we were up to when I texted him from Jack's phone earlier so I didn't think twice about replying that we were heading here.

'You guys are ridiculous,' Agnes states. 'Why don't you just come clean?'

'Dudes!' Brandon's shout prevents us from answering. I sit up straighter as he drags over a chair from another table. 'Man, that YouTube shit is nuts!' he exclaims with a grin.

'What did you expect?' Agnes asks him, before smiling at me. 'Johnny singing to you was crazy cute,' she says. 'Did you see Margarita's Twitter feed?'

'No?' I give her a questioning look.

'She posted a pic of you, Gina, Rafe and Johnny and got, like, six thousand retweets or something.'

I presume she means Rafael Rios, the male model.

'How funny,' I say with a giggle.

I can't believe all these famous kids are in my class.

'So listen,' Jack says, sitting forward and resting his elbows on the table. 'I was contacted again by Owen from *Muso* magazine today. We've set up next Friday for the interview. That cool?'

'Fine with me,' I reply, feeling a buzz of excitement at the thought of doing an interview with a proper music journalist. I remember Jack talking to him after the gig in San Francisco.

'Are we sticking to Mondays, Wednesdays and Thursdays for band practice?' Brandon asks.

'I can't do Wednesdays,' I say. Jack throws me a glance. 'Driving lessons,' I explain. 'And I think Harry wanted to change my singing lessons to Mondays, going forward, but maybe I can stick to Tuesdays.' Harry is my singing tutor. 'I was going to try to fit in piano lessons, too,' I muse.

'You're gonna be busy,' Brett comments.

'Don't forget homework,' Agnes chips in.

I groan and slump down in my seat.

'Tuesdays, Thursdays and Saturdays?' Jack suggests.

'Works for me,' Brandon replies. 'I'll check with Miles.'

'Where is he this arvo?' I ask. He didn't reply to the message I sent from Jack's phone.

'Work,' Brandon replies.

Jack, Brandon and Miles all finished school last summer, but they were more interested in pursuing careers in music than going off to college. They have part-time jobs to keep their parents off their backs while they focus on the band. Jack and Miles work in a record store and Brandon does some music PR for his dad's company. He and Jack also do a bit of DJ-ing. None of them *need* to work, but I'm kind of glad that they do. There's nothing attractive about a waster.

Brandon hangs out with us while we finish up our drinks and then we wander back outside to our cars, Jack carrying my new keyboard.

'I'll catch a ride home with Sam,' I say, smiling at the man in question as he leans against his car, waiting for me.

'You sure?' Jack asks, seeming disappointed. 'Miles is coming over after work if you wanna join us?'

'I can't. Eddie's doing a "first day of school" dinner,' I tell him. 'Johnny and Meg are going to totally grill me. See you on Thursday, though?'

'Yeah.' He glances at Brandon and then gives me a small, regretful smile.

I jerk my head towards Sam and Jack carries my keyboard over to put it in the car boot.

'Bye,' I say, stepping forward and hugging him. I hope the embrace looks platonic to Brandon, even though the feeling of Jack's chest against mine makes my pulse race.

I call goodbye to the others and climb into the car, glancing out of the window in time to see someone who looks just like Charlie Hunnam walking into Intelligentsia.

I smirk to myself. Just another typical day in LA.

Chapter 7

The next day at school, Jenna reminds me that I'm invited to her and Justin's sixteenth birthday party. It's on Saturday night and it sounds like everyone is going, everyone except Agnes.

'I'd rather spend my last weekend with Brett,' she tells me at lunchtime as we wait in line for our food. What's on offer looks a damn sight more appetising than what they used to serve in the cafeteria back home. 'You should go, though,' she urges, sliding her tray along the counter.

'Yeah, I suppose so.' The thought of going without her is not very appealing. 'Do you know what Jack's up to?' I ask.

'Don't you have a direct line to him?' she responds with a smile.

'Sorry.' I don't want her to ever feel like she's caught in the middle. She was one of the people who warned me that her brother was trouble, but she also sort of encouraged our relationship. She can be contradictory like that.

'I'm sure Jenna and Justin wouldn't mind if you invited him,' she says.

'Really? I'd feel a bit cheeky.'

'Everyone knows Jack. He's probably invited, anyway.'

I soon find out that she's right.

'Why didn't you tell me?' I ask with mild irritation when I arrive earlier than Miles and Brandon for band practice on Thursday. I felt awkward earlier, when I finally bit the bullet and asked Jenna if Jack could come with me to the party, and she replied that all three of my bandmates were already on the guest list. She'd invited them last weekend at my house.

'It hadn't occurred to me,' Jack replies casually, leading the way into the games room. Brett picked up Agnes from school today in his campervan and they've gone for a drive to Malibu beach so Davey brought me here.

'Are you going?' I ask, feeling a bit miffed.

He shrugs. 'I dunno yet. You?'

'Yeah. I am.' I try to sound as flippant as he does.

'Then I guess I am, too,' he says, flashing me a grin. Why do I get the feeling he's teasing me? *And* testing me?

I think I might need to keep Jack on his toes. The thought is depressing. I don't like having to play games. I never had to with Tom. I wonder how he's been getting on with his dad. I make a mental note to call next week when he's back in England.

'Hey,' Jack says. I return my attention to him as he jerks his head towards the back of the room, indicating that I should follow him.

'Why?' I ask, staying where I am.

'Miles and Brandon'll be here in a minute. Let's hang in a dark corner until they arrive… Don't make me come get you,'

73

he warns when I don't instantly oblige. He slowly starts walking towards me. My face breaks into a grin as I back away.

'Oh, you do *not* wanna do that,' he says meaningfully.

I turn and run out of the games room doors, laughing.

His family's property is set into a hill and there are three flat expanses, divided by small, steep hills as the land slopes down. I run straight down the first hill, laughing as he chases me. He catches me easily at the beginning of the next hill, grabbing my waist and whizzing me round. I'm panting as he spins me to face him, and then we're falling on the sloping ground. He traps me beneath his body and my whole head fizzes and sparks as his tongue enters my mouth. I feel dizzy as I kiss him back with just as much fervour.

We freeze at the sound of a car driving through the front gates. Jack sighs and rests his entire body weight on top of me. It feels so good, even if I'm momentarily unable to breathe.

Reluctantly, he gets up, holding out his hand to pull me to my feet. I smooth down my hair and flash him a cheeky grin as we walk over to greet our bandmates.

Maybe I like playing games after all.

Saturday comes around quickly and, with it, Jenna and Justin Kelly's sixteenth birthday party. There's been a buzz about it all week at school and, as far as I know, everyone who's anyone is going. I'm disappointed that Agnes can't be there, but at least Lottie is coming, and Jack, Miles and Brandon, too. We've had a couple of really good band sessions this week, including today, which saw us working on a new song. I even suggested a few lyrics myself that seemed to go down well.

Eve, the last All Hype singer, didn't write any lyrics, which is something I feel hugely relieved about. Jack and Brandon write most of their stuff, so she doesn't have any ownership over their songs. That would have really bothered me. It's hard enough to compete with her voice, but she was super cool, too.

I hate that she had sex with Jack – at least, I think she did. He told me that they weren't really boyfriend and girlfriend, that they just had 'a thing' going, but then he later told me that he 'broke up' with her because of me.

I'm not sure it makes me feel any better.

But I'm still buzzing after today's session when we arrive at the party together, which is being held in the Kellys' mansion in West Hollywood. Davey has driven all four of us, but Johnny was satisfied with the Kellys' security measures so he let me come without Sam.

When we climb out of the car, several flashes go off in our faces. I pose with my bandmates for a few photographs, and my head is spinning as we walk through the gates.

The whole garden has been decked out like a winter wonderland, with fake icicles hanging from the trees and real snow being sprayed out of machines into the air. Waiting staff wander around with trays of colourful cocktails and canapés and they're all dressed in extravagant, icy-looking costumes that wouldn't seem out of place on a film set. Even their over-the-top make-up looks like it's been done by proper make-up artists. One guy's hair has been spray-painted white and slicked up into an enormous quiff and his eyebrows have been frosted blue.

Jenna and Justin are welcoming guests so we go over to say hi.

'Hello,' I say warmly. 'Happy birthday.'

'Thank you!' Jenna gushes. She looks somewhere between

a princess and a bride in a sparkling white ballgown. Justin is rocking an electric-blue, sequinned suit.

As for me, I'm wearing an Alexander Wang minidress that's black with draped, ruched detailing. Meg gave it to me yesterday when she found out I had a party to go to. I couldn't believe it when I googled the price.

I still feel underdressed, though, and I'm not sure Jack's crumpled suit jacket over ripped jeans is up to standards, either.

Not that I mind. He looks so sexy.

We each take a cocktail and head further down the garden, where I notice with amazement that an ice rink has been set up on the grass. People are gliding across the length of it and I watch with fascination as one girl spins on the spot like a professional ice dancer. I flash Jack a grin.

'I so want to do that.'

'Can you skate?' he asks.

'No, but I'll give anything a go at least once.'

'I'll keep that in mind,' he says quietly enough that Brandon and Miles can't hear him. The hairs on my arms stand up and then I hear an unfamiliar voice speaking from a few metres away.

'I will if you will.'

I turn to see Sienna Victor, the daughter of supermodel Courtney Victor. She's tall and stick-thin with thick dark eyebrows, blunt dark hair cut to just above her shoulders and piercing blue eyes. It's no surprise that she's following in her mother's footsteps.

She flashes me a grin. 'I overheard. You tempted?' She nods again at the skating rink. 'It'll only get busier.'

'OK,' I decide on impulse, downing half of my drink in one go and dumping my glass on a nearby table.

I haven't seen much of Sienna this week in school. We don't share many classes, but I met her briefly at my party. As she leads the way, her gangly, high-heeled feet treading carefully across the soggy grass, I start to have second thoughts. Do I really want to make a complete tit out of myself in front of this girl? Though if I worried about that all the time I'd have no fun at all. I decide to stick with my convictions and follow her to the boot hut, which is covered with fake snow.

'Only got guy boots in that size,' the man tells Sienna.

'Fine,' she says abruptly, looking embarrassed.

'I really hope you can't skate well,' I say, trying to sound upbeat.

'Are you kidding? I'm about to fall flat on my face.'

'Phew! Me too!'

Once we've laced up our boots, she offers me her arm and we walk carefully across the artificial lawn to the ice-rink entrance.

'OK,' she says, taking a deep breath. 'Let's do this.'

I shoot a look across the rink and see that Jack is nowhere to be seen. *Good*, I think to myself before launching forward.

'Argh!' I scream and she does the same as she follows me, her gazelle-like legs scooting this way and that as she tries to stay upright.

'Crap!' she gasps, as I crack up laughing.

I'm surprised at how much fun I have in the next twenty minutes, but, by the end of it, we are actually doing some semblance of skating. As we do a last lap round the rink, we even manage a conversation.

'Where's Agnes tonight?' Sienna asks me.

'She's with her guy, Brett. He's over here from Australia,' I explain.

'Aah,' she says knowingly. 'I saw them together at your birthday party. Great night, by the way.'

'Thanks,' I reply, touched. 'Not that I had anything to do with organising it.'

'I love that your dad's All Hype song went viral.'

'Me too! So funny.'

'And you have some serious lungs on you, too, girl.'

She flashes me an impressed look and my insides fizz with pride.

'Why didn't you sing another song?' she asks curiously.

I'm not sure I want to get into it with her, but then I think, why not? We've bonded over our shared lack of skating skills and it's not like it's a big secret.

'My birthday was the first anniversary of my mum's death,' I tell her.

'Oh, God.' She looks shocked and actually stumbles a bit.

'So I was a bit of a mess that day.'

'No shit,' she says, falling silent.

I try to think of a lighter subject, but then someone bumps into me and I grab Sienna's arm to stop myself from falling and inadvertently pull her down with me. We both burst out laughing as we sit on our backsides on the cold, wet ice. The temperature is so far from freezing in LA and the ice is rapidly melting.

'I need a drink,' she splutters.

'Me too. I hope we can get a proper one,' I find myself adding.

'I heard Gina used to go out with one of the barmen. Let's go find her!'

The party flies by. Sometimes I spy Jack talking to various people, but I'm not missing him as I laugh and chat to my new schoolmates. Gina Miranda is fun – she reminds me a little of

78

the singer Jess Glynne, with her curly red hair and beautiful alabaster skin. Margarita Ramirez is super friendly, too, but it's Sienna who I find I really like.

'We should get a selfie,' Margarita says at one point, shouting out to a passing Jenna. I spy Lottie and call her over. She joins us, smiling.

We have to give Margarita's phone to the barman to take the picture because there are so many of us to fit in.

'Let's see how many retweets this one gets,' Margarita says with a grin as she posts the picture. 'What's your username, Jessie?'

'I don't have one.'

'What?!' she gasps. 'We have *got* to rectify that before I post this. Where's your phone?'

I smile and get it out, luckily not minding that I'm being railroaded into embracing social media. She talks me through what to do, but I hesitate when I'm asked to write down my name. Am I Jessie Pickerill or Jessie Jefferson?

A couple of days ago, Annie – Johnny's PA – gave me my social-security number and informed me she's already well into the process of getting me American citizenship. The name we agreed to file is Jessica Pickerill Jefferson.

I feel a pang of guilt as I type out Jessie Jefferson, but that's already taken. I try Jessie Pickerill, but that's gone, too, and I feel strangely relieved that the decision has been taken away from me. Eventually I compromise and settle on JessiePJeffers. I'm satisfied with that.

Margarita tweets the pic and tags us all. I feel a little flurry of excitement.

'Now we need to get you on Instagram,' she says, tucking her glossy black hair behind her ears and flashing me a smile.

At least I'm already on Snapchat…

'I love your dress,' Sienna says to me later, after we've media maxed out. 'Alexander Wang, right?' she says.

'How did you know?' I look around. Is someone else wearing the same thing as me?

'I'm a model. I need to know about these things,' she explains with a shrug, as though reading my mind. 'Hey, we should go shopping some time.'

'I'd love that,' I say with a smile.

'Next week?'

'That'd be great. I can't do Mondays, Tuesdays, Wednesdays… Jeez,' I say, as it dawns on me. 'The only free days I have are Fridays. And shit! No, I can't even do Friday next week!' We have our *Muso* interview at four o'clock.

She wants to know why I'm so busy so I tell her about my singing lessons and band practice and driving lessons, which I only started on Wednesday. She laughs as I describe the look on my instructor's face when I went a little too fast along Mulholland Drive. I persuaded him to let me drive my new Fiat 500, but he told me we'd be using his instructor vehicle next time so he can slam the brakes on with his dual pedals…

'And Friday?' she asks.

'Jack, Miles, Brandon and I are doing an interview with a magazine.'

'Which one?' she asks with interest.

'*Muso*. Do you know it?'

'I've heard of it, but music magazines are not really my scene. Give me fashion mags any day of the week. I liked you guys, though. Have you got any gigs coming up?'

'Hopefully we'll be doing one in San Francisco next month.'

We've been invited back by the same venue as last time and I've asked if we can make it the weekend of half-term in mid-February when Stu's visiting. Stu suggested it, actually.

'Cool, maybe I'll come,' she says.

'That would be great,' I reply with a grin, spying Jack across the terrace. He raises one eyebrow at me and jerks his chin towards the edge of the garden. I give him a minuscule nod of acknowledgement and, a moment later, make my excuses.

I check over my shoulder as I duck behind a cluster of palm trees, but I can't see anyone looking this way and, the next thing I know, Jack is tugging me further into the darkness. He presses me up against a palm tree and proceeds to kiss me passionately. The trunk is rough and spiky against my back, but I barely notice. I feel dizzy and I'm pretty sure it has nothing to do with the couple of drinks I've had.

'Jack,' I gasp, putting my hands on his chest. I can feel his heart pounding against my palms.

He breaks away from me, breathing hard against my mouth. 'What?'

I don't know what to say. I don't want him to stop, but I feel completely out of my depth. I'm not even sure he knows I'm a virgin.

'You're scaring me,' I whisper.

He tenses and immediately steps backwards, looking shocked.

'Not like that,' I explain, realising he's taken me the wrong way. '*This* is scaring me.' I motion to the two of us. 'I'm scared how much I like it.'

His shoulders sag with relief.

'What if it all goes wrong?' I ask.

He frowns. 'What do you mean?'

'With Miles and Brandon. All Hype.' I love singing and being a part of this band. I want to be more than just Johnny Jefferson's daughter. 'I don't want to be another Eve.'

'I don't want that, either,' he states. 'But I can't keep my hands off you.'

'I don't want you to keep your hands off me,' I whisper.

'Good,' he says meaningfully, closing the gap between us.

'I just hope we can be cool if it doesn't work out,' I murmur, as he presses his lips to my neck. 'I really, *really* don't want to screw up the band…'

'We won't,' he whispers between kisses. And then I can't think about anything else apart from kissing him back.

Chapter 8

The next morning, I groggily come to at the sound of Johnny's voice outside my bedroom door.

'Can you get up and come to the studio?' he calls.

I frown. 'Sure,' I reply. *Am I in trouble?*

I remember with a lurching stomach that last night I kept Davey waiting on the road outside Justin and Jenna's house for half an hour.

I get dressed as quickly as I can with a pounding headache. I didn't even drink that much last night, did I? Maybe I did. Those cocktails slipped down way too easily.

I emerge bleary-eyed from my bedroom and wander along the landing to Johnny's music studio. The door is ajar so I go straight in.

Johnny is sitting on a stool behind the glass with his acoustic guitar in his hands. The mixing desk with its control panels is in front of me, flanked by big speakers. Johnny's voice comes through them now.

'Afternoon,' he says drily.

'What time is it?' I ask, rubbing at my eyes.

'Eleven thirty.'

'Oh, is that all?'

He raises one eyebrow at me. 'Get in here.'

I push open the glass door and walk into the soundproofed room. There's a full-size drum kit in here, and a keyboard, too, but Johnny's various guitars are hanging on the wall in the control room outside. The walls in here are covered with yellow foam, made of miniature pyramid shapes. Apparently the sound bounces off the walls and improves the acoustics.

'Close it,' Johnny says, nodding at the door.

He reaches forward and flicks a switch to turn off the microphones and then indicates the stool in front of him. 'Sit down. We need to talk.'

Shit. This sounds serious.

'Sorry about keeping Davey waiting last night,' I say quickly.

'That's not what this is about.' He tucks his chin-length hair behind his ear. I notice he hasn't shaved for a couple of days, judging by the dark-blond stubble gracing his jaw. 'But try not to do it again.'

'I won't,' I promise.

'Did you have fun?' he asks, regarding me steadily.

'Yeah.' I can't help but grin. 'It was great, actually.'

His small corresponding smile morphs into a look of apprehension and I tense up again. He digs into his pocket and pulls out his phone, pressing a few buttons before passing it over to me. His display is showing the photo we took of all of the girls last night, and my jaw hits the floor when I realise it's made it onto one of the biggest online celebrity gossip sites.

'Pictures from the party are all over the net,' Johnny says.

My brow furrows as he takes the phone back and searches for something else before handing it over again. This photo is of Sienna and me clutching each other's arms and laughing our heads off as we ice-skate. We went for round two towards the end of the night. It was such a laugh.

I grin up at Johnny, but he's not smiling. 'What's the problem?' I ask with confusion.

'She a friend of yours?' he checks.

'I hope so. I really liked her. We're going to go shopping sometime. Her name's Sienna Victor.'

'I know her name,' he replies heavily. 'I recognised her from your party, but I didn't know who she was until today.'

I'm extremely confused now.

'Jessie, do you know who Dana Reed is?' he asks seriously.

I swallow and nod. Dana is Johnny's druggie ex-girlfriend. She was a singer-songwriter and marked for great things, but I haven't heard anything about her for well over a year. She and Johnny infamously met in rehab and got up to all sorts of crazy, scary shit together. It was like one of those terrible, twisted relationships that usually end in disaster. They both overdosed – Johnny could have died before I even found out he was my dad. It's a chilling thought.

The press planted most of the blame for what happened on Dana's doorstep, re-embracing Johnny when he married Meg, a sweet, ordinary girl whom he claimed was the love of his life. If the press painted Dana as the devil, Meg was their angel.

Seeing how settled Johnny is with her now, I have to concede that the press had Meg pretty well pegged. But what has Dana Reed got to do with my new friend? I'm shocked when Johnny tells me.

'Sienna is Dana's half-sister,' he reveals. 'She didn't mention that to you?'

I shake my head, gobsmacked. No, she didn't, which is a bit surprising, considering her sister's horrifying history with my dad.

'Dana used to talk to me a bit about Sienna,' Johnny reveals. 'Dana's dad had an affair with Courtney, and Sienna was the result of that. She and Dana weren't close when we were together. I don't know about now.'

'Sienna is nothing like Dana,' I say quickly. 'She's not into drugs or anything like that—'

Johnny cuts me off. 'Jessie, Dana is Meg's worst nightmare,' he states. 'If Meg knew that you were hanging out with anyone even remotely connected to her, she'd go mental.'

'But Sienna is really nice!' I defend her. 'I promise you, you have nothing to be worried about.'

He gives me a long, weary look and then sighs heavily. 'I hope so, chick. I guess I can't tell you who to be friends with, but I can warn you to be careful. The same goes for Jack Mitchell.'

Damn. I thought the heavy conversation was over, but, from the look on his face, my dad's just getting warmed up.

'I didn't want to get into this with you last weekend, but I've gotta tell you, I'm sorry Tom's no longer on the scene. He was a better option than Jack.'

'He lives in another country!' I squawk.

Johnny shrugs and purses his lips. 'Exactly.'

'Come on,' I say with annoyance. 'Tom and I weren't working out. And I really like Jack. I *really* like him,' I emphasise.

I don't like the look he's giving me. It's almost... pity. 'Just be careful,' he reiterates quietly, his green eyes piercing mine for a long, uncomfortable moment.

My face warms and I nod and look away. 'I will,' I mumble. *Are we done now? Can I go?*

'Sixteen is underage in California,' he adds.

I shoot him a sharp look, momentarily forgetting to blush. Is he talking about sex now?

'Google it,' he adds.

'OK!' I say, trying to sound breezy. 'Do you mind if I go and get a shower? I've literally just rolled out of bed.'

'Not yet,' he says. 'There's something else I need to talk to you about.'

Oh, God. What now?

'Don't look so worried. This bit's good news,' he says with a grin, before adding, 'at least, I hope it is. You remember when you did a few harmonies for me before Christmas and we put it on a demo for Nick?'

I nod. Nick is from his record company.

'Well, he wants us to lay the track down properly. You OK about featuring on my new album?'

I nearly fall off my chair. When I'm done screaming, he laughs softly. 'I'm going to take that as a yes.'

There's no time to waste. Johnny's next album is coming out at the end of February, well in time for the world tour that kicks off in April. I'll have to postpone tomorrow's singing lesson so we can go to the studio downtown after school.

I can't believe it. I'm going to sing on his album! I'm even going to get paid for it. I am beside myself with excitement.

Finally I get up to go, desperate to wash away last night's cobwebs, but, on my way out of the door, Johnny speaks.

'And Jessie?' I look over my shoulder at him to see a crease between his eyebrows. 'Don't mention anything about Sienna or Dana to Meg. I don't want to stress her out if I can avoid it.'

Now I realise why we had our conversation in a soundproofed booth.

Chapter 9

'I hope you're not getting carried away with it all,' Stu says a few days later when we finally manage to catch each other for a chat. It's so difficult with the time difference. 'I keep hearing your name being bandied around school.'

I can't help giggling. I find it surreal but also kind of hilarious that people at my old school are talking about me.

The press attention has gone a bit mental this week. Today I got my ten thousandth follower on Twitter, and yesterday Johnny's publicist, Hannah, was contacted by two journalists requesting an interview with me – not All Hype: me! After the initial excitement, I felt a bit uneasy. Johnny has asked Hannah to handle my publicity, going forward, but she's going to wait until I've spoken to the guys before getting back to the journalists. I'm on my way to see them now for Thursday afternoon practice. We haven't got together since Saturday night. Unfortunately I had to cancel band practice on Tuesday because Johnny and I were still in the studio.

Not a sentence I ever thought I'd say.

'Just try not to get too swept up,' Stu warns.

'I won't.' I catch Sam's eye in the rear-view mirror. He collected me from school today.

'Listen, I want to talk to you about something.'

First Johnny, now Stu. It's not easy having two dads in your life.

'GCSEs,' Stu says. 'I think you should still do them.'

The American school system is very different to the British one. Over here, there are no GCSEs or A levels – your teachers give you tests and grade you. The big 'examining board' style exams happen at the end of Eleventh Grade – but they're not even compulsory. You have to pay to take them so most people only do them if they want to go to college. They're called SATs and ACTs. Some colleges prefer SATs results, others ACTs, so people choose which exams to do, depending on where they want to go. Some students choose to do both. The results are what the colleges rely upon when they're accepting admissions.

As I'm in Tenth Grade here, I'm not due to do my SATs until next year – if I choose to do them at all. I'm not sure I want to go to college. I'm thinking I'd rather pursue my music, like Jack.

But Stu thinks I'd be doing myself a disservice by not taking my GCSE exams along with my British classmates.

'How can I?' I ask with confusion. 'I go to school here.'

'From what I understand it, school in California breaks up for the summer before exams in the UK start, so I would suggest you fly over in time to do them,' Stu says. 'You'd have to take extra lessons in the meantime, to make sure you're learning the same curriculum.'

'You've got to be joking,' I say flatly. I am so not liking this idea.

'I just think you should keep your options open. What if you decide you want to go to a British university?'

'I won't!'

'You don't know that for sure. Libby, Lou, all your friends here will be going. You might want to do a sandwich year in the UK. You just don't know. This will make life a whole lot easier. Get all your ducks in a row so whatever happens, whatever's around the corner, you have possibilities.'

I let out a loud, dramatic sigh.

'I'm pretty sure your mum would've agreed with me,' he adds quietly.

'That is *not* fair!' I raise my voice. 'You can't bring her into this!'

'Sorry.' For once, he's the one apologising. But it's too late: the damage has been done. He can't take back his words and the simple fact is I know that he's right. I groan and slump further down in my seat, reluctantly agreeing.

Agnes has seemed a little down this week and she wasn't at school today, so when Sam drives through the gates belonging to Jack and Agnes's Spanish-villa-style home, I'm delighted to see her standing in the tiled courtyard, waiting to welcome me.

I say bye to Sam and climb out, going over to give her a hug. 'Hey, you,' I say warmly.

She grins and hugs me back and, when I withdraw, I narrow my eyes at her. 'You don't look ill.'

'Doesn't a broken heart count?' she murmurs, the usual spark gone from her eyes.

I regard her with sympathy. I take it she's talking about Brett. 'It's tomorrow he's leaving, isn't it?'

She nods disconsolately, then whispers meaningfully: 'I've got so much to tell you.'

I give her an inquisitive stare, but, from her expression, I think I know what her news is.

'You've *done it?*' I whisper, taken aback.

She nods ever so slightly. 'Come and knock on my bedroom door when you've finished practice,' she urges.

'OK.'

She squeezes my arm and then leads me round the corner of their home, past fat palm trees and a multitude of tropical-looking plants to the games room.

'Delivery for you,' she says to her brother, pushing me inside the room.

We don't waste time talking.

Later, when Brandon and Miles have joined us, I bring up the subject of my interview requests.

'Who wants to interview you?' Miles asks with a frown.

'One is a British tabloid newspaper. Johnny vetoed that one.' He really doesn't trust the tabloids and he feels it would be a slippery slope for me. 'But the other is for a weekly celebrity magazine called *Hebe* – also British. They want to fly over and do a photoshoot and stuff. Obviously I'll talk about the band, but it does feel a bit wrong with it just being me.'

Jack shrugs. 'It's no big deal.'

'Yeah, I mean, all publicity is good publicity, right?' Brandon chips in.

'Are you sure? Because I don't want to do it unless we're all agreed,' I state firmly. This time I look at Miles to gauge his reaction.

He seems nonplussed. 'Fine by me.'

'OK.' I feel a flurry of nerves, which strengthen when I remember we have to get tomorrow's interview out of the way, first.

After band practice, Jack takes me inside to find Agnes. His mum and stepdad Tim have very different tastes to Johnny and Meg. Instead of a minimalist pad, here the rooms are crowded with dark-wood, antique-looking furniture, the floors dotted with intricately designed colourful rugs and the walls covered with old-fashioned paintings in ornate frames.

'Is your mum here?' I ask Jack, looking around.

'Somewhere,' he replies.

'I should say hi. Shouldn't I?'

He shrugs, not seeming to care either way. 'Mom?' he calls out.

Her voice comes back from a room off the living room. I follow him nervously.

'Jessie wanted to say hello,' he says, as I look past him to see his mum, Lucille, sitting at a large desk, surrounded by paperwork.

'Well, hello there!' she gushes warmly, getting to her feet. She's slim and attractive with a wide smile and long dark hair that comes all the way to her waist. 'How are you, Jessie? It's been a while since I've seen you.'

I've barely spoken to her at all, truth be told. I get the feeling she's very laid-back about what Jack and Agnes get up to. I'm not even sure she knows I'm going out with her son.

'Does your mum know about you and me?' I whisper a few minutes later, after we've exhausted the small talk with Lucille and I feel free to wander upstairs.

'Yeah. Agnes told her.' He comes to a stop outside my friend's room. 'Come and say bye to me before you go.'

93

I nod and knock on the door.

'Come in,' Agnes calls.

I walk in to find her lying on her double bed, atop her hot-pink bedspread. Fairy lights are twirled round the white iron bedhead behind her, but they're turned off and the only light in the room is coming from two burning, vanilla-scented candles.

She likes a lot of the same actors and bands that I do and I pause to admire the posters of Harry Styles, Justin Bieber, Liam Hemsworth and Joseph Strike looking all sexy and ripped. I express my appreciation as I shrug off my jacket.

'Didn't Meg go out with Joseph Strike once?' she asks, furrowing her brow as she sits up.

I shoot her a startled look. 'Are you serious?'

'I'm sure I heard that somewhere,' Agnes says. 'Maybe she can get us tickets to his next premiere.'

'Oh my God, can you imagine?' I say with wide-eyed excitement as I perch on the end of her bed. 'I bet she keeps it quiet because Johnny gets so jealous.'

Agnes screws up her nose. 'He doesn't, does he?'

'Yeah.' I smirk. 'He's so into her.'

Shame he didn't love my mother like that… I push the thought away. Some things aren't meant to be and, if Johnny hadn't met Meg, Barney and Phoenix wouldn't exist.

'Did *you* know Sienna was Dana's Reed's little sister?' I ask Agnes with a frown, now that we're onto the subject of my dad's love life.

Her eyes widen. 'God. Yes, I did, but I had *completely* forgotten. She never talks about her.'

'I hung out with her a bit on Saturday night and she didn't mention it.' I don't reveal that I've sort of been avoiding her this week. I've said hi, of course, but I do feel strange about the whole thing. 'I just thought that maybe that would have been something she'd think to bring up,' I add.

'Maybe she's embarrassed,' Agnes says with a shrug.

'Anyway, let's change the subject.'

Agnes's cheeks flame as it becomes clear what that subject is.

'So you guys had sex?' I whisper.

She nods, squirming.

'When?'

'Last night,' she replies.

'Oh my God.' I have so many questions. What was it like? Did it hurt? Where were they when it happened? How does she feel now? I barely even know how to start.

'I thought you'd decided not to,' is what I come out with.

She chews a snag off her thumbnail. 'We sort of had,' she says in a small voice. 'What you said in San Fran, about me giving my virginity away to someone who's not going to be around afterwards... That got to me. And it bothered him, too. But things have been getting so heated. I've seen him practically every day for the last few weeks and we almost went the whole way in his car that day we drove to Malibu. He stopped it, and again on Saturday night. Then, last night, Mum and Tim were out and Jack was, too, and we had the whole house to ourselves.'

Where was Jack? I try to shake the question out of my head and focus on my friend.

'So he came over?' I prompt.

She nods. 'Things were getting pretty heavy and I told him I didn't want him to stop. So he didn't.'

'God. Are you alright?' I ask.

She nods slightly, but then her eyes fill with tears.

'Oh, Agnes,' I say with dismay, gathering her in my arms. 'Was it OK? Did it hurt?' I ask tentatively – and curiously, if I'm being honest.

'Yes, but it was bearable. And lovely. What's killing me is that he's leaving tomorrow.'

'Maybe he'll come back? I mean, you'll stay in touch, right?'

She nods. 'Of course we will. But he's starting a new job soon and, I don't know, Australia is just so far away.'

'I'm sorry,' I say, rubbing her back. This is what I was afraid of. Brett won't be around to pick up the pieces.

'I don't regret it,' she whispers. 'I love him. It was so special. I wanted it to be him.'

I squeeze her tighter, wishing I could protect her from the pain I'm certain is to come.

Before I go home, I ask her if Jack knows. I'm relieved when she says that Brett confided in him earlier. From the age of twelve, Brett lived with his mum in what is now the Mitchells' games room. His mum was a housekeeper here and Brett and Jack were the same age. Although Brett didn't go to the same exclusive school as the Mitchells, he never felt threatened or uncomfortable around them. He and Jack were like brothers, Agnes told me.

Jack's bedroom door is closed when I go to say goodbye and I can hear the familiar riff of The White Stripes' 'Seven Nation Army' playing inside. Retro. I knock and the music stops. When I go in, I'm surprised to see him holding his electric guitar in his hands.

'Was that you?' I ask, impressed.

'Yeah.' He plays the riff again.

Jesus, I fancy him.

96

He goes to put his guitar down.

'Wait, can you teach me how to do that?' I ask impulsively.

'Lead vocals, keyboard *and* guitar? Are you planning on going solo?'

'Don't say that. I hate the thought of not being in All Hype.'

'I'm teasing.' He picks up his instrument again and edges backwards, leaving a space on the bed between his legs for me. My breathing accelerates as I sit where he wants me, my back snug against his chest as he brings the guitar across my front. I'm in his bedroom, and we're alone.

OK, so Agnes is next door and his mum is downstairs and Sam is going to be coming for me any minute, but I still feel on edge when I'm this close to him.

His cheek is against mine as he shows me how to play the riff, talking me through the different frets on the neck of his guitar and then letting me have a turn.

'How long have you played your guitar?' I ask, pausing a moment.

'Ever since I can remember,' he replies.

'How did you learn?'

'My dad taught me. It was the one good thing he did.'

'Are you close to him, though?' I ask, eyeing Jack over my shoulder.

He shrugs. 'We're pretty cool. He's probably closer to Drew than Agnes and me. We wanted to stay with Mom when he left. Here,' he says, moving my left hand with his to the tenth fret. I take the hint that he's done enough talking about his dad.

'Your fingers are so rough,' I murmur, as he shows me how to play the riff once more.

'Only on my left hand,' he says. 'It's from years of holding down the strings. But my right hand is smooth.' He runs the tips of his right hand along the side of my face, his thumb coming to rest on my bottom lip, leaving a ribbon of skin sparking with electricity. Every nerve ending in my body is on edge as I melt into him, turning to offer my mouth to his. Our kiss is warm and wet and makes me feel so very tingly. He takes the guitar out of my hands and props it up against the bed, pulling me to lie on top of him. A moan escapes my lips as he pulls me against him. He's breathing heavily as he gently eases me upwards so I'm sitting astride him, looking down at his face.

'What are you doing to me?' he murmurs.

My heart seems to be making an attempt to crash out through the bars of my ribcage. We stare at each other for a long few seconds and then jolt simultaneously as the downstairs buzzer sounds. That'll be Sam.

As I climb down from the bed, I notice him adjusting his crotch. His cheeks brighten as he meets my eyes.

'You might have to see yourself out,' he apologises, casting a quick look south. 'I don't want your dad to have me castrated.'

I giggle. I did that to him. The realisation makes me feel kind of powerful.

But, as I walk down the stairs alone, I muse that surely it's only a matter of time before he wants – maybe even needs – more from me. And what's going to happen if I'm not ready to give it to him? Will he get it from someone else?

As Sam drives out through the gates, I also realise that I forgot to ask Jack where he was last night.

Chapter 10

It's a ridiculous twenty degrees and sunny the next afternoon when Davey drives me to Soho House in West Hollywood to do the *Muso* interview. I'm meeting my bandmates there and I'm a bit gutted to receive a text from Jack telling me that the journalist has already arrived. I would have liked a moment to get my nerves under control.

As it is, the view distracts me from my jitters as I head along the walkway to the roof garden, listening to the sound of car horns honking below, helicopters whirring up above and my heels *click-clack*ing across the stone tiles. Soho House is on Sunset Boulevard on the top two floors of a fourteen-storey building and the view stretches across LA with downtown in the distance. I round the corner to see olive trees in large plant pots and lanterns in spherical wicker lampshades hanging from the underside of their branches.

I manage to avoid the temptation of scanning the crowd, looking for famous faces – I should try to be cooler than that – but I do have a quick search for my friends, locating them on a couple of sofas near the window.

'Hi!' I exclaim, attempting to sound confident as the journalist gets to his feet to shake my hand. 'Owen, right?'

He seems pleased that I remember his name. I recognise him from our San Fran gig. He's in his mid-twenties and he's wearing a crumpled black jacket over blue jeans. His brown hair looks recently slept-in.

'And I remember you, of course,' he replies with a friendly smile. 'You look just like your father.' He motions to a wicker garden chair situated between the two sofas. 'What can I get you to drink?' he asks, as I sit down.

'I'm happy with water.' I nod at the bottle of sparkling that rests on the table, flashing my bandmates a quick smile.

'You mind if I turn this on?' Owen asks, indicating the recording device on the table.

'Go for it,' Jack responds.

My eyes linger on him for a moment. He looks so cool, calm and collected, lazing back on the sofa. Brandon seems pretty relaxed beside him, but Miles is sitting forward with his elbows resting on his knees and his foot tapping an unheard beat. The tips of his black hair are dyed orange, and they look even more vibrant than usual. I'm guessing he's just had them redone.

'So let's get a few specifics out of the way first,' Owen says. 'When did you guys form?'

Brandon takes the lead, talking about how they got together when they were still at school. Someone is discussing a new TV show at the table next to us, saying that the pilot has been picked up. I try to concentrate on our interview and not eavesdrop on the conversations going on around me.

'Your original singer quit, right?'

My ears prick up.

'That's right,' Brandon replies, casting a long, accusatory look at Jack.

'What's that all about?' Owen asks with a grin, sitting up straighter.

'It's not important,' Jack says, glaring at his so-called friend. 'Things didn't work out with Eve, but we're in a better place now,' he says steadily.

'Why didn't things work out?' Owen asks, not about to let it drop. The seconds tick by. 'You got involved?' he asks Jack, as realisation dawns on him.

Jack shrugs, but doesn't deny it. I very much want to kick Brandon.

'And it went sour,' Owen sums it up. 'So where is she now?'

'In another band,' Jack replies.

I stare at him in surprise. *Is she? How does he know that? Has he seen her? Are they still in touch?*

'What's it called?' Owen asks.

'I can't remember,' Jack replies, scratching his chin. Owen looks dubious, and I am, too, but I imagine he'll find it out if he wants to.

'So, Jessie...'

I start as he fixes his attention on me.

'How did you come to be in All Hype?'

The interview gets easier after that, but I'm still mortified when Miles and Brandon rib Jack about the way he flirts with me.

'Luckily she's got a boyfriend,' Miles states jokily, 'otherwise we would've had to stick to our plan of getting a guy.'

I try to cover up my shock at the fact that my break-up with Tom has gone unnoticed.

'That's not true, dude,' Brandon interrupts. 'As soon as we heard her sing, it was a done deal.'

Miles nods, conceding, and my insides expand with warmth.

'So it had nothing to do with who her dad is?'

'Definitely not,' Jack says. The strength in his voice startles me – in a good way.

'It helps, though, right? I mean, you guys are gonna get more attention this way.'

'That's not always a good thing,' Jack points out calmly.

'Yeah, I mean, we want it to be about our music,' Miles chips in.

'Sure, your music's great,' Owen says, nodding. 'But it doesn't hurt that one of your songs has gone viral because Johnny Jefferson sang it at his daughter's birthday party. His daughter that he didn't even know existed until a year ago. That's a great story, man.' Owen looks at me. 'You've been on some journey.'

'You could say that,' I reply.

'And I hear you're gonna be singing on his new album?'

'How did you know that?' I ask with a frown.

'So it's true, then?' He raises one eyebrow.

'I don't think it's a secret...' I hope not, otherwise I'm in big trouble.

'Have you guys heard the track?' Owen asks my bandmates.

'I haven't even heard it myself yet,' I chip in before they can reply.

'Are you all doing solo stuff?' He looks around the table.

'I wouldn't say I'm doing solo stuff,' I quickly say, feeling tense at the expressions on my bandmates' faces. 'I'm just helping out my dad.'

'Right...' he says, moving on.

Luckily there aren't too many difficult questions after that and the interview flies by. I wish I could travel home with Jack – I really want to ask him if he's still in contact with Eve – but Davey is waiting and I'm still trying to make amends for messing him around after Jenna and Justin's party.

'See you tomorrow,' I say, touching my fingertips to Jack's when Brandon and Miles aren't looking.

'Four o'clock,' he replies, glancing at his friends. 'Guys, can we do four o'clock tomorrow? I'm having a late lunch with my dad and Drew.'

'Sure,' they reply.

'See you then,' I say meaningfully, turning to walk towards Davey, who's holding the door open for me. I climb in and he shuts the door, but I still feel on edge, even though the interview is over.

'I'm so glad I don't have to rush out of the house today for school,' I say the next morning, revelling in being able to come downstairs in my PJs for breakfast and find my family sitting round the table and dressed accordingly.

'Me too,' Meg says. 'Well, I mean I'm glad I don't have to rush to get Barney ready.'

Bee started back at nursery this week and he's been in a foul mood every evening because he's been so tired. Now he's chattering away quite happily and Phoenix is also trying to get a babbled word in edgeways between mouthfuls of Rice Krispies.

Johnny looks like he has a bit of a headache. He's resting his head against his palm and he smiles groggily up at me as Meg places two pills and a glass of water in front of him.

'Take these,' she says wryly.

Phoenix is around a year and a half old now and his vocabulary is coming along in leaps and bounds. I pull up a chair next to him and ask him what a cow says.

'Moo,' he replies obligingly.

I reach into his highchair and tickle his ribs. He lets out a squeal and spits Rice Krispies all over the place.

'Whoops!' I say with a laugh, grabbing a napkin.

'Dezzie,' he says in a silly voice, giggling.

'Jessie,' I correct him, my face close to his. 'Je, je, je.'

'De, de, de,' he tries to mimic me.

'Jessie, will you play with me today?' Barney asks, seeking my attention.

'Of course I will, buddy. What do you reckon – Lego?'

'YEAH!'

'Haven't you got band practice?' Meg asks me, smiling.

'Not until four.'

'Maybe we could all go somewhere this morning?' she suggests hopefully.

'No, I want to play here!' Barney complains.

'I've got to be in the studio, anyway,' Johnny tells Meg reluctantly.

The corners of her lips turn down. 'On a weekend?'

'Afraid so.'

He's putting the last touches to his album, but his schedule is not going to let up. He has to start rehearsing for his tour on Monday so the next couple of months are going to be really full-on, apparently.

'Nick sent our track over late last night if you want to hear it?' he asks, looking at me.

My eyes light up. 'I'd love to!'

We go upstairs to the studio straight after breakfast.

'How's this week at school been?' he asks, pushing the door shut behind me.

'Good,' I reply with a nod. 'Everyone's really friendly.' I sense his unspoken question so don't make him vocalise it. 'I haven't seen much of Sienna,' I tell him.

He looks relieved. I imagine he's hoping it was a flash-in-the-pan friendship – one that lasted only a night. I wonder if he's mentioned it to Meg. I don't want her to be upset.

'Hey, how did your interview go?' he remembers to ask, as he pulls up a chair and pushes one towards me. He worked late at the studio downtown last night so I didn't see him.

'Fine,' I reply. He sits with his hands clasped between his knees, listening intently as I fill him in on some of the things we were asked. I avoid talking about Eve.

'You're going to get more requests, but make sure you run them past me before agreeing to anything.'

I frown at him. 'Sure, that's fine if they come through your publicist, but I can't control what comes directly to the guys.'

'You can ask them not to agree to anything until you've checked with me,' he says, and it's not a request, it's a demand.

'Why?' I ask, bristling.

'Jack, Brandon and Miles are eighteen. But you're sixteen and I'm responsible for you. I'm not going to let you walk into anything unless I'm sure about it. OK?'

If Stu spoke to me like that, I'd feel patronised and pissed off, but right now Johnny's words have the opposite effect. It's still so strange to have a cool, connected dad whom I respect and who actually cares about me.

Chances are my bandmates won't appreciate him interfering, but I'll have to convince them that it's for the good of us all.

So I nod in compliance. Satisfied with that response, he gets on with what we came in here for: to play 'Acorn', our track.

I'm on the edge of my seat as Johnny's electric guitar comes in first, then a laid-back drumbeat follows and, soon after, his vocals. My head prickles as the room is filled with his deep, soulful voice, and then my own voice comes in and the prickling rushes all over my body. Oh my God. I can't believe that's me. I stare at Johnny in shock. He's avidly watching my reaction, a small smile on his lips. I press my hands to my face as a blush spreads across my cheeks. I have goosebumps all over. I look down at my arms and can actually see the hairs standing up on end.

'Me too,' he says, showing me his arm.

I let out a laugh, but stop abruptly. I want to focus on listening to the rest of the song.

As soon as it's finished, I jump up, unable to keep still.

He laughs and gets to his feet, too, wrapping his arms round me and giving me a brief kiss on top of my head.

'You like it?' he asks.

'It's amazing,' I whisper, staring up at him.

'I'm glad.'

There's so much warmth in his gaze. Tiny bubbles of happiness are popping inside my stomach, as though someone has shaken a can of Coke and opened it in there. 'When can I show my friends?' I ask.

'This is the only copy,' he replies, taking a CD out of the player. 'And it cannot, under any circumstances, leave this room.

The album is embargoed by the record company, so no one's supposed to hear it until nearer release and only then under strict regulations. But, if your lads are coming over anytime, you can play it to them.'

'Thank you!' I can't wait.

I listen to the song three more times before leaving the studio, and then I'm on such a high that I don't know what to do with myself. I've told Barney I'll play with him, but he's is in the pool with Meg and Phee, judging by the squealing and splashing noises carrying up the stairs from the open living room doors. I suddenly remember that I promised to call Tom. I emailed him earlier in the week and we agreed to touch base today. Annie doesn't work on the weekends so I have the office to myself. I pull up a soft, padded black chair on wheels and dial his number, feeling odd when I realise that I know it by heart.

'Hello?'

My heart clenches a little at the sound of his familiar voice.

'It's Jessie,' I reply. 'Are you OK to talk?'

'Sure.'

'Cool.' I settle back in the chair and put my feet up on the desk. 'So what are you up to? How was America?'

He starts to tell me about the week with his dad. It was the first time he'd met Riley, his dad's girlfriend – the woman his dad left his mum, sister and him for.

'What was she like?' I ask.

'Young.' He sounds on edge. 'She didn't seem that much older than me. She's really pretty, and *really* over-the-top friendly. She was trying so hard. I reckon I could've asked her to drive me to New York and she would've jumped at the chance.'

'Was she nice?'

'Yeah. I mean, I don't know how much of it is false, but she seemed pretty desperate for me to like her. I don't think she's going away anytime soon.' He pauses. 'Do you know, this is the first time I've been able to talk properly. Mum has been driving me insane with her questions.'

'It must be so hard for her,' I say.

'Yeah, it is. It's bad enough for me, seeing my dad kissing another woman. I hated it. I was so angry when I first went there, but after a few days I realised that I needed to chill out if I still wanted him in my life. And I do.'

'When will you see him again?' I ask.

'I'm not sure. He really wants Becky to go with me next time, but I don't think she will. She's finding it a lot harder to forgive and forget.' Becky is his older sister by three years.

We chat for ages about school, his trip and our mutual friends. He's blown away when I tell him about the track Johnny and I have recorded, and in the end I take the phone with me up to the studio and play it to him. I'm astonished when I check the time and realise we've been on the phone for over an hour.

'Yeah, I'd better go, actually,' he says. 'Chris will be here in a minute to pick me up.' They're heading to the pub, and I suddenly feel sad that I can't just hop in the car and go with him. I've missed talking to him. This conversation has felt like old times.

'Hey, did you know your stepdad and my mum have been hanging out?' he asks out of the blue.

'*No.* Really?'

'Yeah. They went to see a movie together the other night.'

'Did they?' I frown. 'Well, I suppose they got to know each other when they were over here.'

'Yeah, I get the feeling he's been looking out for her. Mum was so upset when I said goodbye to her at the bus station in LA.'

'Do you think they're just friends?' I ask warily.

'Yeah, I think so. I dunno. Would it bother you if it was more?'

I swallow. 'Yeah, it would,' I admit quietly. 'But I'd hate the idea of Stu moving on with anyone. The thought that my mum is replaceable...' My voice trails off.

'Hey, I'm sure it's nothing,' he says gently. 'I'm sorry I brought it up.'

'I miss you.' As soon as the words are out of my mouth, I wish I could take them back.

There's a long silence, and I'm about to wrap up our conversation and go bury my head in the sand, when he brings up the one subject that we've so far avoided.

'So are you and Jack official yet?'

'No. Not yet,' I reply, shrinking into myself a little.

'OK, Jessie, well, I've really got to go. Chat again soon?'

'Yeah. I'd like that.'

I'd like it a lot more than I should, I realise, as we end our call.

Chapter 11

Jack is distracted when I turn up for band practice later that afternoon.

'Will you go check on Agnes?' he asks, concern etching his brow. 'I think she needs a friend right now.'

I find her in her bedroom, curled up into a ball on her bed. 'Hey, you,' I say gently, going to sit beside her. Her face is puffy and her eyes are red from crying. She's clutching a sodden tissue and she breaks down again as soon as I place my hand on her back.

'I can't believe he's gone,' she sobs, shaking violently.

I hold her while she cries, my heart breaking for her.

Eventually she pulls herself together and assures me that she's fine, that I should go join my band, but I'm reluctant to leave her.

'Come to the games room with me,' I urge. 'We'll take your mind off him. And maybe we could do something later? Go out for dinner or catch a movie or something? In fact, I've got spa vouchers that Johnny and Meg gave me for my birthday! Why don't we plan a spa day?'

She smiles at me sadly. 'Thank you for trying to cheer me up. A spa day sounds great, and a movie tonight, too. I'll join you guys in a bit. Just let me sort out my face first.'

Brandon and Miles don't really know how to handle a downhearted Agnes, but Jack's concern for her is touching. He sets her up on the beanbags at the back of the games room with Diet Coke and snacks and keeps calling back to her as the afternoon spills into evening. She soon perks up.

We don't make a whole lot of progress with our songwriting, though, and Brandon makes a point of reminding us that our next gig is fast approaching. He also plans to line something up here in LA, but Jack wants to make sure we have some new songs ready first.

After our last session, I've become braver at suggesting lyrics. I used to write lyrics in England, but I never showed them to anyone. Everything we're doing now is new, though, and I love working as a team and batting ideas around. I've been toying with the keyboard Jack gave me for my birthday, but I haven't brought it with me today. I start my lessons on Monday, straight after singing, so for the moment I'm just messing about with different sounds and melodies.

Finally we call it quits and grab drinks from the fridge.

'Hey, I meant to tell you guys that I heard the track that I'm doing on Johnny's album,' I say casually.

'When can we hear it?' Jack asks with interest, so I explain about the embargo.

'Maybe we could do band practice at mine sometime so I can play it to you?' I suggest.

111

They all nod and agree, but I sense a lack of enthusiasm from Miles in particular. I hope I didn't sound like I was boasting.

Miles is seeing a friend tonight, but Brandon is up for a movie, as is Jack.

'Where's Maisie?' I ask from the back seat of Jack's car, trying to stave off my disappointment that Brandon's joining us. I can't kiss Jack in front of Agnes, anyway, I rationalise. She doesn't need me rubbing my love life in her face when she's upset about Brett.

'She's away with her parents,' Brandon replies, distractedly looking at his phone. 'Hey, Lottie's just texted me. Shall I see if she wants to join?' He looks over his shoulder at Agnes.

'Sure,' Agnes replies with a nod.

Lottie, it turns out, has promised her dad that she'll have dinner with him and her stepmother tonight, but she begs us to head to hers after the movie. We go for a burger first, followed by the ArcLight cinema in Hollywood. It's a far cry from the multiplex in Maidenhead, with its cushy, reclining chairs, fancy snack bars and in-house cafe-bar.

I sit between Jack and Agnes in the film – a horror movie, which was Agnes's choice – and, when all the lights go out, I'm in a state of edgy anticipation, knowing that Jack is so close, but I'm not allowed to touch him. Brandon is sitting on the other side of him, so we can't even hold hands, but Jack rubs his knuckles against the side of my leg, and even that small contact makes my skin burn. At one point, when Brandon bends over to put his empty popcorn bucket on the floor, Jack leans across and whispers in my ear: 'I hope you know how much this is killing me.'

His words make me shiver.

We head over to Lottie's house afterwards, and I'm not at all surprised to see six cars parked up on her driveway. It's typical of her to have impromptu gatherings.

'How was dinner?' I ask when she's done squealing her hellos. She's been drinking – that much is obvious.

'Such a bore,' she groans, rolling her eyes. 'C wouldn't shut up about this stupid show Mike's just cast her in. She drives me insane.'

C stands for Colleen, her stepmum, and Lottie can't bear her. In fact, her dad – the man she bizarrely refers to as Mike – now lets Lottie live in a log cabin in their enormous garden, rather than in the house. Even a huge mansion isn't big enough when Lottie wants space, apparently. I don't know a lot about what Colleen is like, but I do know that she's not much older than Lottie. She's also a budding actress, it seems. She certainly married the right man. Michael Tremway is a hotshot producer.

There are three fire pits flaming with warmth and I'm pleasantly surprised to see Gina and Margarita sitting around one of them, sipping cocktails.

'Jessie!' Gina cries, waving. I look over my shoulder to check Agnes is OK and spy her talking to a sympathetically nodding Lottie. I'm about to go and join Gina and Margarita, when I see Sienna exiting the log cabin.

'Hey!' she exclaims, as she catches sight of me. My heart lifts and then sinks. She seems genuinely pleased to see me, but I still feel uncomfortable as I give her a hug.

Jack joins us. 'You wanna drink?' he asks, resting his hand on my hip.

'Yeah, thanks,' I reply, smiling at him.

'He is so hot,' Sienna says dreamily, as he walks away. 'Does he have a girlfriend?'

'Er, yeah, I think he's seeing someone,' I reply, my stomach contracting unpleasantly.

She collapses into giggles and then tries to control herself by clapping her hand over her mouth. 'The look on your face.'

'What?' I ask, frowning.

'You think I didn't see you guys sneaking into the bushes last weekend?' she whispers with a mischievous smile. 'I won't tell a soul,' she vows, suddenly serious, but a moment later she's grinning again. 'Why is it a secret?'

I narrow my eyes at her, but, a moment later, I'm reflecting her grin. Bugger it. I do like her. Sorry, Johnny. Her light-hearted teasing is reminding me of how much fun we had at the Kellys' party.

I give her a brief lowdown on Jack and, by the time the guy in question returns with my drink, she's pretty much up to date.

'Thanks,' I say, aware of Sienna's gleeful expression as her eyes dart between us. Jack gives her an odd look and raises one eyebrow enquiringly at me. I shrug, smirking.

'I think I'll go chat to Morgan,' he says drily, leaving us to it.

I turn back to Sienna. It's time for an explanation on her part.

'Why didn't you tell me Dana Reed was your sister?'

She looks instantly uncomfortable, and then something seems to dawn on her. 'So *that's* why you've been avoiding me this week.'

I don't even try to deny it.

'I'm sorry,' she says, flashing me a repentant look. 'Maybe I should've said something, but she's been the bane of my life ever since I was born. I didn't want her ruining this for me, too.' She indicates the two of us. 'I like you. I wanted us to be friends. And I knew your dad would be against the idea after what went down between him and my sister.'

I feel a stab of pity for her. 'Well, I want us to be friends, too.'

'Are you two joining us or what?' Margarita calls out.

'Coming!' Sienna replies. I follow her towards the group.

'Hey, Jessie!' I look across the flames to see Peter, one of Lottie's *Little Miss Mullholland* co-stars, waving at me. Every time I see him now I'm reminded of when he was dressed like Fred from *Scooby-Doo* at Lottie's Halloween party: all blond and buff. He looks better as the brunette he really is, with his short dark hair, brown eyes and stubble. He plays Lottie's character Macy's long-lost brother in the show and all my friends back home fancy him. I met him last summer and he shared a few show secrets. He rises to give me a kiss on my cheek and I pull up a log seat next to him.

'I didn't get to talk to you on New Year's Eve,' I say warmly. 'What's the latest gossip?'

He sweetly obliges me with news of his upcoming storyline and I'm on the edge of my seat, listening to him. Eventually he turns the conversation around to me.

'I hear it was your sixteenth birthday recently?'

I cock my head to one side. 'You couldn't come?'

'I wasn't invited,' he replies with a shrug.

'Why not?' I'm aghast.

'Don't worry. You can't invite everyone to these things.'

'Maybe Agnes just stuck to schoolfriends,' I muse. Peter doesn't go to our school. 'I'm sorry,' I say, leaning in to give him a quick, apologetic hug. 'I would've wanted you there if I'd known anything about it.'

'Hey there!' Gina calls for our attention. I look over to see her holding her phone aloft. 'Smile!'

Peter throws his arm round me and pulls me close as we oblige.

While Gina adds filters to the shot, Margarita leans in to study the results. 'Wow, you guys look awesome with the fire in the foreground. That's a great shot.'

'Let me get one of you three,' I offer, nodding for Sienna to get into the frame, too.

Gina hands over her phone. Margarita and Gina are tiny and Sienna is tall, but, sitting next to each other, they're the same height and they look so beautiful: Sienna with her dark eyebrows and piercing blue eyes, Gina with her green eyes and curly red hair framing her face, and Margarita with her caramel-coloured eyes and glossy black locks falling over her right shoulder. I try not to look fazed by them as I take the photo.

'Straight to Instagram,' Gina says with a smile after I return her phone.

I really do get such a thrill at the thought of people back home hearing about me hanging out with these famous people, especially the girls who were a bit mean to me at school. It's exciting, going from being a nobody to a somebody. Maybe it's naïve of me, because I hope I don't get sick of it. I couldn't hide from the spotlight, even if I wanted to. Not as Johnny Jefferson's daughter.

After a while, I go to use the bathroom inside the log cabin. When I come out, I catch Jack's eye. He jerks his head, beckoning me over. He's still talking to his friend Morgan, but Morgan excuses himself to get a drink.

'Having fun?' Jack asks.

'Yeah,' I reply, perplexed at the edge I detect in his tone. 'You?'

116

He shrugs, glancing towards the fire pit. 'You two were looking pretty cosy.'

'Who, me and Peter?' I ask, bemused. 'We're friends.'

'Is that how he sees it?'

'Of course it is.' I stare at him. 'We've already established how many female friends *you* have,' I add accusingly. 'Christ, are we even exclusive?'

He stares at me in disbelief that quickly morphs into anger. 'You need to ask?'

'Yeah, actually, I do.' Heat spreads across my cheeks as I glare at him, demanding clarification. 'Am I your girlfriend, Jack? Or just someone you like to kiss from time to time?'

He casts a quick look over the crowd and then tugs me round the side of the cabin, out of sight of everyone.

'Are you serious?' he demands to know. 'Of course you're my fucking girlfriend. I'd be shouting it from the rooftops if it weren't for Brandon and Miles giving us crap.'

I gawp at him for a long moment and then have a sudden uncontrollable urge to laugh. He still looks thoroughly pissed off as I guffaw, but his anger evaporates and he smiles sweetly, stepping forward to take my face in his hands. My lips part as his mouth closes over mine and soon my knees are wobbling and I'm finding it hard to stay upright. I pull away, gasping. His chest is pressed up against mine and we're both breathing hard, competing to inhale the same air.

'Man, you can kiss,' he murmurs.

That's about all I can do, I think to myself uneasily. I really should mention that I haven't gone the whole way with anyone before.

'You're not so bad at it yourself,' is what I say instead, inhaling sharply as he runs his hands over the curves of my body.

'I should go and check on Agnes.' I have to force out the words because I really don't want him to stop.

'Next weekend,' he murmurs, drawing away and staring down at me intently. 'Let's do something, just the two of us.'

I nod up at him and feel a flurry of nerves. 'OK.'

Chapter 12

But my date with Jack has to be postponed because the next weekend is Johnny's birthday and, on Friday afternoon, I find myself sitting next to Barney in the back of a helicopter. This could be Johnny's last free weekend before he goes on tour, so he and Meg decided to take all of us to one of their favourite places to get away from it all: Big Sur.

Even Gramps is coming – Johnny's father. I never banked on getting a grandfather when I found out who my real dad was, so I can't wait to hang out with him properly.

This week has been mental. Between keyboard lessons, singing lessons, GCSE tutorials, homework, driving lessons – both behind the wheel *and* online – not to mention school and band practice, I haven't had a minute to myself.

Then yesterday morning Johnny landed this trip on me. Jack was pretty gutted when I had to cancel our date – I was, too – but it'll be good to have some quality family time, even if I do have a stack of homework to get through this weekend.

The closer we get to Big Sur, the more beautiful the scenery below becomes. One side of the helicopter looks out at the impressive Santa Lucia Mountains, and on the other is a rugged stretch of coast and the Pacific Ocean. I think I'm going to appreciate the view more from solid ground, though. This journey is making me feel a little queasy.

It's not long before the pilot is landing in a big field, and I look out of the window to see the long grass being flattened by the wind coming from the whirring rotor blades. When the noise dies down, Johnny's voice comes over the headphones in my ears, telling me that I can unclick my harness and Barney's, too.

The field turns out to be part of the property, which stretches all the way from the high cliffs overlooking the vast blue ocean, to a gently sloping hill that ends in a redwood pine forest. The mountains form a backdrop to the forest and I stare up at them in awe. I've never seen anything like this, apart from in the movies. I take a deep breath of the crisp sea air and follow the rest of my family towards the house.

It looks like a log cabin, but its size is deceptive. From the field, you'd think it's only one storey, but, when we go inside, I realise there are three built in tiers down the cliff with floor-to-ceiling glass offering the most breathtaking views of the ocean.

It's at moments like these that I have to pinch myself.

'Wow,' Meg utters, and I glance at her to see that she seems to be as blown away as I am. Barney has already gone in search of his bedroom, completely unfazed, but Meg flashes me a wide-eyed look and I feel a surge of warmth towards her. Barney and Phoenix were born into this lifestyle, but she's just an ordinary girl like me.

Johnny comes over and throws his arm round her shoulders, pressing a tender kiss to her forehead.

'Did Annie do good?' he asks, gazing down at her.

'Did she ever,' Meg replies, looking around.

'Cuppa?' Johnny says. 'I'll make them.'

'Yes, please,' she replies. 'I need one after that helicopter ride. Come on, Jessie, let's go and explore.'

I don't need to be asked twice.

Later, the whole family convenes in the living room on the bottom level, which has unspoilt views of the ocean. Big, comfy, fawn-coloured suede sofas packed with cushions surround a large glass coffee table and there are shaggy rugs underfoot. I sigh happily as I watch Johnny help Barney finish a jigsaw puzzle.

'This is the life, eh, kiddo?' Gramps says, nudging me conspiratorially.

'It's incredible!' I exclaim, before my thoughts drift guiltily towards Mum...

The main reason Mum didn't want to tell me about Johnny was because she was scared she might lose me. We didn't have much in Maidenhead – a shabby 1970s townhouse and a crappy car. I had a Saturday job so I could afford to buy my own clothes, though things were always tight. It's no wonder Mum worried that, if I had a choice between that life or this, I might be tempted. But I never would have left her.

Wouldn't I?

Tom still wants a relationship with his dad, even though it's hurting his mum. How can I honestly say that I wouldn't have wanted to spend time with my dad if I'd known years ago that he existed? I adore being with him.

But then Johnny hasn't always been as he is now. He went

through a really rough patch in his twenties, first when he split up with his band, Fence, and later when he was a solo artist and Meg was working for him. There was also the whole Dana hell.

I googled her the other night and felt sick to my gut at some of the articles I read and the sight of her hanging off my dad's arm, both of them looking pale-faced and half dead with the amount of drink and drugs they'd consumed. I looked Dana up because I'd been feeling guilty about Sienna – and yes, also because I was curious – but what I saw and read made me feel so uneasy that I ended up slamming down my laptop lid.

I already knew about my dad's history with Dana, of course, and I'd even seen a lot of the same pap shots, but he's no longer just a random celebrity. Looking at those pictures and reading those articles now, knowing Johnny's my dad, felt completely different.

Johnny has been on a tough ride, that's for sure, but thankfully he's in a better place than he's ever been. I'm not sure he could have handled me when he was younger – and I'm not sure that I could have handled him. I'm still struggling to blot out the *images* I saw of him and Dana – if I'd actually been there to witness what a screw-up he was, I probably would've ended up hating him.

So maybe Mum saved me from heartache. Maybe she knew what she was doing because she was well aware of what he was like. She was protecting me.

The thought gives me some comfort.

Stu told me that she'd intended to tell me about Johnny on my eighteenth birthday. I wish with all my heart that she'd lived to fulfil her promise.

'Right, I'd better check on the boys' dinner,' Meg says, getting to her feet. 'Johnny, can you bring them through?'

'You're very quiet,' Gramps says when they've left the room.

'I'm just thinking,' I reply softly.

'Johnny tells me you've been hanging out with Billy Mitchell's boy.'

This comment jolts me out of my reverie. The way he says Jack's dad's name makes me think that he knows the lead singer of Casino Girl personally.

'That's right. Have you met Billy?'

'A few times back in the day,' he replies. 'Partied hard, that one. I hear his son is a chip off the old block,' he adds slyly.

'Johnny doesn't know what he's talking about,' I state, jumping to Jack's defence.

'Steady on, lass.' He grins. He's only teasing me. I settle myself back in my corner. 'Young love, hey?' he says. 'You can't beat it. What am I saying? I still fall in love at the drop of a hat. No better feeling.'

'How is your love life?' I ask with amusement.

'Oh, you know. Still searching for the one.'

He winks at me.

Gramps looks exactly how you'd expect an ageing musician to be: tanned and a little leathery, with slightly too long, greying, light-brown hair. He's in his mid-sixties and he's thin and wiry, but you can see that he was pretty good-looking once. He's been around the block a few times.

The next morning we all go for a walk to the forest and gaze up at the towering redwood pines soaring into the sky. There are birds singing all around us, despite the noise of Barney jumping from fallen log to fallen log. Phoenix is on Johnny's back in a rucksack-style baby carrier and Meg smiles at them fondly before leaning in close to me.

123

'He used to refuse to even push a buggy, so this is a big step,' she whispers, nodding at her husband walking ahead of us.

I return her smile.

She's so pretty, so natural and kind-hearted. But, if I'm being completely honest, I wouldn't have placed my dad with her. It makes me feel sick and wrong to even *think* this, but in some of the pictures of Johnny and Dana – not the horrible ones of them looking wasted – they actually looked kind of right together. They suited each other. Dana's a fashionista rock chick with a real talent for music. Insiders used to call her the Next Big Thing before she screwed it all up. She couldn't be more different from sweet, stable Meg.

Dana gave one interview after the news about Johnny and Meg's engagement broke and I wish I could forget it, but unfortunately I remember it word for word: *'When Johnny's done playing mummies and daddies with Meggie Poppins, he'll come back to me. He knows we're soulmates. He knows we belong together. He may have issues with drink and drugs, but I'm his biggest addiction and I'll be waiting for him when he cracks. And he will crack. It's just a matter of time…'*

Her words sent a chill down my spine.

My conscience pricks me again about my friendship with Sienna. I have a strong feeling that Johnny hasn't told Meg that Dana is back in her life – in a roundabout sort of way. I can't say I'm surprised he's keeping it to himself. If *I* feel tainted by those articles and pictures, how must she react when she thinks about the hell she went through with Johnny? They've only been a proper couple for about two and a half years – the last pap shots of Johnny and Dana were taken around six months before that.

124

'I hope you don't mind that we sprang this trip on you,' Meg says, interrupting my thoughts. We've been walking side by side since her comment about Johnny refusing to push a buggy, but I fell quiet after that.

'Not at all!' I say enthusiastically, keen to banish my dark thoughts.

'I know you had a date planned with Jack,' she says.

'I'll see him next weekend,' I reply with a shrug, kicking at the carpet of pine needles under our feet as we walk.

'How are things going there?' She raises one eyebrow at me.

'Pretty well,' I reply.

'He's very good-looking.'

'He is,' I agree, smirking. 'I seem to have a thing for bad-boy rock stars.'

She laughs drily. 'I guess I do, too, although I didn't know it until I met your dad.'

I cock my head at her, thoughtfully. 'So you haven't always gone for bad boys?'

'God, no! No, it was just Johnny who had that effect on me.'

'What are you two talking about?' Johnny asks suddenly, looking over his shoulder at us.

'Never you mind!' Meg calls back at him.

He shakes his head and returns his attention to the front, but I'm pretty sure he's still listening.

'It seems to work for you both, in any case,' I say, inwardly wincing at the memory of Dana's claims in that interview.

She smiles affectionately. 'Yeah. It does. I guess sometimes opposites attract.'

I hear Johnny chuckle. He turns round to face us, walking a couple of steps backwards and grinning widely as he speaks.

'You're not my opposite, Nutmeg. You're the missing pieces of my jigsaw puzzle,' he says in a teasing tone. 'I wouldn't be complete without you.'

He winks at her and flashes me a cheeky look, spinning back round as she bursts out laughing. Warmth surges through me. Dana must've got it wrong. My dad is exactly where he's meant to be, now and forever.

After our walk, I go to my room to do some homework, but, when I glance over at my phone recharging on the side table, I decide to give Jack a quick call first. His phone rings out and goes to voicemail, so I try Agnes instead.

'Hey, you,' she says. 'How's Big Sur?'

'Amazing. So beautiful.'

'It is pretty up there,' she agrees.

'What are you up to? I just tried calling Jack, but he didn't answer.'

'He stayed out last night,' she says casually. 'Just over at Drew's,' she clarifies quickly. 'I'm sure it's nothing to worry about.'

So why am I still feeling uneasy minutes after we end the call?

I don't like this feeling. I usually feel confident, not insecure. Aren't your boyfriends supposed to bring out the best in you, rather than the worst?

I don't know why, but I have a sudden intense longing to speak to Tom, so, before I can think any more about Jack, I'm dialling his number. Some of the ice in my stomach thaws at the sound of the pleasure in his voice.

'Guess what?' he exclaims after we've exchanged hellos. 'I'm coming to San Francisco for half-term!'

'No way!' I gasp. That's in the middle of February – only three weeks away! 'But I'm going to be there, too! We've got a gig!'

'I know!' He laughs. 'Mr Taylor told me.'

It's funny hearing him refer to Stu as Mr Taylor. He's Tom's old Maths teacher.

'He's coming to visit you, right?' he asks.

'Yes! Wow.' My delight is suddenly tinged with apprehension. 'Hey, is Stu still hanging out with your mum?'

'Mmm. They went for dinner last weekend. I think they're seeing a movie tonight.' He sounds on edge.

My insides clench. 'What, just the two of them?'

'Yeah.'

'They're definitely dating, then.' My voice sounds flat.

'I'm not sure it's like that,' he tries to assure me. 'They just seem friendly. I haven't seen them kiss or anything.'

I swallow. I still don't like it. Aside from the fact that Stu might be moving on with his life after Mum, does he really have to hook up with my ex-boyfriend's mother?

'So will you come to my gig?' I ask, trying not to overthink it.

There's a moment's silence. 'Maybe,' he replies, and the enthusiasm has diminished from his voice. 'If I don't, perhaps we could catch up before or after.'

'I'll probably only be there for the one weekend. They don't have half-term here.'

'Really?'

He listens with interest as I tell him about the differences between schools here and at home. They don't even have time off for Easter. You just get one week off around the third week of March called Spring Break. School finishes much earlier for

127

summer and, a whopping two and a half months later, it starts up again – in the middle of August. So strange.

'Did Stu tell you that he wants me to do my GCSEs?' I ask Tom.

'No?!'

Once more, the time flies by as we chat. After a while, he divulges that everyone at school is still talking about me.

'What's this I keep hearing about a teen girl squad?' he asks and I can picture the look of bemusement on his face.

'It's just a bit of fun,' I reply with a giggle.

Celebrity gossip blogger Samuel Sarky coined the term, saying we're like a mini, much less famous, version of Taylor Swift's girl squad. A few other gossip sites have picked up on the phrase and run with it, which is pretty hilarious.

The Instagram pictures that Gina posted online got a crazy amount of attention this week, and three more tabloids have been in contact with Johnny's PR, Hannah, requesting interviews with me. Johnny told me to stick with *Hebe* magazine and turn the newspapers down, so I didn't even mention them to my bandmates. It's all very surreal. The team from *Hebe* are flying over on Tuesday so I have to skip band practice. But I'll be squeezing as many mentions of All Hype into the interview as I can to make up for it.

'How many followers on Twitter and Instagram do you have now?' Tom asks.

'I don't know. I haven't checked for a few days.'

'I hope you're having as much fun as you look like you're having,' he says. 'I went to a club last night and saw this girl sitting at the bar looking totally miserable. Then she got out her phone, plastered a completely false smile on her face, held up her drink and took a selfie, trying to make it look like she was having the time of her life. It was ridiculous,' he says scathingly.

'Well, I'm not doing that,' I tell him, feeling stung that he might think that I am.

'I'm not saying you are.' He's quick to put me right. 'At least I think I know you better than that.'

'You do,' I say in a small voice.

We both fall silent for a long moment.

'So are you official yet?'

I know what he's talking about and I'm instantly uncomfortable. 'Yes. He calls me his girlfriend, just not when our bandmates are around,' I clarify.

'Why?' His tone is disparaging.

'I've told you why,' I reply. 'It would complicate things. Can we not talk about Jack? How's *your* love life?'

The question spills off the tip of my tongue, but, as soon as I ask it, I dread his answer.

'What love life?' he responds.

I let out the breath I'd been holding, knowing I have no right to feel tense.

I try to sound light-hearted as I say, 'Are you telling me that the hottest boy in school doesn't have dozens of girls chasing him around?'

My joke falls flat on its face when he doesn't answer for a long time. Eventually he says, 'Yeah, right,' sarcastically.

We wind up our conversation soon after that.

I try Jack's number once more and, when he doesn't answer, I do my best to get on with some homework, but I'm preoccupied. My fingers are twitching, but I manage to resist calling him again. After a while I give up on what I'm doing and return to the living room, seeking a distraction in the form of my half-brothers. I find them sandwiching Gramps on the sofa, watching a Disney movie.

'Come and join us,' Gramps offers, patting the space beside Phee's cuddly body.

As soon as I sit down, Phee gets up and clambers onto my lap. I wrap my arms round his chunky waist from behind and press my cheek against his. He giggles and I instantly feel a lot better.

When the movie is finished, Barney drags me over to the enormous box of Lego that he found in the children's bedrooms here, while Meg takes Phoenix for his nap. I help Bee to build a couple of cars and we race them round the sections of the floor that aren't covered in plush rugs.

'What do you want to be when you grow up?' he asks me later when we're lying on our stomachs with a mound of Lego between us, building stuff.

I stare into his solemn green eyes and fight the urge to giggle. 'Well, I really like singing.'

'I wanted to drive a train, but now I don't know,' he confides.

'It's a long time before you have to make any decisions like that,' I tell him.

'Mummy says that I can't be a singer like Daddy.'

'Does she?' I ask, surprised.

'So you should probably think about what else you can do, too,' he finishes seriously.

'I didn't say that.' Meg casts her eyes to the ceiling as she enters the room, closely followed by a smirking Johnny. They obviously overheard. 'I just said that it's good to have a couple of alternatives. Right, Jessie?' She looks at me for help.

'Definitely,' I reply. 'Always good to keep your options open.'

'I think I would've been an architect if I hadn't been a singer,' Johnny muses, collapsing on the sofa.

'You've always said you would have been a racing driver,' Meg says, as she sits down beside him.

He grins at her sideways. 'I mean a normal job.'

'An architect? Really?' I ask with interest.

'Yeah, I love design and I love houses. I reckon I would've liked to combine the two as a job.'

'What would you do if you couldn't sing?' Meg asks me.

I shrug and sit up, thinking. 'I don't know. I mean, now that you've said that, Johnny, I do quite like the idea of designing houses. But I really hope the singing works out,' I add quickly.

'I reckon it will,' Gramps says encouragingly. 'You've got a stunning voice, you really do.'

'Aw, thanks, Gramps,' I say warmly.

'Why do you get called Gramps and I'm still Johnny?' Johnny asks with annoyance, frowning at his dad.

'Aah,' Meg interjects sympathetically, giving her husband's leg a tender squeeze.

Is he being serious? 'Does it bother you?' I ask with a furrowed brow. I know he's teased me about it in the past, but is there more to it than that?

'It does a bit,' he admits, and he looks quite vulnerable as he crosses his arms in front of his chest. Barney is still knee-deep in Lego and Phoenix is asleep in his room, but everyone else is staring at me.

'I guess it's because I've only just met Gramps, but I've known you as Johnny Jefferson for my entire life. It's harder to get used to calling you Dad.'

He nods, accepting my explanation, but I still feel bad.

131

'What are you making?' he asks, nodding at the Lego construction.

'A garage.'

He gets up and comes to lie on the floor beside me and we work in contented silence while Meg and Gramps chat between themselves.

'What are you after?' Johnny asks me, as I rummage through the pile in search of the largest-sized bricks. I tell him and he helps me look, throwing a few my way.

'Thanks.' Pause. 'Dad,' I add cheekily.

He purses his lips, but doesn't comment, making me giggle. The central heating is turned up and he's only wearing a short-sleeved T-shirt so his tattoos are visible. The B one catches my eye. He sees me studying it.

'Guess I'll have to get a J one soon,' he says under his breath.

My stomach flips. 'Would you?' I ask with surprise.

''Course I would,' he replies, making my heart swell.

'Can I get a tattoo?' I ask eagerly.

He throws his head back and laughs. 'I don't think so, no,' he replies, as I scowl at him.

'Is that your phone ringing, Jessie?' Meg asks suddenly.

My ears prick up. Yes, it is. I race to my room to see a missed call from Jack. I ring him straight back.

'Hey,' he says in his sexy, deep voice. 'You called earlier.'

'I did. Agnes said you stayed out last night.' I try not to sound as on edge as I feel.

'Yeah, crashed at Drew's. I did a gig with him last night.'

'DJ-ing? I didn't know you had anything lined up.'

'I didn't. He called me yesterday afternoon,' he explains.

'Was anyone else there that you knew?'

132

He pauses, then says warily, 'Have you got a sixth sense?' Before I can ask what he's going on about, he continues. 'I saw Eve.'

A wave of nausea crashes through me. 'Did you speak to her?'

'A little, unfortunately.'

'Why unfortunately?'

He falls silent for a long moment, as though trying to decide whether to tell me. 'She was being a bitch,' he says eventually. 'You don't wanna know.'

'Well, now I really do.'

He sighs heavily. 'She was giving me crap about you.'

'In what way?' I ask, my stomach clenching.

'She says we only chose you because of who your dad is.'

'Oh,' I say flatly. I thought he meant she was giving him grief about our relationship. It feels oddly worse that it's about All Hype and Johnny. Somehow that makes it even more personal.

'You wanted to know,' he reminds me.

'Does she know you and I are together?' I ask.

'Probably.' He doesn't divulge details. On second thoughts, he's right. I don't want to hear whatever catty comment she came out with.

'Don't let her get to you,' he adds.

'Do you think she wants you back?' I find myself asking.

'Probably,' he replies. My eyes widen, then he continues. 'I'm a catch,' he teases.

'You're such a dick,' I say with a laugh. He doesn't deny it, but I know he's smiling. 'So what is her band called?' I ask.

'Gold Leaf,' he replies.

'You lied to the journalist, then.'

'I knew it was Gold something, but I couldn't remember what. Anyway, why should we give her any press?'

I hate that now it feels like even more of a competition.

'What are you doing tonight?' I ask, trying to change the subject.

'Now that my girlfriend has cancelled my date?' he replies drily, and I get a thrill at the sound of him calling me his girlfriend. 'Aggie and I are gonna catch another movie.'

'Are you really?' I ask with a smile. 'You're such a good big brother.' I was an only child growing up. It was lonely. 'I wish I'd had a brother like you.'

'You wish I was your brother?' he asks, jokily startled.

'No!' I laugh. 'There's nothing sisterly about the way I think about you, Jack.'

'I should hope not.'

A shiver goes down my spine at the underlying meaning in his voice.

'Man, I really wish you weren't so far away,' he murmurs.

'Next weekend,' I say significantly, and my stomach twangs with nerves as I realise that that sounded like a promise. We seriously need to have a conversation about the sex thing.

It's Johnny's birthday tomorrow, and when I hang up I remember that I haven't yet written in his card. It was hard enough knowing what to get him – Jack helped me in the end. He came across a rare B-side record at work and I could have kissed him when he suggested it. I did kiss him, actually. Johnny might already have it, but then what *do* you get the man who has everything? Hopefully the thought will count.

I go to fetch a pen and the card out of the back of my suitcase and open it up, staring at the blank space. What do I write? Sudden inspiration strikes for my opening line and, after that, it's easy...

Dear Dad,

You'll smile at that, I think. And do you know what?
It came out surprisingly effortlessly, which is pretty nuts,
considering I didn't even know you a year ago.

I'm so glad I know you now. Thank you for welcoming
me into your crazy life. I love being a part of the Jefferson
family and I can't wait to celebrate loads more birthdays
with you.

Love Jessie xxx

That evening, Gramps goes off in search of a pub, accompanied by Lewis, and Meg jokes that he can only do the doting grandfather routine for so long before he cracks and needs a drink. I hang out with Johnny and Meg for a bit before finally calling it a night myself. I'm in my bedroom getting ready when I remember that I left my phone on the coffee table, so I set off back to the living room to retrieve it, halting in the darkened corridor when I hear Meg and Johnny talking.

'I'm going to miss you so much,' I hear Meg say. 'I can't get my head around the fact that you're going on the road without me.'

'I'm going to miss you, too,' Johnny replies in a strained voice. 'But you'll be there for some of the dates.'

I take it they're talking about his upcoming world tour. I poke my head round the corner to see them cuddling on the sofa in much the same position as I left them.

'Yes, but not enough of them,' she replies fretfully. 'I want to be there for all of them. I want to support you. I hate the idea of you doing this on your own.'

'I won't be on my own. I'll have my team around me,' he says calmly, before falling silent. He presses a kiss to her forehead, looking apprehensive. 'You're going to have to trust me, Meg.'

Is he talking about women or drugs or both? It *must* be drink and drugs. I can't believe he'd cheat on her – he dotes on her too much.

She withdraws and stares up into his face. 'Can you one hundred per cent honestly say that you trust yourself?'

He doesn't answer her and my heart races. *Come on, Dad!*

'I'm taking Barney out of school,' she declares suddenly, firmly, as though her mind has just been made up. 'We're coming with you.'

He sighs and tucks her hair behind her ears. 'What about Jessie?' he asks quietly.

She stares at him for a long moment and then her shoulders slump.

I can't bear this. Without even thinking, I walk into the room. Meg looks shocked when she sees me.

'I came back for my phone,' I say, sitting on the sofa next to Johnny. 'It's OK,' I try to reassure them. It's pretty obvious I was eavesdropping. 'I don't want you to stay behind because I'm here.' I stare at Meg. 'I couldn't bear that. I'm sixteen. I'm more than capable of looking after myself.'

Johnny shakes his head in disbelief. 'If you think that we're leaving you without a proper guardian, then you're out of your mind. There is *no way...*'

Meg looks drained, but clearly agrees with him.

'Yeah, but it's not Meg's job to look after me,' I state.

I'm only just settling in here, only just becoming accepted. I don't want to be the bane of her life, and, if she feels that she still needs to support Johnny while he's on tour, then I don't want to be responsible for stopping her from doing that.

'Maybe Stu could come over?' I suggest, and almost instantly dismiss the idea. He won't be able to leave his job.

'We'll think of something,' Johnny says, and then a commotion from the top of the stairs makes us all jolt.

'What the—' Johnny starts, but doesn't finish his sentence.

'Couldn't help overhearing,' Gramps says, stumbling slightly as he starts to walk down the stairs. 'How about *I* come over and look after the little blighter?' he says with a grin, opening his arms wide with a flourish as he reaches the bottom of the stairs.

I giggle. He's slurring his words.

'I don't think so, Dad,' Johnny says wryly. Meg looks completely unimpressed.

'Why not?' he asks spiritedly, swaying slightly. 'We'd have a laugh, wouldn't we, kiddo?'

'You bet we would,' I reply with a grin, nodding. I bloody love this idea.

'I think we might talk about it some more when you're sober,' Johnny states, getting to his feet. 'That OK, Jess?' He squeezes my shoulder.

'Sure,' I say with a nod, standing up, too. 'But we'll have to think of something, because I don't want to be a burden.'

'You're not a burden,' Meg says quickly.

I flash her a small smile. Even if her heart is in the right place, we both know that's not true.

Chapter 13

'What's your new school like?' the interviewer from *Hebe* magazine asks conspiratorially.

His name is Russ and he reminds me of Ed Sheeran with his short ginger hair and a generous sprinkling of freckles. I liked him as soon as he introduced himself.

It's Tuesday afternoon and we're sitting in the Mondrian Hotel's Skybar on a cushioned bench seat framed by large windows overlooking LA. This is one of Agnes's favourite places to grab a coffee – the open-air bar is full of beautiful people lounging around a central swimming pool. We've already done the photos – up in Beverly Hills with the Hollywood sign in the background – and now we're onto the words.

Johnny decided it was too much of an invasion of privacy to have them photograph and interview me at home, even though he sniggered at the sound of our clichéd Hollywood backdrop. That made me smile, too, but there's no denying it was exciting being photographed in public with that famous sign in the background, even if it was a little cheesy.

'It's different,' I say in answer to Russ's question. 'You don't have to wear school uniform, for a start.'

'I was thinking more along the lines of what it's like to go to school with so many famous teenagers?'

I laugh. 'There are a fair few of those.'

He wrinkles up his nose and leans in closer. 'What are they like? Is Margarita Ramirez as much of a diva as they say?'

'Not at all,' I reply adamantly. 'She's been nothing but nice to me. On my first day of school, she offered to show me to the office, which was really sweet of her because I was nervous.'

'I bet you were.'

'My dad gave me a lift on his motorbike and she said, "That's one way to make an exit," or something like that.'

I almost said Johnny, then, but remembered to refer to him as my dad.

'You get lifts to school on the back of Johnny Jefferson's motorbike? That is so cool!' Russ effuses.

'Only on my first day. He wanted to take me, but mostly I go in a car with their driver.'

'Your life has changed so much—'

'You're telling me,' I interrupt him.

'Do you ever just want to pinch yourself?'

'Every day. I had to pinch myself at the weekend when we went to Big Sur for my dad's birthday. The house we were staying in overlooking the ocean was incredible.' I describe it to him. 'It's hard to believe I'm just an ordinary girl from Maidenhead.'

'Do you miss anything about your old life?' he asks.

I shrug and swallow. 'Of course,' I reply around the sudden lump in my throat. 'I miss my friends and seeing my stepdad every day. I miss the familiarity of my old school. And I miss my home and my bedroom. We didn't have much, but it was mine and I have a lot of happy memories there.'

He nods, seriously, and I can tell that he's thinking about asking me about Mum, but he doesn't.

'So what's the best thing you've bought with your new-found wealth?' he asks with a grin.

We're sticking to the fun stuff and I can't say it's not a relief. This is *Hebe* we're talking about, after all. We're not on *Oprah*.

Because the interview is about me and the way my life has changed personally, I don't get to talk about All Hype as much as I'd like to. Luckily, the *Muso* magazine interview hits the shelves on Thursday, so at band practice the guys are all over it.

It's a good, strong piece – half a page, which is amazing for an unsigned band, even if they did miss out loads of stuff. It flags up our upcoming gig in San Francisco, thankfully, and it also makes a lot out of the fact that I'm Johnny Jefferson's daughter. I'm worried about that sort of publicity at first, especially remembering what Eve said, but then Brandon reads aloud Owen's verdict on our last gig, saying that I: 'more than hold my own as a front girl'.

I'm bursting with pride as Brandon wraps his arms round me and lifts me from the ground.

'That's cool,' Miles says with a laugh, patting my back as Brandon puts me down again.

'*Very* cool,' Jack adds, and I purse my lips as he hooks his arm round my neck and plants a kiss on my cheek, knowing how tame the gesture is compared to what he'd like to be doing.

On Saturday evening, Jack turns up in his Audi to collect me. I had an argument with Johnny earlier about security measures for tonight. He's agreed that Jack can drive me on the condition that Sam follows and comes into the venue with us. I'm gutted.

He came out with his usual, 'you won't even know he's there,' line, but he's wrong. It was supposed to be just Jack and me tonight.

Still, I'm trying not to let it get to me. Gramps left to go back to the UK yesterday after he and I spent the week trying to convince Johnny and Meg that he's capable of being my guardian while they're away on tour. Johnny is still thinking about it, so I don't want to rub him up the wrong way by making his life difficult.

As we're going to a gig, I've dressed down tonight in skinny black jeans and one of Agnes's cool neon-on-black graphic tees, but I've spent ages getting ready. I've scrunched my hair and I'm wearing it down so it's got a tousled effect, and my eye make-up is dark and sultry. This is the first time Jack and I will be out together without our friends around. Who knows what the night has in store?

Again, I have to remind myself that Sam's going to be there…

I jump when the doorbell goes, even though I'm expecting Jack. I have to force myself to walk steadily and calmly down the stairs.

Johnny is sitting on the living-room sofa, watching telly. I still call him Johnny most of the time in my head, even though I'm trying to call him Dad to his face.

141

'Ask him in,' he calls.

'I think we'll just get going,' I reply edgily.

'No, ask him in.' He looks over his shoulder at me. 'This is your first proper date, right?' Damn me for telling him that. 'I should meet your boyfriend,' he adds.

'You've met him loads of times,' I point out with a frown.

He raises his eyebrows at me.

'Fine,' I mutter, going to the door.

My heart flips at the sight of Jack standing there. He's so gorgeous. His black hair, longer and messier on top, has been pushed back from his face, offering a clear view of his blue-grey eyes and his long dark lashes.

'Hi,' I say, feeling shy all of a sudden.

'Hey.' He smiles down at me. 'You ready?'

'Johnny, I mean, my dad, wants you to come in.'

He cocks an eyebrow. 'Really?'

'Mmm-hmm,' I say ominously.

He shrugs. 'OK.'

I lead the way back inside.

'Hey, Jack,' Johnny says casually, getting up from the sofa.

'Hi,' Jack replies.

Johnny leans against the back of the sofa and crosses his arms. 'You guys are going to see Contour Lines tonight, hey?'

'That's right.' Jack nods.

'My friend Christian wrote their biography not that long ago. Should be a good gig.'

'I hope so,' Jack replies, shoving his hands into his pockets. His shoulders are hunched and he seems a little awkward.

'You know Sam is coming.'

I roll my eyes. *Of course he does.* I had to break it to him earlier.

142

'He'll stay out of your way as long as he can keep Jessie in sight,' Johnny says. 'So don't go sneaking into any dark corners.'

'Johnny!' I squawk. 'I mean, Dad,' I mumble.

Johnny flashes me an amused look. The combination of Jack's mortified expression and me calling him 'Dad' seems to lighten his mood.

'Have you heard Jessie's track on my album yet?' Johnny asks Jack, unfolding his arms. He instantly seems more open and friendly.

'No, no, I haven't,' Jack replies, shaking his head.

I had planned to host band practice here one day so my bandmates could hear it, but that hasn't come about yet. I'm still worried about sounding like I'm boasting, and no one else has brought it up.

Johnny jerks his head towards his studio at the top of the stairs. 'You got time?'

'Definitely,' Jack replies eagerly.

Johnny leads the way up the stairs. I pinch the tips of Jack's fingers with mine as we walk side by side. He flashes me a quick smile, but he's clearly on edge.

It's kind of cute that he's fazed. I'm not sure how much of it is because Johnny is famous and how much of it is because he's my dad.

Jack seems properly impressed by the song and my cheeks flush as he smiles at me. I look at Johnny to see that he, in turn, is watching Jack's reaction, and there's something about his expression – a certain satisfaction – that makes me think that Jack is passing whatever test he's unwittingly being put through.

'OK, well, you guys have fun,' Johnny says when we're leaving the room.

'Thanks, we will. Hey, can I just show Jack my bedroom?'

Johnny recoils and Jack looks horrified. I have to laugh.

'You said you wanted to see it,' I say, looking at Jack.

'Yeah, but—' He glances at Johnny.

Johnny's face breaks out into a grin as he turns and jogs down the stairs. 'Leave the door open,' he calls back over his shoulder.

'Did you have to say that?' Jack hisses, as soon as we're inside my room.

I'm trying to stifle a fit of hysteria. 'The look on your face,' I say, giggling.

He roughly shoves his hair back and clamps his hands at the back of his head.

I grin and wave my arms at our surroundings. 'Ta-dah!'

Finally he chills out enough to look around. 'You weren't kidding when you said it was called the White Room.'

The plush carpet is white, the bedspread, pillows and cushions on the enormous bed are white, and the shiny, lacquered wardrobes lining the back wall are also white. But I've been trying to accent the white with colour – posters, fairy lights, photo frames. I've got a long way to go.

'I think I need to get a new bedspread.' I sit down and bounce lightly on the bed. Jack stares at me. I pat the space to my right. He glances at the door, then shakes his head.

'I think I'll stand.'

I screw up my nose. 'Are you honestly freaked out about my dad?'

I spoke in a whisper, but he still looks alarmed and tells me to 'Shhh!'

I grin and get to my feet, walking over to him and looping my arms round his neck. His shyness is making me feel bold. He's tense as I press my lips to his.

'We should get going,' he murmurs, looking down at me out of the corner of his eye.

In the end, we decide to ride with Sam. There's no getting away from the fact that he's coming with us, so it seems a bit pointless taking two cars.

The concert is brilliant, but it's a while before Jack loosens up. He's sexy as hell when he's hot and sweaty – we've both been jumping along to the music – but, when I turn to face him, he tenses. We just can't get away from the fact that we're constantly being watched.

'No one's going to shoot you for kissing me, you know!' I shout in his ear, sounding sardonic.

'I'm not taking any chances!' he shouts back.

I don't think this is his idea of how he was expecting our first date to go, and neither, frankly, is it mine.

I doubt Jack's other girlfriends have put him through this, and that thought makes me feel uncomfortable. As the night wears on, I'm beginning to realise we need some proper time alone.

'How about I ask Sam to drop me at yours,' I whisper when we're sitting in the back of the car, on our way home. His mum and stepdad seem to be a whole lot more laid-back than mine are.

'My car's at your place,' he reminds me.

'You could get a lift over tomorrow to collect it,' I suggest. 'In fact, Agnes and I are going for our spa day – maybe she could drop you over in the morning?'

He stares at me for a long moment and then nods. I lean forward to tell Sam of our change of plans.

'I've got orders to get you home by midnight,' he replies in his deep drawl. I swear he reaches lower octaves than anyone else I know.

'That's fine.' It still gives us an hour.

I've completely forgotten about Agnes, of course, but, as soon as we're out of the car, I remember.

'She's probably asleep,' Jack says, but, when we pass her room, the lights are spilling out from under a crack in the door frame. My heart sinks. I love my friend, but she'll have me for the whole day tomorrow. Still, it feels wrong to sneak past and my conscience gets the better of me. Jack sighs as I knock on her door.

'Who is it?' she calls.

I open the door and poke my head round. 'Me.'

'Hey!' She's lying in bed with a book and she sits up, looking happy to see me. 'Come in!'

'I'll be in my room,' Jack says, turning away. I flash a rueful look at his departing back, then go inside and shut the door.

'How was the concert?' Agnes asks. 'Nice T-shirt,' she adds with a smirk.

'I love this one of yours.' I tell her, perching on the end of her bed. 'The gig was awesome. They had the most amazing laser display. How are you? What have you been doing tonight?'

'FaceTiming Brett,' she replies downheartedly.

'Is he missing you?' I ask.

She nods sadly. 'He had to go and do something, but he's calling me back in a bit.'

'You still on for our spa day tomorrow?'

'Definitely. I can't wait.'

'Me neither.'

146

She smiles at me and nods at the wall that she shares with Jack's room. 'It's OK. You can go.'

I grin and get to my feet, pressing a kiss to her cheek. 'It's been killing us that Sam had to babysit tonight,' I confess in a rush.

She grins at me as I back out of the room.

Jack is playing The Strokes when I walk down the hall. I knock on his door softly, but don't wait for him to tell me I can go in.

'You were quick,' he says, seeming surprised. He's lying on his bed with his arms folded behind his head.

'Your sis is pretty switched on. She could tell I needed some alone-time with you.'

He props himself up on his elbows. 'Come here.'

I don't need to be asked twice.

'At last,' he whispers, when I'm finally in his arms. I tilt my face up to his and we kiss, slowly and languidly. His tongue brushes against mine, making me shiver all over. He places one hand on my hip, his thumb slipping beneath my T-shirt to trace the curve of my waist. I breathe in sharply and then my hands are on his taut stomach, wanting to feel the skin under his T-shirt. His kisses become more frenzied, more urgent, and then he roughly manoeuvres me so I'm sitting on top of him. His hands slide up the back of my top and brush over my bra strap. I gasp into his mouth.

'Jack.'

He doesn't stop kissing me.

'Jack,' I say again and he pauses, realising I have something to say.

'What?' He pulls back so he can look at my face.

I've got to tell him.

147

'I haven't gone the whole way with anyone before,' I whisper.

His attention sharpens. 'You're a virgin?'

I nod.

'But Tom...'

I shake my head. 'We never did it.'

'When you said you were serious about him, I thought... Damn.' He takes his hands out from under my top and rests them lightly on my hips.

'I'm only fifteen. Well, sixteen now,' I correct myself, blushing.

'I forget you're not older,' he admits with a furrowed brow.

I tuck my hair behind my ears, looking at him uncertainly, and then I decide that yes, I do want to know, even if I'm not going to like the answer.

'How many girls have you slept with?'

He takes a deep breath.

'Yes, we really are having this conversation now,' I tell him drily, mimicking his comment at my birthday party just under a month ago.

'Six,' he replies on an exhalation of breath.

'*Six?!*' I exclaim. 'Who?'

Too uncomfortable now to continue sitting astride him, I slide off, perching on the bed at his side.

'Eve,' he replies, folding his hands behind his head again. 'You don't know the others.'

I feel a small flood of relief. 'Not Lottie?'

'No!' he scoffs. 'Sure, we've messed around a bit, but nothing like that.'

'Great,' I say sarcastically, still not happy to hear from his own lips that he's made out with her, even though Agnes did warn me. 'Who was your first?' I ask.

'A friend of Drew's,' he replies.

'Was she older?' His brother is two years his senior.

'Yeah.' He shrugs, then frowns, thinking. 'They've all been older, actually.'

'How old is Eve?'

'Nineteen,' he tells me.

'How old were you when you lost your virginity?'

'Fifteen.'

That's younger than I am now, I think dolefully. 'Were any of the girls you slept with virgins?'

'No.' He stares at me directly.

'God,' I mutter, looking at the wall. That's going to make me seem so inexperienced.

'Are you done with your questions?' he asks, raising one eyebrow at me as I look back at him.

'I think so.' *For now.*

He gives me a small, thoughtful smile and opens his arms up. I lie down beside him and rest my face against his chest.

He was surprisingly forthcoming about his answers. I have to give him credit for that. 'We'll take it slow,' he murmurs, holding me tight.

The scary thing is, I'm not sure I want him to.

Chapter 14

'How did it go last night?' Agnes asks with a significant look.

We're sitting in the cafe at the spa, both dressed in white dressing gowns and having our second mint tea of the day. I reach for a biscuit and shrug. 'Fine.'

'I know he's my brother, but I won't tell him anything we talk about.'

'Does he confide in you about me?' I ask candidly.

'No,' she replies with a shrug. 'But I can tell he likes you. More than some of the other girls he's gone out with.'

I sigh. 'I like him, too.' *Really* like him. 'But I'm freaking out a bit. If we break up, I can't see me staying in the band, and that seriously upsets me.'

'God, can you imagine them having to go through that audition process again? Rock on.'

The thought makes me smile, but I'm morose a moment later.

'Aw,' she says. 'Listen, don't worry about it. Everything works out for a reason, right?'

I used to think so. But then my mum died and nothing anyone ever says will make me think her death was for the best.

I don't say this out loud to Agnes. I just nod agreeably and say, 'Sure,' before moving the conversation on.

Agnes has been noticeably absent from most of the teen girl squad pictures that our famous classmates have posted online. I've been wondering if she minds.

She shakes her head and rolls her eyes when I ask.

'No offence, but most of it's bullshit. Margarita and Gina are all about the publicity.'

I'm a little hurt. Is that all Agnes thinks I am to them? A publicity stunt? I thought they liked me.

'Sienna's not like that, though,' I say defensively. 'She's pretty cool. We're going shopping this week, actually.'

'When?'

'Wednesday. I'm not doing my driving lessons after school any more so I have some more free time during the week.'

I say free, but I should be at home revising for my GCSEs, doing my online Driver's Education course or practising my singing and keyboard skills, but jeez, a girl's gotta have a break sometime.

'Why have you stopped your driving lessons?' Agnes asks with a frown.

'I haven't stopped them. But from this week I'm going to be doing them on the way to school instead.' I've been practising on the driveway in my cool little car and I'm really starting to get the hang of the clutch now. Most teenagers here learn on an automatic, but Johnny was insistent I master 'a stick' – the

151

American term for manual cars. Anyway, earlier he suggested I move my lessons to the morning so I can make the most of the journey to school. My driving instructor is an ex-Navy Seal, so Johnny just about trusts him to get me there safely. By the end of this week, I will have clocked up all six of my required hours, but Johnny wants me to keep going. The more practice I get, the better I'll be when I actually get my provisional licence. I'm lucky he's happy to pay for my lessons.

'Well, I imagine Sienna can be trusted when it comes to helping you pick clothes,' Agnes says, pretend huffily. 'As long as she doesn't get any ideas about being your stylist.'

'Never,' I vow.

A woman in a pristine white uniform comes into the room. 'Miss Jefferson and Miss Mitchell?'

I tense at the sound of my name. I know Annie made the booking under Pickerill-Jefferson, but I feel like I'd be making too much of the issue by correcting the woman.

'Yes?' we say in unison.

'We're ready for you now.'

Time for our massages…

'You're not bothered about Sienna's sister any more?' Agnes asks as we follow her.

'A bit,' I admit. 'But Johnny hasn't mentioned her for a while, so I think I'm off the hook.'

'Until the next photo of the two of you gets posted online,' Agnes points out wryly.

That's exactly what happens a few days later when Sienna and I finally make it out for our shopping trip.

We're in a gorgeous little boutique called Elodie K on Melrose

Place and Sienna is holding up a pair of black stiletto-heeled boots with gold butterflies coming out of the back of them.

'These Sophia Websters would look *amazing* on you.'

'I'm not sure I could carry them off,' I say with trepidation.

'Are you kidding? Of course you could,' she insists. 'You should try them on.'

I shrug and take them from her. I don't suppose it could hurt. Sienna has great taste, but she's into high-end fashion, whereas I'm more of a rock chick.

'And these,' she says, passing me a pair of red stiletto sandals with a lace, fanned detail around the heel and ankle.

'They're not very me,' I say. 'Why don't you try them on?'

She checks the price. 'Why not?'

I take a quick look at the price of the boots and gulp at the sight.

How much money? I hope Johnny doesn't think I'm taking the mick.

'Your dad can afford it,' Sienna says drily, seeing my expression. 'Mine too, for that matter.'

'What does your dad do?' I ask, as we take a seat on a padded black sofa and wait for the shop assistant to come back with our size.

'He's a talent agent.'

'Is he very successful?'

'Not as successful as my mom.' She notices my quizzical look and shrugs. 'My dad owes me. He wasn't around for a lot of my childhood.'

Suddenly she's on her feet and making a beeline for a sparsely filled clothes rack. I watch as she flicks through the pieces hanging there. She pulls out a tiny dress with a white puff skirt and colourful dragonfly wings printed onto it. The bodice is fitted and strapless.

'This?' she asks me.

'It's pretty, but I can't think when I'd wear it...'

'What about Gina's launch party?' She holds it up against her body and cocks her head to one side.

The launch party for Season 3 of *Blood Ten*, the crime drama that Gina stars in, is this Saturday. Gina cornered me outside my locker this afternoon and said that an invitation from the show's publicity team would be making its way to me via Johnny's PA. She said she was only inviting a few people from school, so not to mention it to anyone else. I felt very honoured, even if Agnes is right about her just liking the publicity of this whole teen girl squad thing.

'It is kind of cool.' I stand up and walk over to Sienna, my heels clipping across the polished dark-wood floor. The lighting in here is like an art gallery and the merchandise works of art. There are only a few pairs of shoes and handbags on the glass shelves. I hold the dress up against myself and look in a mirror.

'Sure, I'll give it a go,' I say.

Half an hour later, we walk out of the shop. It's sunny again, despite being early February. Sienna slips her glasses back onto her nose and hooks her arm through mine.

'Paps,' she whispers, grinning. She swings her shopping bags and broadens her smile, then acts as though the paparazzi are not even there as she continues to chat merrily away to me. I follow her cue, ignoring them, but right behind me is the big bear of a man that is Sam.

Why is it that so few of my friends have bodyguards?

Even Margarita and Gina get to walk around pretty much unaccompanied unless they're going to be in crowded public places. I suppose it's a testament to the level of Johnny's fame that even his 'part-time daughter' chalks up a need for security.

Sometimes I want to ask how much of it is really necessary, but then I remember that someone tried to kidnap me last year and that shuts me up.

Johnny is back late that night after tour rehearsals, but he hunts me out soon after he arrives home. I'm in my bedroom, messing around with melodies on my Yamaha. I still can't believe Jack bought it for me.

'I thought you weren't taking it any further with Sienna,' Johnny says, pulling a chair out from my new desk and sitting down to face me. Annie ordered the desk earlier in the week because the downstairs office isn't always quiet or private enough for me to do my homework. Sometimes she has to work late to make phone calls abroad.

'How did you kn—?' My voice trails off. Of course he knows. Sam or Annie would have been onto him immediately. 'We just went shopping,' I say instead. 'I like her, Joh— I mean, *Dad*. She's nice. She's not like Dana.'

His eyebrow twitches even at the *sound* of Dana's name.

'I'd prefer you to stay away from her,' he says, folding his arms and sitting back in his seat.

This makes me angry. As if I don't have enough on my plate! The one time I get to do something as ordinary as shopping, he has a go at me!

'Seriously, do you know how ridiculous you're being? Sienna doesn't even speak to Dana! I need to let my hair down. She's nice to me. She's funny. We get along. I'm so busy at the moment with school and GCSEs. God, why am I even bothering with GCSEs? It's crazy!'

'OK, OK,' he says, holding his palms up and looking taken aback. 'Forget I said anything. Fine, if you're sure about her. Just be careful.'

'I will be. You have nothing to worry about.'

'I won't bring it up again,' he promises, but he's still eyeing me with trepidation.

'Good.' I let out a frustrated sigh and press the off button on my Yamaha. I've had enough for one day.

'Did you have a good time with her?' Johnny asks, raking his hand through his hair.

'It was great,' I reply reluctantly, only slightly appeased by the change in his tone.

'You looked like you bought a lot of stuff.'

My face falls.

'Samson Sarky,' he adds, to explain how he knows. Pictures of Sienna and I must already be online. That was quick.

'Do you mind me spending your money?' I ask warily.

He pulls a face. 'Of course not.'

My shoulders sag with relief, but then he adds, 'On one condition.'

'What?' I ask cautiously, tensing up again.

'I don't want you to quit doing your GCSEs.'

I sigh. 'Why do you care about that? You didn't even do A levels.'

'I didn't, no, but I do care about your schooling and Stu does, too. You should do it for him, if not for me, if not for yourself.'

My mind shows me a mental image of Stu's face, his eyebrows

pulled together over the top of his horn-rimmed glasses. He would be so disappointed if I quit.

'Fine,' I say morosely. 'Guess I'd better get on with some studying, then.' I nod at the desk he's sitting at and he gets to his feet, giving my shoulder a sympathetic squeeze before leaving my room.

But the first thing I do when I open my computer is check out the online celebrity gossip sites. I can't resist.

I snort with amusement at the sight of Sienna and me walking laughingly along the pavement, arms hooked together as we swing our shopping bags. She's wearing a minidress and is absolutely stunning with her blunt-cut dark hair, big sunglasses and tanned legs, but I don't look so bad myself with my tousled blonde hair, jeans and heels. She's wearing flats so luckily she doesn't completely dwarf me.

Seeing myself in pictures like this and on online gossip sites is very surreal. It's like I'm not looking at me, only my public persona. It would be easy to get caught up in that persona, but I think I'm doing a pretty good job so far of staying true to myself. I hope so, anyway.

Chapter 15

A few days later, Davey drives me into West Hollywood, where Gina's launch party is taking place.

I'm meeting Sienna there and I'm nervous about arriving on my own. I was shocked on Thursday afternoon at band practice when I found out Agnes hadn't been invited. I know Gina asked me not to mention it to anyone, but I couldn't believe Agnes wouldn't be on the guest list so I casually asked if she and I could head there together. She was a little taken aback that I was going and she wasn't – I felt so bad.

I told her I'd text her and Jack later, thinking that maybe I could swing by theirs on the way home, although Jack did say he'd meet me in town instead. I loved this idea, until Johnny told me I had to stay put in the venue if I wanted to go without Sam.

The party is taking place in the penthouse suite at hip hotel The London. A red carpet has been laid out at the front and a huge crowd of people lines the barriers, screaming and shouting for autographs and selfies with celebrities. At the other end of the carpet is a roped barrier, behind which a horde of photographers is snapping off shots.

I'm wearing the dragonfly dress with my hair in a loose, tousled bun, high up on my head, and as I walk down the red carpet, trying not to slouch, I spy Sienna at the end with Rafael – the male model from our class who's just landed the CiaoCiao campaign. She's wearing a fitted dark-red dress and is staring sultrily at the cameras while she hangs off Rafael in his well-cut black suit. He's tall, tanned and gorgeous and has the most gravity-defying cheekbones I've ever seen. He and Sienna look amazing together – they're totally working the cameras.

I smile fondly as I approach, enjoying the opportunity to watch my model classmates in action. I'm preparing to walk straight past into the venue, but, to my surprise, one of the paps calls out my name. As soon as one person says it, others join in, and then Sienna notices me and her eyes light up as she beckons me over. I stand between her and Rafael and try not to look like all my Christmases have come at once.

Our photo session is over pretty quickly because Joseph Strike arrives. I force myself to walk inside, resisting the overwhelming urge to throw myself at his feet, screaming hysterically, but my heart is hammering with adrenalin. I never did pluck up the courage to quiz Meg about what Agnes had said: that she and Joseph used to date. She and I don't really have that causal sort of relationship – not yet, anyway. Maybe I can ask *him*, I think with a cheeky smile. As if I'd be able to get anywhere near him without dissolving into a gooey mess...

Sienna, Rafael and I take the lift up to what claims to be LA's largest hotel penthouse suite. Sienna tells me that the interiors were designed by Vivienne Westwood, and you can see her kooky style everywhere you look.

There's a large, open-plan living room with quirky gold-and-white floor lamps, and an enormous geometric-patterned turquoise-and-grey rug covers much of the marble floor.

I try not to gawp at all of the recognisable faces in the room. *Blood Ten* started out with a cult following, but now it's so big that it's become mainstream and everyone wants a piece of it.

The show is rated 18 and is extremely gory, but that didn't stop my friends or me from watching it. I gulp as I walk past one of the lead actors – he's short and stout and his bulging eyes would look more appropriate on a pug dog than a person. He stars as an evil lawyer who gets people to do nasty things, but right now he's gaily laughing his head off and affectionately tweaking the cheek of another sexy-as-hell actor who plays a gruesomely violent drug lord. It's a bizarre business.

'Let's go to the roof,' Sienna says as Rafael veers off to talk to someone he knows. I follow Sienna through the crowds to the far corner of the room where stairs lead up to the outdoor terrace.

The roof terrace is open to the sky, which is a deep mauve colour above our heads, changing to pale orange the closer it gets to downtown's jagged skyline. There aren't as many skyscrapers here as in New York – the earthquakes are the main reason for that – but the view is still awesome.

Sienna barely bats an eyelid as she leads me to the marble counter where barmen are busily mixing cocktails.

There are so many famous people up here that I'm trying not to stare. Gina is chatting away happily to her onscreen mother not far from us and I feel a surge of pride for her. I'm so lucky to have such interesting, talented friends.

Guilt pricks my conscience as that thought crosses my mind. I've barely spoken to my old friends back home in weeks. I've been so busy. Libby rang me a week ago and I haven't even had time yet to call her back. I remind myself to do so tomorrow.

We grab a couple of drinks and make our way over to the glass balustrade, standing beside a large potted palm and chinking glasses.

'You and Rafael looked amazing downstairs,' I tell her. 'I've never seen you in work mode before.'

She grins. 'Can you keep a secret?'

'Of course.'

She leans in close. 'I'm in line to be the next CiaoCiao girl. I'll be working alongside Rafe.'

'No way!' I squeal. 'That's amazing!'

She beams at me, her blue eyes sparkling. 'Thanks! I'm so excited.'

'So you're going to have to get up close and personal with him, then?'

CiaoCiao is known for its sexy young models wearing surprisingly little clothing considering it's in the business of selling them.

She shrugs and grins wickedly. 'I guess so.'

'It's a hard life! I find it difficult enough to concentrate in English.' Rafael sits one table in front of me to my right, and his profile is very distracting.

She pulls a face. 'No. We have chemistry, sure, but I don't like him like that. Anyway.' She arm-bumps me. 'You only have eyes for Jack Mitchell, remember?'

I narrow my eyes at her. 'True, but we're still a secret so—'

'My lips are sealed,' she finishes my sentence.

'I was really surprised Gina didn't invite Agnes,' I say, now that we're on the subject of the Mitchells.

She cocks her head to one side, thoughtfully. 'I'm not,' she says at last.

'Why?' I ask with a frown.

'Gina and Margarita are all about the publicity,' she tells me bluntly, echoing what Agnes said. 'They like what's in fashion. *I* don't think that,' she adds quickly, seeing my appalled expression at the idea of friends being somehow *unfashionable*. 'I adore Agnes, but, you know, her dad *is* a washed-up rock star.'

My mouth drops open.

'Again, it's not me who's saying that!' She looks alarmed and places her hand on my arm, trying to reassure me. 'But you can't deny the facts: Johnny Jefferson and Courtney Victor are still cool.'

It's weird hearing her refer to my dad and her mum like this. They don't sound like real people, let alone normal, everyday parents.

But then they're *not* normal, everyday parents. Johnny is Johnny and Sienna's mum is a supermodel who hit the big time over ten years ago as an underwear model and is still working the catwalk today.

I suppose Sienna's right, but I really don't like the thought of anyone calling Jack and Agnes's dad a washed-up rock star, even if he hasn't done anything in a while. A long while. Well, OK, she's got a point; there just must be a better way of putting it.

Talking about Sienna's mum makes me think of her dad again.

'What's your dad like?' I ask her. 'If you don't mind me asking,' I add.

'Not at all. He's, well, he's…' She wrinkles her nose. 'I don't

162

really know him that well, to be honest. He left my mom when she got pregnant with me. Mom ranted about it once when she was drunk.'

Oh. 'So he and your mother had an affair?' I remember Johnny saying this.

'Yeah, for five years. My dad's still married to Dana's mom. They live in a ranch in Montana, but Dad comes to LA to do business. He has an apartment here. Sometimes we'll grab lunch, but his wife is insanely jealous so he tries to keep his relationship with me pretty quiet.'

'That's sad,' I say.

'I'm used to it now,' she says lightly.

'Still, it must hurt.'

I see her swallow and wonder why I'm pushing her. 'Yeah, it sucks,' she admits in a choked voice. 'I don't know why I didn't just come out and admit that.'

'Sorry, I shouldn't have brought it up.'

'It's OK.' She gives me an uneasy look.

'What is it?'

She sighs. 'I wasn't going to say anything, but I don't want to lie to you so I should probably tell you that my sister has been in contact with me.'

'What?' My stomach contracts.

'She's always been a total bitch to me, but yesterday she called me out of the blue and said that maybe we should get together and have a coffee or something. She sounded OK, you know? I think that maybe she wants to be friends.'

'Oh. Right.' This makes things tricky.

'You look worried,' she says.

'I am a bit. I mean, this shouldn't affect me or our friendship at

163

all.' And it really shouldn't. 'But my dad was really worried that we were friends, because of your sister.'

'My sister is my sister. She's not me and I'm not her, so why should that impact on our friendship?' Her dark brows have pulled together.

'You're right, it shouldn't,' I say firmly. 'So are you going to catch up with her?'

'Yeah, later this week. She's in town meeting up with her record label so she said she'd swing by after school and take me out for a coffee.'

'Good luck.'

'Thanks.' She takes a sip of her drink and scans the crowd.

'I didn't know Dana was still making music,' I say casually.

'She's had some time off, but I think she's got her shit together now so hopefully she can get back to being the Next Big Thing.' She shrugs and grins at me.

The next couple of hours fly by. When my phone buzzes to let me know I have a text, I'm surprised to see that it's already ten o'clock. I'm also surprised to see that it's from Jack, telling me that he's in the bar downstairs.

My heart jumps. I'm desperate to see him, but Johnny told me I had to stay put, otherwise he'd send Sam with me tonight. Surely I'm still staying put if I'm in the same building, though?

I text him back to say that I'm on my way, grabbing Sienna to tell her of my intentions.

'Perhaps I'll see you down there later,' she says.

Jack is sitting on a gold stool at the white marble bar of the cocktail lounge. The bottles of spirits on the glass shelves behind him sparkle like jewels in the low-level light, making me think of old Hollywood as I walk towards him. He's wearing a slim-fitting black blazer tonight over skinny black jeans and, with his dark hair partly falling down across his forehead, he looks like he should be on the big screen. My pulse starts to race when he looks over his shoulder, a lazy smile tipping the corners of his lips as he sees me approaching.

'Hey,' he says, swivelling in his seat as I come to a stop in front of him.

'Hey,' I reply, giving him a kiss. 'This is a surprise.'

'A surprise that I wanted to see my hot girlfriend?' He raises one eyebrow.

I shrug at him and glance down at my outfit. 'You like the dress?'

'I like you.'

A shiver goes down my spine.

He nods behind me. 'Go grab a table. What are you drinking?'

'Just a mineral water, thanks.

'Where's Agnes?' I ask when he slides into the bench seat beside me rather than taking the free seat opposite.

'Last I heard, she was FaceTiming Brett.'

'She didn't want to come out?' I ask, as he drapes his arm round my shoulder.

'Nah.'

'I feel bad that she wasn't invited.'

'Why? It's not your fault.'

'No, it's just…' I think of what Sienna said about Jack's dad and decide not to elaborate. 'Never mind.'

'She'll get over it,' he assures me. 'You been having fun upstairs?'

I nod. 'I'll never get used to this life.'

'Yeah, you will,' he says drily.

We both fall silent and then he takes my chin between his finger and thumb and turns my face towards him.

I'm tingling all over as he kisses me and I know I could sit here doing this all night, but it feels like a long time since we've been able to chat openly, to have a proper conversation for once. I bring him up to date with what's been happening and go on to tell him that I feel bad for not speaking more to my friends back in the UK.

'They'll understand,' he says. 'You gotta lot going on.'

'I just don't want them to think that I've changed.'

'You have changed,' he states. 'It's inevitable. There will be people that you'll leave behind.'

I frown at him. 'But I don't want to leave my friends behind.'

'You can't bring them with you,' he says reasonably.

'Maybe I can. I mean, it's half-term in the UK in a couple of weeks. Maybe my dad would fly them over again.' A bubble of excitement bursts inside my chest at the idea. 'Oh my God, he really could do that. It's our gig in San Francisco! They could come to that!'

He shifts in his seat. 'Who would you ask?'

'I don't know. Nat, Libby, Lou...'

He looks relieved. 'Not Tom, then,' he says.

'Well, he's coming, anyway,' I say with a shrug that freezes into tension.

Whoops. I haven't actually told Jack that we've been speaking.

He pulls away to look at me directly. 'What?'

'His dad lives in San Francisco,' I say defensively. 'I'm sure I mentioned that. He left Tom's mum for another woman so Tom's coming over for a week to see him. I'm going to catch up with him when we're there for our gig.'

Jack looks put out. 'When did you decide this?'

'A couple of weeks ago.' I try to sound more casual than I feel.

He stares at me levelly. 'Why didn't you say anything?'

I guess I should be honest... 'Because I thought you'd be pissed off about it.'

'Glad we're getting somewhere.' He takes his arm out from around my shoulders and edges away from me.

'Hey, it's nothing. I told you Tom and I are friends. Why are you being shitty about it?'

'If it was nothing, you would've mentioned it. Do you speak to him often?'

'A few times.'

'Does he call you or do you call him?'

'A bit of both.'

'So you're telling me you rarely call your friends, but you make time for Tom?'

I swallow. That's about the crux of it.

'If you really want to know,' I say, trying to offload some of my guilt, 'I rang him from Big Sur when you stayed out all night and I couldn't get through to you.'

He blanches. 'Hang on, you called him because you couldn't get hold of me?'

I shift in my seat. 'Well, yes. I didn't know where you were. I wanted to take my mind off it.'

'So you called your ex-boyfriend?'

He looks thoroughly peed off, and I guess that's understandable.

'I didn't know where you were,' I say again, dejectedly.

'So you don't trust me.'

'Well, no, now you're asking, not really.'

His mouth drops open.

'Are you surprised?' I ask him. 'We didn't exactly get together under the most honourable of circumstances. You were still seeing Eve.'

'Eve and I weren't serious.'

'That depends on your definition of serious, doesn't it?' I say with a spark of irritation. 'You were having sex with her.' And I wasn't with Tom. That doesn't need repeating.

'I'm talking about how we felt about each other. You and Tom, well, *you* said *you* were serious.'

'We were.'

'Yet you kissed me when you were with him.'

Now he's looking at me almost accusingly.

'What's that got to do with anything?' I wish I hadn't had that last cocktail upstairs because my mind would be a lot clearer.

'You cheated on your boyfriend once. What's to stop you from doing it again?'

I stare at him, gobsmacked. 'Are you saying you don't trust *me*?'

He shrugs. 'You're the one who cheated. Eve wasn't my girlfriend. I told you that she and I just had a thing. She knew that I played around.'

'Ha!' I erupt. 'You've just said it yourself! You play around!'

'I thought we'd established that I don't any more,' he says, his eyes flashing.

'You won't even tell your bloody bandmates that we're together.' I lean back on my seat and fold my arms. 'How am I supposed to know how much you care about me?'

He reaches for his drink and takes a large gulp.

I've had enough of this. I get my phone out of my bag and send Davey a text.

'What are you doing?' Jack asks warily.

168

'Going home,' I reply flatly.

'You've gotta be kidding me.' He gives me a hard stare.

My phone buzzes almost immediately with a text from Davey, letting me know he'll be out front in two minutes. I shove my phone back into my bag and edge out from my seat.

'You're leaving. Just like that?'

I feel a pang of remorse. Do I really want to do this? No, but I'll lose face if I back down now.

'See you at band practice,' I call over my shoulder, as I walk out of the bar.

Chapter 16

On Sunday morning, the first thing I do when I wake up is reach for my phone. I wanted to call my friends in England last night, but the time difference meant that it would be the middle of the night for them, so I've had to wait. I return Libby's call first.

'Hi!' she exclaims when she realises it's me. 'How are you?'

'I'm sorry it's taken me this long to call you back,' I say, feeling bad.

'It's OK. I know you're busy.'

'I am, but it's no excuse. The time difference makes it hard.'

'I know what you mean. And your life is so full now.'

'Full-on, you mean. Yeah, it is.'

'Well, don't forget about us,' she says cheerily, but there's an edge to her voice.

'I won't.'

We talk for a good half an hour, catching up on everything that's been happening, both in her life and in mine. She wants to hear about all of my celebrity gossip, so it's a while before I get around to confiding in her about Jack.

'Trust your instincts,' she says. 'If you think he's a player, he probably is.'

It sounds like something she could have read in *Cosmo* magazine.

'I don't think he's a player. At least not with me,' I say defensively.

'OK, if you're sure.'

'Well, no, I'm not entirely sure. We haven't been going out for long. I don't know what to think.'

'I know Lou wasn't keen on him,' she reveals, to my annoyance.

'What do you mean Lou wasn't keen on him? She didn't say anything like that to me!'

'It was just an impression she got,' Libby tells me, and I'm peeved to think about my *new* friend confiding in my *old* friend like she's her *best* friend.

'Yeah, well, Lou goes out with Tom's best mate so I don't imagine her perceptions are skewed *at all*,' I say, unable to keep the sarcasm from my voice.

Libby falls silent.

'Forget it,' I say, realising that maybe she's not the person to confide in about Jack.

For some reason, this thought leads me to think of Sienna and whether I could talk to her about him. I texted her last night to let her know I'd left the bar and she said she'd call me today. Despite what Agnes says about me being welcome to confide in her about Jack, I don't really feel that comfortable. He is her brother after all.

'Are you looking forward to seeing Tom in a week?' Libby asks me.

'It'll be closer to two by the time I see him, but yeah,' I reply. 'How is he?' I ask.

'He's great.'

An alarming thought strikes me. With me gone and Libby and Lou hanging out, have they become a foursome?

'You don't fancy him, do you?' I find myself blurting out.

'Of course not!' she scoffs. 'If anyone fancies him, it's Nina. I keep seeing her talking to him in the courtyard at school. Probably trying to console him over your break-up.'

Nina is – *was* – one of my classmates and, before the news about me being Johnny's daughter came out, she teased me that I looked like him. It wasn't done in a funny way – more a mean, bullying way. I hate the thought of her getting her claws into Tom.

We end our call soon afterwards. I'm not really in the mood for another big conversation, but I know I shouldn't wait any longer before returning Natalie's call.

'It *is* you!' she exclaims when I say hello. 'I thought I was seeing things when your caller ID flashed up.'

Ouch. 'I spoke to you a couple of weeks ago,' I say, slightly hurt that that's not good enough for her.

'Yeah, but I'm always the one to call you.'

Is that true? I cast my mind back to our rare conversations and realise that my friends *are* always the ones to instigate the calls.

'Well, I'm sorry,' I say. 'I'll try to make more of an effort.'

My head feels like it's going to explode with all of the pressure I'm under at the moment.

To say that I feel rubbish over the next couple of days is an understatement. Jack doesn't call me and I don't call him, so the next time I see him is at band practice on Tuesday and I'm nervous when Sam drops me there straight after school.

Unfortunately, Brandon and Miles are already in the games room when I arrive so Jack and I aren't going to get a chance to clear the air.

'Hey,' he says to me, barely meeting my eyes.

'Hi,' I reply, steeling myself.

I'm not sure the atmosphere is frosty enough for our bandmates to pick up on it, but this will be a challenge for us both. Can we make this work for All Hype, even if it's not working for Jack and me? Let's see.

I adjust my microphone stand to make myself look busy and then turn round to see Jack crouching down in front of his pedalboard. A pedalboard lets a guitar player change the sound coming out of their instrument by turning a dial or pressing a pedal with their foot during a song. It's how bands can create such different sounds within the same track.

Jack has collected a few different pedals over the years and Miles and Brandon often tease him that it's his fetish.

'Don't tell me you've got another pedal?' Miles grins at him.

'Yep,' Jack replies, glancing up at his mate with amusement. 'Thought I'd try it on "Blue Tuesday".'

'Shall we do that first?' Brandon asks me.

'Sure.' I nod, instinctively flashing Jack a playful look, but he doesn't meet my eyes as he stands up again and I feel slightly sick. I turn away and face my mic.

Miles takes his place behind his kit and starts to bash out a beat, but I'm distracted and the words fly from my mind. We only wrote this song a week ago.

'Hang on,' I say, holding up my hand as Brandon and Jack kick in with their bass and electric guitars.

The music dies in a cacophony of sound.

'Sorry,' I apologise, blushing as I flip through the pages of my notepad. 'I haven't had enough time to practise this one.'

No one says anything, but I feel like I'm being judged as I quickly glance over the lyrics. 'OK, I'm good to go,' I say, stepping back towards the mic.

Miles starts up again and Brandon and Jack kick in. In the chorus, a new sound comes blaring out of Jack's amp – it's almost keyboard-like – and I jolt with surprise and look over my shoulder to see him grinning at Brandon.

Brandon throws his head back and laughs. 'Awesome!' he shouts.

Jack stamps on one of his pedals and the sound reverts to dirty and raw.

He catches my eye and I nod hearteningly, but he lowers his gaze and my stomach feels flat.

'We should definitely commit that one to the playlist,' Miles states afterwards.

'It needs practice,' Jack replies.

I bristle. 'Sorry, guys,' I say again, figuring that Jack's comment is directed at me. 'I'll step it up, OK?'

'Maybe we should meet daily for the next couple of weeks,' Miles suggests, looking at each of us in turn.

I shift on my feet. 'That could be difficult.'

'You can't scale back on your other activities?' Brandon asks me, his brow furrowing slightly.

'Of course I can. My singing lessons and driving lessons can be put on hold for sure, but my stepdad is arriving on Saturday. I want to spend some time with him.'

'Saturday?' Jack clarifies.

'Yeah, it's half-term in England. He's a teacher so he has a week off.'

'What's half-term?' Miles asks.

'It's a holiday we have halfway through each of the three school terms.'

'Sweet,' he says.

'Anyway,' I continue, 'much as I'd love to practise more, I'm going to be in school all day and I want to see Stu in the evenings while he's here.'

The look on their faces tells me this is just not good enough.

'I'm sorry!' I say, feeling like I'm being demonised. 'It's alright for you guys. You already drive, you don't go to school and you don't have homework. You play your instruments really well and—'

'How about we practise at yours?' Jack cuts me off, meeting my eyes at last. 'That would shorten your travel time. Stu could watch. If Johnny's OK with it, that is.'

I breathe a sigh of relief as the others shrug and nod. 'That's a great idea. I'm sure my dad will be cool. I'll practise my vocals at lunchtimes. I promise I'll be ready for the gig.'

Towards the end of our session, Agnes comes in.

'Have you seen this?' she asks me with interest, holding up a copy of *Hebe* magazine.

'Is that my interview?'

'Yeah.' She grins and hands it over.

Miles is chatting to Jack, but Brandon ambles over, peering over my shoulder as I flick through the pages, looking for my interview. Suddenly there I am, standing in front of the Hollywood sign.

I snort. 'It's so cheesy,' I say, glancing at Brandon to see him smirking.

'You still look hot,' he says with a shrug.

'What's this?' Jack asks, glancing over. His bandmate got his attention with that comment.

'Jessie's magazine interview.'

He and Miles join us and I feel on edge, remembering how little I managed to mention the band. I wish I could read this in private. Knowing Annie, she'll have a copy waiting for me at home. I put the magazine down, hoping they'll lose interest in a moment, but Jack picks it up and buries his nose in the article, with Miles on his left and Brandon on his right. I turn to Agnes.

She was a little quiet yesterday at school and I wondered if it had anything to do with her not being invited to Gina's launch party. I chose not to bring it up, which was a bit cowardly.

'So two weeks until our gig. Have you decided what I'm wearing yet?' I ask impertinently.

'I've got some ideas,' she replies with a smile at my tone. '*You OK?*' she mouths, nodding at Jack.

I shrug at her.

'Want to come and see what I've got for you in my wardrobe?' she asks at normal volume.

'Sure. That OK, guys? Are we done now?'

They wave me away, barely looking up from my interview as I leave the room.

'What's wrong?' Agnes asks, as we walk into the house.

'Jack and I had an argument on Saturday night,' I say morosely.

'So that's why he's been like a bear with a sore head,' she comments, as she leads the way upstairs.

I sigh. 'It's pretty stupid. I don't know why I haven't just called him to apologise.'

'It was your fault?' she asks with surprise. 'That's new.'

I sigh, as we walk into her room. 'Mmm.'

I'm a bit sick of everyone thinking it's Jack who's going to screw this up. No one has any faith in us as a couple. We don't have any faith in us as a couple. 'I told him I'd been speaking to Tom,' I say.

'Your ex-boyfriend?'

'Yeah. We're friends,' I say firmly. 'He's going to be in San Francisco visiting his dad when we're there for our gig. Obviously I'm going to catch up with him.'

'Oh.' She turns away from me to rummage in her wardrobe.

'Do you think that's wrong?' I ask with a furrowed brow.

'Well, I wouldn't like it if Brett was still friends with his exes. It just complicates things, doesn't it?'

'Maybe, but I don't want to lose Tom from my life.'

She turns round and gives me a significant look.

'I still care about him,' I say. 'It doesn't mean I want to be with him like that any more.' *Does it?*

'Are you sure you're not just keeping him sweet so if things with Jack don't work out—'

'No!' I exclaim. 'Definitely not. Anyway, Tom never goes back. He was totally in love with his last girlfriend when she cheated on him, and she begged him to give her another chance, but he never once cracked. He stuck to his guns. Even if I wanted Tom back, he'd never go there.'

'Hmm,' she says.

'Show me what you've got in mind,' I prompt, nodding at her wardrobe. I think it might be a good idea to change the subject.

I'm trying on my third outfit when there's a knock at the door. Agnes opens it to reveal her brother standing there.

'You gotta minute?' he asks me, leaning against the door frame.

'You can have her in five,' Agnes replies inflexibly. 'We're in the middle of a styling session.'

'I'll come and knock for you,' I tell him, smoothing my hands over the skin-tight skirt I'm wearing. It's black with gold thread and fits tight to my hips, all the way down past my knees. I'm wearing a black, fitted bodice top.

Jack's eyes graze over the length of my body before meeting my eyes. Electricity crackles between us. Then he pulls the door shut without another word.

'That's the one,' Agnes says, pursing her lips as she nods at my outfit.

'Are you sure?'

'Just take it off now before he tears it off you.'

'Agnes!' I squawk. 'Not likely!'

'It's only a matter of time, though, right?'

'Not if we can't stop arguing,' I reply truthfully. 'And I can't believe I'm having this conversation with my boyfriend's sister,' I mutter, as she giggles and passes me my jeans.

As soon as I knock on Jack's door, it opens.

'I'm just going for a smoke,' he says, joining me in the corridor and patting his jeans pocket. 'Come with.'

I follow him downstairs and outside to the garden.

'Do your mum and stepdad mind you smoking?' I ask. He's pretty blatant about it.

He shrugs. 'They'd prefer that I didn't.' He sits on one of the sunloungers beside the pool. The floor is covered with peach-coloured tiles and there are enormous palms dotted around in huge terracotta pots.

I take a seat opposite him and watch as he lights up, blowing smoke away from me.

'I guess I should quit,' he says, regarding the cigarette he's holding. 'But some habits are hard to kick.'

'Does the same go for you being a player?' I ask drily.

'What do you want from me?' he asks outright. 'I've told you we're exclusive. I'm not messing around.'

'I'm not, either.'

'So what's the problem?' he asks, flicking his ash into a nearby pot plant.

'The problem is that you don't trust me to be friends with Tom,' I remind him.

He sighs and looks away from me. 'I trust you,' he says eventually, meeting my eyes.

'You do?' I ask with surprise.

'Yeah. I don't have to like it, though, do I?'

'No,' I reply with a grin, getting up and going to sit beside him. He stubs out his cigarette and leans back on the sunlounger, patting my leg and indicating for me to straddle him. I breathe in sharply as he manoeuvres himself beneath me so he's more comfortable. I wouldn't like his mum to look out of the window and see us in this position, even though we're fully clothed.

'So your stepdad is coming on Saturday?' Jack asks, eyeing me steadily.

'Yep.'

'You're not gonna be around this weekend, then?'

I shake my head. 'Not really, no. Why?'

He purses his lips. 'You know Saturday's Valentine's Day.'

'Is it?' I reel backwards. I'd completely forgotten, which is odd considering how much they make of it here. The hearts and flowers have been in the shop windows for so long that they've almost become part of the furniture.

'I wouldn't have thought you're the Valentine's type,' I say with a smirk.

He shrugs. 'I'm not, really.'

'Well, you won't miss me, then.'

'Don't be so sure about it.'

We smile at each other for a long moment, and then I lean down and kiss him. He clasps my face in his hands and kisses me back passionately.

I pull away on a gasp of breath. 'Jack,' I whisper, wanting more. I always want more. 'I can still see you while Stu's here. We're going to be practising every day, anyway,' I say hurriedly.

He reaches up and tucks a wayward lock of hair behind my ear, looking thoughtful.

'You sound a little stressed about everything. Do you need to do so much?'

'I keep thinking it's ridiculous that I'm taking my GCSEs on top of everything else,' I grumble.

'I'm talking about your singing lessons, your keyboard lessons. You can already sing, and keyboards will be cool, but they're not gonna happen in time for *this* gig. Maybe you need to cut yourself some slack.'

I bite my lip, thinking. 'Maybe,' I reply with a sigh. 'Do you think Miles and Brandon are OK about doing practice at my house?'

'They're totally cool.'

'What did they think of the interview?' I ask apprehensively.

He shifts beneath me so I sit up again, worried I'm squashing him.

'It's not really their thing,' he says diplomatically.

'I didn't talk about the band as much as I wanted to,' I tell him.

'I think the name's mentioned once,' he states.

'Is that all?' I ask with alarm. 'God, I definitely talked about you guys more than that.'

'Don't worry about it. It's not what the piece was about.'

'Yeah, but—'

'Seriously, don't worry,' he reassures me. 'The gig's already sold out so you're not gonna dampen anyone's mood.'

'Has it?'

'Yeah, the *Muso* piece helped. Anything you can do to raise our profile won't hurt, but it's not a problem if you can't.'

'I wonder if Johnny can help. I mean, he's so well connected. Surely it's only a matter of time before someone wants to sign us.'

Jack raises his eyebrows. 'I hope so.'

Chapter 17

It is so good to see Stu again. I really wanted to go with Davey to collect him from the airport, but the boys came over to have an early band session so I could take the afternoon off. I'm grateful to them, but desperate to spend time with my stepdad.

The LA traffic must've been exceptionally good for a change, because he arrives while we're still in the swing of things.

My dad brings him into the studio.

'Stu!' I yelp, cutting out mid-song. I shove my mic into its stand and rush out through the glass studio door to engulf him in a hug.

He chuckles warmly, pulling away to look at my face.

'You shouldn't have stopped,' Johnny drawls.

'No, that wasn't very professional of me.' I cast a look over my shoulder at my bandmates watching and waiting patiently. 'Coming, guys,' I call, turning back to Stu. 'You want to watch for a bit? We won't be long.'

'Sure,' he says, pulling up a chair.

'Mind if I sit in, too?' Johnny asks.

'Of course not.' I try to sound flippant, but his presence always makes me nervous. I notice my bandmates looking a little less comfortable when I walk back into the studio, too. 'OK?' I mouth.

Jack gives me a small nod.

Johnny leans forward in his seat, resting his elbows on his knees. It's a laid-back position compared to Stu's more upright posture, but I can tell that Johnny is anything but relaxed. He's watching and listening intently as we start the song from the beginning. This is his thing. This is what he's good at.

Stu claps when we're finished, but Johnny just nods. I *think* he's impressed. 'Sounding good,' Johnny says. 'A week today, right?'

'Yeah, you coming?' Brandon asks my dad cheekily.

'Flying in especially,' he replies.

It's so nice to have Johnny in here like this with us. He's been pretty absent from the family in the last few weeks. The only time we're guaranteed to all be together is at breakfast, but Meg really has to kick his butt to get him downstairs in time. He's so tired rehearsing for his tour that he'd sleep in every day if he could. And, if he's going to be home for dinner, we all make an effort to be there.

Anyway, because of his busy schedule, Johnny is not going to bring Meg and the boys to San Francisco for the weekend. Instead, they're going to stay here and he's going to fly in just for the gig. He's not even planning to stay overnight.

Stu and I, on the other hand, are making a proper weekend of it. Johnny has organised for us to fly by helicopter on Friday, straight after school, returning on Sunday night. I can't say I'm desperate to feel helicopter-sick again, but air travel has its benefits and we'll be there in time for dinner with Tom.

I haven't mentioned this plan to Stu yet. Or Jack…

We finish up soon afterwards. Miles played on Johnny's drum kit so all he has with him are his sticks, but Jack has his pedalboard so he takes longer to pack it away in its padded case.

'I'll meet you by the car,' he tells Brandon, who's swung his bass guitar over his shoulder. We used Johnny's amps, too.

'It's OK, I'll wait for you,' Brandon says cheerfully.

'Have you guys heard the song Jessie's doing on my new album?' Johnny asks.

'I still haven't played it for them,' I interject cautiously.

'Let's hear it!' Brandon says, clapping his hands together.

'Yeah, I'd love to hear it myself,' Stu chips in.

Butterflies invade my stomach as Johnny digs out the CD and presses Play. Jack shoots me an encouraging smile.

Brandon reacts with enthusiasm. 'Man, that is sick!' he exclaims. 'What's it called?'

'"Acorn",' Johnny and I reply simultaneously.

Miles nods. 'It sounds cool.'

'Very cool,' Jack says, smiling at me.

Johnny ruffles my hair, proudly.

'OK, you're embarrassing me now,' I say, blushing. 'So are we meeting back here tomorrow evening?'

We all walk downstairs together, but Jack manages to hang back from his bandmates. He arm-bumps me and whispers, 'Back pocket,' jerking his head to indicate he wants me to get something for him. He's laden down with his guitar and pedalboard so I reach into his pocket and pull out a small white box.

'For you,' he mouths.

'What is it?' I whisper, taken aback.

184

He frowns at me, so I shove it into my own back pocket, aware of Stu and Johnny talking between themselves as they follow right behind us.

Jack jogs down the last of the steps. 'See you tomorrow,' he calls over his shoulder, striding after his bandmates.

I come to a standstill at the bottom of the steps. He'll be through the door before I reach him so I decide to let him see himself out.

'Coffee?' Johnny calls, heading into the kitchen.

'Sure,' Stu calls back, joining me. 'I saw that,' he says in a low, meaningful voice.

'Saw what?' I ask innocently.

'What did he give you? Are you smoking again?'

'What? No!' I exclaim, annoyed. 'I don't know what he gave me,' I say with a shrug.

It's obvious from Stu's expression that he's waiting to find out. Feeling nervous, I take a chance and pull out the box. It *is* about the same size as a cigarette packet, and wrapped in white paper, so I can see why Stu might've jumped to that conclusion. I carefully unstick the edges, wondering what the hell it is and whether I'm insane to open it in front of my stepdad, when I realise there's a grey velvet box underneath the wrapping paper. I open it up, my heart in my throat, to see a tiny silver red rose. It's a charm for my bracelet.

My face breaks into the widest grin. 'It's for Valentine's Day,' I say, as my heart melts.

'So you're still together, then?' Stu asks. He's not enthralled by the idea, judging by his tone.

'Yes, we are,' I state adamantly.

'What was with all the secrecy, then?'

'Miles and Brandon don't know we're a couple. It would complicate things with the band.'

I'm getting a bit sick of this explanation – no one understands what the band means to me, how much of my new life is tied up in it.

'I hear Tom is going to be in San Francisco this week,' Stu says, but, although his tone is casual, I notice his cheeks flush slightly.

'We're meeting him for dinner on Friday night,' I reply.

'Are we?' He looks alarmed. 'Are you two in contact?'

'Yeah, we are.'

I presume he reacted like that because, if Tom and I speak, then I'll know he's been seeing Tom's mother. But now is probably not the right time to get into a conversation about whether they're just friends. We head into the kitchen together.

Over the next few days, I can't seem to bring myself to ask Stu if he's moved on from my mum – it hurts too much and I'm too scared of his answer.

In the end, though, it's him who instigates a talk with me.

We're sitting out on the terrace one night after dinner. Johnny managed to get back in time for a change and Meg has taken the boys inside to bed, so it's just the three of us: my two dads and me.

'Jess, there's something we need to talk to you about,' Stu starts.

Both he and Johnny are sitting opposite, staring at me attentively. I have my back to the view and the city lights are casting a dim glow over their faces. It's enough for me to be able to see their expressions, but the anguish in Stu's voice is almost palpable, anyway.

'What is it?' I ask nervously, instantly on edge.

'It's the house,' Stu says. 'I'm selling it.'

My heart clenches. 'Why?' I ask shakily.

Johnny reaches across and presses my hand. 'You know it's not secure enough. You'll be going home to visit. I need you safe, Jess.'

'It's not just that,' Stu says reluctantly, and I watch as his Adam's apple bobs up and down. 'It's hard for me to be there on my own. I need a fresh start.'

'Does that go for Caroline, too?' I ask of Tom's mum.

He looks startled.

'Tom told me that you've been seeing her.'

'We're friends,' he says warily.

'Is that all?' I ask. Johnny shifts in his seat, clearly feeling awkward on Stu's behalf.

'That's all,' Stu replies, swallowing again. 'But—'

'You want it to be more,' I finish his sentence for him.

'Jess…' he starts.

'It's OK,' I whisper, my eyes filling with tears. 'I wish you'd find someone who wasn't my ex's mum, but it was going to be hard for me, whoever it was.'

Johnny takes my hand.

'Do we really have to sell?' I ask with difficulty.

Stu nods and Johnny squeezes my hand. 'It's for the best,' Stu says.

My nose starts to prickle as I think of my bedroom, my bed, my mum lying next to me and keeping me awake with her chatter when I really should have been going to sleep for school the next day. I think of our kitchen and Mum standing in front of the toaster, waiting for the toast to pop up. I remember lying on the sofa with her in the living room while she stroked my hair with her cold hands, and I gulp back a sob.

187

Stu comes round to my side of the table and takes me in his arms, but my hand is still in Johnny's and I squeeze his tightly, not wanting him to let me go.

Thankfully, the very next day I get some news that cheers me up enormously. I'm at lunch, sitting next to Agnes, when Gina and Margarita join us.

'Guess what?' Gina says, as they both slide into chairs opposite.

'What?' I ask, my eyes darting between them.

'We're coming to San Francisco!' Gina blurts, her red hair bouncing around her shoulders.

'You are?' I ask with amazement.

'Not just us,' Margarita says, waving excitedly across the room. I look over my shoulder in time to see Sienna rolling her eyes.

'You already told her?' she berates, as she approaches on her long, gazelle-like legs.

'I didn't know where you were,' Gina replies defensively.

'You're coming, too?' I ask Sienna with delight.

'I sure am. And Rafe said he can probably make it, too. Justin and Jenna are maybes.'

'Oh my God!' I stare at them, open-mouthed.

'Wow,' Agnes says, not sounding anywhere near as delighted as I am.

'We wanted to help,' Margarita says, regarding me in earnest with her caramel-coloured eyes. 'With a bunch of us there, we'll be able to get some cool pics, help to increase All Hype's profile a bit.'

'Guys, seriously,' I say, blown away. 'I really appreciate this.'

As we're walking to our next class, Sienna pulls me aside. 'I'll catch you up,' I say to Agnes.

She puts her head down as she walks on.

'Someone else wants to come to your gig,' Sienna says, looking worried.

'Who?'

'Don't freak out.'

'Who?' I ask again, doing exactly that.

'My sister.'

'What?' The blood drains from my face. 'No!'

'Just hear me out! She's gonna be in San Francisco for business and she loves checking out new bands—'

'Sienna, no,' I say adamantly, rounding on her in the hallway. 'No way. Johnny would hit the roof! Meg's not even going. Oh my God, imagine if the paps caught a picture of Johnny and Dana together at my gig? That would cause all sorts of trouble. She can't come. I'm sorry. I know that you got on well with her last week.' They met after school as planned. 'And maybe she's changed as you say, but if you bring her to my gig then you'll really screw things up for me and my family. Please don't do it.'

She looks completely put out. 'Fine,' she says. 'I'll tell her she can't come. *That's* gonna be an easy conversation,' she adds sarcastically.

'I'm sorry,' I say. 'You can still meet up with her before and after, right?'

'I guess so.'

The bell rings. 'We're going to be late,' I say, hurrying off along the wide corridor.

'What are you doing after school?' she asks, keeping pace with me.

'Band practice.'

'No time for shopping? We could go to Melrose Avenue, check out some gig outfits perhaps?' she asks hopefully.

'Thanks, but Agnes has that covered.' I give her arm a squeeze as we head into the science lab, but I don't think she's very happy with me as we take our seats.

Chapter 18

Two days later, Stu and I touch down in San Francisco. He's looking as green from the helicopter flight as I am, so it's a relief to go to the hotel in a car.

We get ready for dinner quickly, but Tom is already waiting in the hotel restaurant when we come down and the sight of him still makes me jittery. I know this is not good.

He's dressed smarter than usual in a crisp white shirt, and he's gazing out of the window so I can see his profile: his straight nose and his long eyelashes. His brown hair has been styled back from his face, higher on top.

He glances our way, meets my eyes and grins.

'Hello,' I say warmly, as he gets up from his chair and gives me a hug. My heart pounds a little bit faster at the feeling of his chest against mine. He feels familiar yet completely unfamiliar at the same time. He's wearing his usual aftershave and I breathe in as I let him go. He shakes hands with Stu.

'Tom,' Stu says.

'Mr Taylor,' Tom replies.

'Oh, for God's sake,' I exclaim. 'Shouldn't he be calling you by your first name if you're seeing his mum?'

Stu's face flushes. Tom grins at him. 'She has a point,' Tom says sheepishly.

'Call me Stu,' Stu replies with an embarrassed smile, pulling out a seat and sitting down.

With Stu there, our conversation is very general over the course of dinner and neither Tom nor I can completely relax. I appreciate it when Stu decides to call it a night.

'Don't leave the hotel premises,' Stu reminds me.

Miracle upon miracle, it has been deemed unnecessary for me to have a bodyguard this weekend, so Sam is flying here with Johnny and, in the meantime, Stu and I have been instructed to go incognito. We plan to do some sightseeing in the morning, but, with Stu at my side and a baseball cap on my head, it's pretty unlikely anyone will recognise me as Johnny's daughter. Sam will be there at the gig venue so that should be enough.

Finally it seems like they're seeing sense with this bodyguard business. I just have to keep my end of the bargain and not take any risks.

Tom and I relocate to the bar and find a dark corner on a comfy, midnight-blue, padded bench near a circular, central fire.

'So Stu talked to you about him and my mum?' Tom asks with a raised eyebrow.

I nod. 'He's says they're friends, but he likes her more than that.'

'I think it's mutual.'

'How do *you* feel about it?' I ask carefully. I know this isn't all about me. It must be weird enough for Tom seeing his mum move on with any man, let alone his Maths teacher and his ex-girlfriend's stepdad at that.

'I'm OK.' He shrugs. 'I just want her to be happy, and Mr Tay— *Stu*,' he corrects himself with a grin, 'is a good guy.'

'He is,' I state.

He turns to face me, putting his knee up on the bench seat. I reach for my drink and take a sip.

'How are things with you?' he asks pointedly.

I smile and nod. 'They're good. What about you?'

I glance at him and realise with sudden sinking feeling that he's looking very on edge. My first thought is: *Nina*. My next is: *No!*

'What is it?' I try to sound chilled. 'Have you met someone?'

'Not exactly,' he replies, sighing and raking his hand through his hair. He rests his elbow on the top of the seat back and chews on his thumbnail, avoiding eye contact.

'Tell me!' I try to sound light-hearted, but my voice is wobbling.

He sighs heavily. 'It's Isla.'

Gravity takes hold of my sinking feeling and pulls it even lower. Isla is his beautiful ex-girlfriend – the one who cheated on him.

Tom rubs his hands over his face and looks at me wearily. 'We slept together a week ago.'

I feel sick, utterly sick. And I know that I have absolutely no right to at all. It's his business whom he chooses to see – but he told me he and Isla were through, and the thought of him being with her in a way that he wasn't with me... Sorry, but it hurts.

'You had sex with her?' I ask, shrinking into myself.

'Yeah,' he replies, studying my reaction. 'It just happened. We were at a party. You know we still talk. I ended up walking her home and her parents were away and I went in for a coffee…' He doesn't need to elaborate.

'I thought you said you never go back?'

'I guess I was wrong.' He meets my eyes for a long moment before I look away.

'So will you and she get back togeth—'

'No,' he cuts me off. 'We'd both been drinking, but, when we sobered up, I think she regretted it. The next morning I left to come here. I've had some distance and we can't pick up where we left off. Too much has happened.'

It's only a small relief. The fact still stands that he slept with her and the thought of them together like that makes me want to throw up. Yes, even though he's no longer my boyfriend, I'm not over him. That much is clear. And it doesn't matter how much I want to be with Jack, Tom can still affect me.

'Are you OK?' he asks.

'Yeah,' I nod.

He leans forward in his seat, regarding me intently. His gaze is confident and controlled. It's almost as though my shaky reaction is giving him strength.

'How are things with you and Jack?' he asks.

I nod and look down at my drink. 'Good.'

'Are you out in the open now?'

When I shake my head, I feel sort of dirty.

'Can we talk about something else?' I ask, but I can't relax after that, and it's not long before I call it a night.

Tom says he *will* come to the gig the next night, but the following day I can't stop thinking about him. Stu keeps asking if I'm alright and I tell him that I'm feeling a little off colour. It's not a lie.

194

I'm still rattled later that afternoon when Drew, Jack, Brandon, Miles and Agnes drive into the city. Stu and I go to meet them for a snack in their hotel bar, which is a ten-minute walk away. Annie booked Stu's and my rooms. I shouldn't complain about five-star luxury, but I wish I could have stayed in a hotel that had enough rooms available for all of us.

Maybe Jack can sense that my mood is related to Tom, because the looks he keeps giving me are loaded. But we don't get a chance to speak until afterwards when I'm in Agnes's room, getting ready. He comes to knock on her door.

'We don't have a lotta time,' Agnes chastises him.

He ignores her, tugging me into the bathroom and shutting the door behind me, turning the lock.

'What's wrong?' He comes right out and says it, crossing his arms and staring at me with his blue-grey eyes.

'Nothing.' I shake my head.

'Don't lie to me. Tom?' He raises one eyebrow. He is so far from being OK with me seeing my ex-boyfriend.

I sigh and sit down on the toilet seat, staring ahead morosely. 'What did he say? Did he try it on?'

'He slept with his ex-girlfriend,' I say abruptly.

He reels backwards, staring at me with wide eyes.

I look up at him resignedly. 'OK? That's it,' I state firmly.

'It bothers you.'

I don't deny it.

'Really bothers you,' he says, staring at me warily.

'We don't have time for this,' I say. 'We'll talk about it later.'

'The hell we will. Do you want him back? Is that it?'

'No!' I exclaim. 'It's over! I'm with you. I just feel a bit weird about it, OK?' To my dismay, my eyes fill up with tears. 'For God's sake, you're going to ruin my make-up,' I snap. 'I don't want to talk about this any more. Go.'

He glares at me and turns round, leaving the bathroom without another word. I feel guilty, and confused, but I let him leave.

On the plus side, all of the drama with Jack and Tom makes me forget my nerves, so it's not until we're in the limo lent to us by Johnny's record company that it actually hits me that I'm going to be performing to a sold-out audience this evening.

There are four other bands on the bill and we're supposed to be on third, but, when we arrive at the venue, the manager tells us that he's shifted things around a bit and wants us to go on last.

From the way my bandmates are looking at each other, this is good news.

'You must've impressed them last time,' Stu says, looking around at us.

'The extra publicity has helped,' Brandon states, raising a glass of champagne to me as I blush. Johnny popped the cork on a bottle when we got in the car.

'So your *teen girl squad* is coming tonight?' Miles asks, giving me a look that I'm not sure is more teasing or patronising.

'They're not all girls,' I state. 'Rafe is coming, and Justin Kelly, too. Oh, and Lottie is bringing Peter from her show.'

I glance at Brandon when I mention Lottie. He looks pleased. His girlfriend had a family thing on this weekend so she stayed in LA.

'Is Tom coming?' Stu asks me innocently.

I feel Jack's eyes on me as I reply. 'Yeah, he is.' I turn to Agnes.

196

'Could you do me a favour and look after him? He doesn't know anyone here.'

'Apart from me,' Stu chips in indignantly. 'Invisible, am I?'

'No offence, Stu, but I can't really see you up the front in the mosh pit.'

Beside Stu, Johnny stifles a smile.

'What about you?' Brandon asks, looking at my dad. 'Can we expect to see you in the mosh pit?'

'No, I'll be backstage,' he replies.

'Really?' Brandon frowns, and even Miles looks a little put out.

Johnny doesn't respond, just looks at me and raises his eyebrows.

The last time we did a gig here, Johnny said that he'd stay backstage so as not to draw attention to himself. He said the gig was about us and our music and he didn't want to detract from that. But this time I'm not really sure that's necessary.

'Why don't you go out the front?' I ask when we're backstage in the green room. We've just done a soundcheck, and the venue doors are opening in less than half an hour. The green room is packed with four other bands and their friends and it's like a party in here with everyone drinking and chatting away.

'For the same reasons I didn't last time,' Johnny replies, indulging me with an answer where he didn't for Brandon.

'But everyone knows you're my dad now. I've done interviews about it and it's all over the internet. It can only help.'

'You don't need me to help you, chick.' He eyes me levelly with those piercing green eyes of his.

'We need all the help we can get,' I state, begging to differ.

'Trust me. It's better that you do this on your own.'

I can't help but feel annoyed at him. All publicity is good

197

publicity, right? And my dad at the front of our gig would be absolutely incredible publicity. Why is he being difficult about this? Doesn't he want us to succeed?

He squeezes my shoulder as Agnes joins us, and then leaves to talk to Sam.

'You look super hot,' Agnes says. 'Even if I do say so myself.'

'I really love this skirt,' I reply with a smile. It's the black with gold thread number and the bodice is fitted tight over my chest.

'Let's hope it's good enough for Sienna,' she says acerbically.

I purse my lips at her. 'Don't be like that. I told her I couldn't go shopping with her.'

'I'm just kidding.' She smiles, but I can tell that she's not.

'You don't mind that the girls from school are coming, do you?' I ask awkwardly.

'I guess not,' she replies half-heartedly. 'They're right: it will help raise your profile – and theirs, too,' she mutters as an afterthought. 'But I kind of liked it when it was just you and me, you know?'

I smile at her sadly. 'You're still my best friend over here. I don't know what I'd do without you.'

She smiles back at me and we give each other an impulsive hug.

'Are you still missing Brett?' I ask, pulling away to study her face.

'Yeah, but I'm getting used to it. I'm actually thinking about going to Australia for Spring Break.'

'That's a long way to go for a week, not to mention expensive,' I say.

'It'd be worth it,' she replies, brushing at a mark on my cheek.

'Have you got lipstick on me?' I ask.

'Just a touch. At least I'm not wearing red like you.'

I'm wearing a deep crimson shade and my hair is in a loose updo with blonde tendrils falling down around my face.

'Jessie!' Stu says breathlessly. It looks like he's been trying to hunt me out for a while.

'Hi! What's up?'

'Tom texted me. He's outside. Do you want me to let him in?'

'Damn, I turned my phone off! Yes, please, thanks!'

He hurries off and I glance at Agnes. 'You *will* look after him, right?'

'I'll guard him with my life,' she replies, and then we both cast a look to where Jack is standing. He's chatting to a couple of guys from a punk-rock group that happened to be here the last time we played. Maybe he senses our attention, because he glances over his shoulder and meets my eyes. A jolt goes through me and then Brandon joins us.

'Is your dad seriously planning to hang backstage?' he asks.

'Yeah,' I reply, rolling my eyes. 'He won't give. Sorry.'

He tuts. 'So what are we doing after?' He raises one eyebrow at Agnes. 'We gonna hit a club?'

My heart sinks. Clubbing means Sam. *Actually, Sam's supposed to be flying straight home with Johnny...*

'My hotel bar's pretty cool,' I say. Just putting it out there...

At that moment, Stu returns, closely followed by Tom. Tom looks nervous.

He also looks gorgeous.

He's dressed down for the gig in battered denim jeans and a faded black Arcade Fire band T-shirt.

'Hey,' he says, joining me.

I give him a brief hug and step back. 'You remember Brandon, my bandmate,' I say.

'Tom, right?' Brandon says, shaking his hand. 'Glad you could come, dude.'

And then I remember: *Brandon and Miles don't know that we've split up…*

Maybe it won't matter, I tell myself in a panic. *After all, even if Tom and I aren't together, it doesn't mean that Jack and I are.*

I stifle a sigh. At first it was kind of fun, the secrecy. I enjoyed the thrill of sneaking away and kissing each other and trying not to be discovered. But now I'm a bit over it.

I glance back and meet Jack's eye again. He breaks away from his conversation with the other band members and comes over.

'Tom,' he says in a voice laced with meaning, offering his hand.

'Alright,' Tom replies, giving Jack's hand a reluctant shake. They're not exactly disguising their dislike of each other.

'Can I borrow you for a minute?' Jack says to me.

'Do you need me, too?' Brandon chips in, overhearing. He must think Jack wants to discuss the band.

'No, just Jessie,' Jack states firmly. He takes my hand and tugs me out of the green room.

'What is it?' I hiss, irritably. 'You made that a bit obvious.'

He leads me round the corner and out of sight, pulling me into the darkened stage wings.

'Jack, no.' I put my hand on his chest and push him away. He takes a step backwards, looking like I've thumped him. 'You can't kiss me, you'll ruin my lipstick,' I say.

He breathes in sharply. 'Is that the only reason?'

'Yes.' I smirk at him and he looks relieved.

He takes a step towards me, placing his hands on my hips.

'Will it ruin your lipstick if I kiss you here?' he asks suggestively, pressing his lips a centimetre to the right of mine.

'No,' I murmur.

'How about here?' He kisses the underside of my jaw, near my earlobe. My heartbeat spikes. 'Yes or no?' he asks.

'No,' I whisper, shivering.

'And here?' He trails several kisses down my neck, sliding his hands up along the curves of my waist. His thumbs come to rest on my bodice, just beneath the inbuilt bra cups.

My head is spinning as I grab his face and hold him still. His blue-grey eyes stare back at me with amusement.

'You can kiss me wherever you want later, OK? Just don't ruin my lipstick.'

The corners of his lips tilt up as I realise what I've just said.

'Wherever I want, huh?'

My cheeks flame and I let go of his face.

But he grins, raising one eyebrow as his thumbs stroke rhythmically across my ribs, back and forward.

A thrill ripples down my spine and I feel a little less shy and a little more confident as I stare back at him. And then I remember where we are.

I sigh quietly and place my hands on his chest, keeping him at bay.

'Come on, we should go back to the green room. The others will be wondering what we're doing.'

'Let them wonder,' he says, taking my hands and pulling me closer.

'Jack, are you trying to give the game away?' I ask with a frown.

'Maybe,' he replies in a low voice, caressing my cheek.

I pull back from him. 'Do you mean it?'

He shrugs. 'That's what you want, isn't it?'

'They'll be angry.'

'So?' He raises one eyebrow.

'What if you and I split up?' I ask.

'I think this is heading the other way, don't you?' He gives me a significant look.

'What do you mean?' I ask. 'If you're talking about—'

'I said we'd take it slow,' he interrupts me. 'Didn't I?'

'Yes, but…' My thoughts jump to Tom and Isla. I still feel stung that he slept with her recently, but at least they were in love when they lost their virginity to each other.

'Tell me what you're thinking,' he states.

I look at him, square in the eye, and force myself to open up to him. 'Jack, I don't want to do that with someone who doesn't love me.'

His eyebrow twitches as he stares down at me.

'Come on,' I say downheartedly, stepping away from him. 'We really should join the others.'

'Hey, we're not done here,' he states, as I begin to walk away.

'I think we are. For now, anyway,' I reply, casting a regretful look at him as I approach the green room.

He strides over and places his hand on the door handle, his eyes flashing as he stares down at me.

'I've never been in love, so I don't know if this is it, but what I feel for you is pretty fucking intense,' he says in a low voice, yanking open the door. 'Just so you know,' he throws back at me before stalking into the room.

Chapter 19

My mind is reeling as we wait backstage for the band before us to finish their fifth and final song. Jack's last words to me keep replaying over and over inside my head. He doesn't know what love is, but he more or less said that this could be it.

I've been on edge in the green room. He didn't come and stand with me when I returned to Agnes and Tom, choosing instead to mingle with the other bands. I tried to catch his eye a couple of times, but, if he felt me staring, he didn't show it.

Now I'm standing with Johnny, and Jack's talking to a roadie. He feels so far away, but he's only three metres to my right.

The crowd outside cheers and applauds as the last band finishes up, and then they're coming offstage.

'Ready?' Johnny asks me.

I nod and glance at Jack again.

'Everything OK?' Johnny asks.

I nod and look back at him. 'Better than OK,' I reply with a small smile.

He raises one eyebrow at me quizzically, but I don't elaborate, instead turning to watch the roadie hooking Jack up to his electric guitar. Jack glances my way and a jolt goes through me as he meets my eyes at last. I hold his gaze as the seconds tick by.

I want to be with him.

A moment later, his lips tilt up at the corners. Can he read my mind?

He jerks his head, beckoning me over.

'Good luck,' Johnny says.

'Are you sure you won't go and watch from the front?' I ask him one last time, coming out of my Jack-induced trance to give him a pleading look.

He shakes his head and purses his lips, then taps my elbow and nods towards Jack.

I sigh and walk away, but my spirits lift as soon as I'm beside my boyfriend.

'OK?' he asks, swinging his guitar behind him so the strap stretches across the front of his chest. He slips his hand round my waist and pulls me flush to his side.

'Ready, All Hypers?' Brandon interrupts. I jolt, but Jack's grip on me tightens. I'm pretty sure Brandon notices, but he's used to his bandmate being tactile.

Miles joins us, too.

'Is Tom out front?' he asks me, glancing at Jack's hand around my waist.

'I think so. He's with Agnes,' I reply edgily.

'He doesn't like *you* much, does he?' Brandon says to Jack with a cheeky grin.

'The feeling's mutual,' Jack replies drily, reaching out to finger a lock of my hair with his free hand.

Brandon stares at the ceiling and shakes his head. 'Oh, well, you'll get over it.' He pats Jack's chest and glances in the direction of the crowd. 'Better let her go now, dude. You don't want to cause a scene if he sees you like that.'

'I'm not letting her go,' Jack states.

Our bandmates freeze, regarding us with trepidation.

'Tom and I broke up at Christmas,' I say guiltily. 'He and I are just friends.'

They look taken aback at my belated revelation, their eyes darting between Jack and me, and then it dawns on them – and they are not happy.

'You better be fucking kidding me,' Brandon says furiously.

'Sorry, I'm not,' Jack replies, deadly serious. He appears relaxed from the outside, standing there with me in his arms, but I can feel the tension radiating from him.

'Can we talk about this later?' I desperately interject. 'Now is not the time.'

'There will never be a good time for *this*,' Brandon snaps, throwing us both a look of disgust.

'You're unbelievable!' Miles shakes his head at Jack before turning his back on us.

I stare at Jack in dismay. Did he have to do this now?

The stage manager indicates that it's time for us to go on and I feel sick as Miles and Brandon stalk out on stage to the sound of the crowd cheering.

'It'll be OK,' Jack says, clasping my head to his hard, warm chest so he can plant a kiss on top of it. It's a fast, sweet gesture and it does make me feel marginally better, but then he lets me go. He flashes me a grin and swings his guitar round to the front, then strides out onstage as Miles starts to hammer his drum kit. I take a deep breath and join them.

Nothing prepares you for the adrenaline of being in front of a big crowd of people. The venue is even more packed than last time – there must be at least five hundred people here. I don't think I'll ever feel ready to perform – the nerves will never vanish completely – but will it always be such an incredible rush?

I step up to the mic. The lights are blinding – I can't see Stu or Tom or my friends. All I can do is sing.

The bass and beat of my bandmates' instruments reverberate through my body and my voice fills the venue.

Despite what happened only moments ago, I feel on top of the world.

The first two songs fly by. Sometimes the lights on the stage turn on the audience instead and then I seek out my friends, right near the front. I can't see Stu, but the others are all there, jumping up and down and getting hot and sweaty in the crowd. It is the most amazing high, but it's so hard to describe. It makes me want to do better. It makes me want to succeed.

By the third song, I'm totally in my element. I have time to take in my surroundings and I notice Johnny backstage, standing in the wings with his arms folded, smiling at me.

I glance at Jack. His dark hair is damp with sweat and falling down across his forehead. He's wearing a dark graphic T-shirt and his POW! tattoo stands out on his right arm, his biceps lean and muscled. His other tattoo, an intricate criss-crossing bracelet of black ink running round his left wrist, is usually hidden by a series of leather straps, but not today. He is sexy as hell. He grins at me before jumping in the air and pounding his guitar with boundless energy.

I look over my other shoulder and catch Brandon's eye. He still doesn't look amused as he gazes back at me, but even he manages a wry smile, and then I turn and walk towards Miles, singing directly to him and trying to make him smile. It works. He's still angry, but finally he gives in and grins back at me.

I only just manage to stop myself from laughing into the microphone as I turn round and see Brandon shaking his head, entertained.

Nothing can dampen our enthusiasm while we're playing. And I have a sudden surge of faith that everything is going to be alright.

The boys play a longer intro to our last song, while I address the audience. I'm slightly stunned at the noise from the crowd when I introduce myself. The stage manager raises the lights so I can see my friends at the front. I introduce the band, starting with Miles and moving onto Brandon. It doesn't escape my notice that Jack gets the loudest screams. I imagine most of the girls in the audience would give anything to get up close and personal with him.

I don't know how I'm supposed to feel about that, but, as we launch into our final song, I mostly just feel proud.

I don't want the gig to end but end it does. We walk offstage to raucous applause and shouts for more, and then we're in each other's arms in a four-way, sweaty hug, squeezing the life out of each other.

Brandon shoves Jack gently and prods him in his chest.

'Don't fuck it up,' he warns.

Jack takes it on the chin, but I notice he doesn't make any promises.

I turn away from them and look for Johnny.

'You were unbelievable,' he says, laughing as he holds his arms open. I run into them and they close around me.

'Really?' I ask hopefully, smiling up at him.

'Even better than last time.' He shakes his head at me. 'Seriously, chick. You really didn't need me.'

I purse my lips at him in amusement.

'So what now?' he asks. 'Back to the hotel bar for a quick drink before I fly home?'

'Sounds great. Can I see if the others can come?'

''Course. There's a tour bus waiting outside.'

'You mean limo?'

'Nah, swapped it for the tour bus. I didn't realise how many people you had coming.'

'Nice one!' I hold up my hand to high-five him and he raises his eyebrows at me as he drily obliges.

'Jess?' Jack calls, nodding towards the stage. 'They want us to do one more.'

'Are you serious?' I glance from him to the stage manager. Nobody else did an encore.

'Go for it,' Johnny says with a grin. I'm stunned as I follow my bandmates back into the light.

Chapter 20

'You look tired,' I say to Stu. We've taken over a whole corner of the hotel bar and everyone is in high spirits. 'You should probably call it a night,' I add solemnly.

'You trying to get rid of me?' he asks.

'Yes,' I state.

He shakes his head good-naturedly. 'OK, Jess, but you know what Johnny said. Stay—'

'—in the venue!' I finish his sentence for him.

Johnny and Sam left half an hour ago, but not before reiterating the rules.

'I know.' I nudge Stu's ribs with my elbow. 'I'll see you at breakfast.'

'Text me when you're upstairs,' he replies. 'So I know you're safe. No later than midnight.'

'Come on!' I squawk.

'One a.m., then.'

'OK. One it is. Thanks.'

209

That was easier than I thought.

I grin at all of my friends as the last of the adults finally leave us. I'm not including Jack's brother Drew in that description, although he has recently turned twenty-one.

Agnes and Drew are deep in conversation, her dark head and his blond head pressed together. Brandon is, as usual, getting up close and personal with Lottie. I watch them uneasily. He's a fine one to talk, telling Jack not to mess things up. He has a girlfriend, yet he flirts with Lottie every time he sees her – and she's affected by it. I don't know what he's playing at.

Tom is surrounded by Gina, Margarita, Sienna, Rafe, Jenna, Justin and Peter. They've all gone nutty over his English accent.

And Jack is on the other side of me, talking shop to Miles.

I never did ask Johnny about flying my other friends over from the UK. They were all a little off the last time we talked, and I didn't feel comfortable asking my dad to splash out again so soon after the last time. I was only going to be here for the weekend, so I wouldn't have seen much of them. Stu has asked me to go home for Spring Break, and that *would* be nice, but right now I think I'd rather stay here with Jack.

I squeeze his leg.

'You OK?' he asks, reaching over and stroking his thumb across my lips. 'It's wearing off,' he notes of my lipstick.

'Shall I reapply some?'

'Not if it means I can't kiss you.'

We smile at each other. I notice Miles taking a sip of his drink and realise that I've interrupted their conversation. I nod pointedly at Miles for Jack's benefit and pat his leg again. 'See you in a bit,' I whisper.

He nods and lets me go.

I've barely spoken to Tom tonight. As soon as I approach the huddle he's in, everyone sits back and merrily makes room for me. It's still a squash, though, so I end up completely flush with Tom's right-hand side.

'You having fun?' I ask him with a grin.

'It's a bit surreal,' he replies under his breath.

I giggle. I know what he means. We're surrounded by Gina and Peter, two of the country's hottest up-and-coming actors; Margarita, child star turned sexy pop starlet; Justin and Jenna, tween music TV hosts; and Sienna and Rafe, who are well on their way to supermodel stardom. And then there's Tom and me.

'Do you like them?' I whisper. 'They're nice, aren't they?'

He smirks at me. 'A bit full of it,' he replies.

I frown. 'What do you mean?'

He cocks his head to one side, a curious expression on his face.

'What's that look for?' I ask, bemused.

'You *are* keeping your feet on the ground, Jessie Pickerill, aren't you?'

My insides flutter as I stare back at him. It's been a long time since anyone's used my name like that. My real name.

'Of course I am,' I whisper, wanting it to be true, but not entirely sure that it is.

'I hope so,' he says, not once taking his brown eyes from mine.

Considering all of the people around us, it feels like we're alone in the room. I jolt suddenly and look away, instantly locking Jack in a stare.

I force a smile, but he doesn't smile back, so I impulsively stick my tongue out at him. He returns to his conversation with Miles.

'So what did you think of the gig?' I ask Tom, trying to perk up our conversation a bit. It was getting kind of heavy.

'Incredible,' he replies, nodding. 'Bit of a change from SingStar.'

'I rocked SingStar,' I tease. 'When I was drunk,' I add offhandedly.

'Exactly.' He laughs. 'Seriously, you're like a proper rock chick now. It's pretty nuts.'

'Aw, thanks.' I bump his arm with mine. 'So you fly home tomorrow?'

'Yep, tomorrow evening.'

'Maybe we could catch up for lunch?'

'Maybe. I'll have to see what my dad and Riley are doing first.'

'OK, cool. Listen, I've got to head to the bathroom. See you in a bit.'

As I'm washing my hands, I note that my lipstick has indeed worn off. I have a sheer lipgloss with me so I apply some of that instead, smiling as I remember Jack's earlier words.

'Hell, yeah, let's do it!' I hear Rafe saying as I return.

'What's this?' I ask, sitting back down opposite Jack.

'There's a club around the corner,' Sienna tells me. 'Let's go!'

'Oh. I can't. I have to stay here,' I reply with regret.

'Come on, it's literally a minute away,' she tries to persuade me. 'Don't you feel like dancing?'

I really *do* feel like dancing, actually. 'Absolutely, but…'

'No selfies,' Margarita interjects. 'Your dad will *not* know that you've left this hotel.'

'Scout's honour!' Gina says, holding her hand up. 'I've already posted a dozen pictures tonight, anyway.'

'You know you want to,' Sienna urges. 'Anyone would have to get through all of us to get to you,' she points out. 'We can be your bodyguards.'

I look at Jack. He shrugs, leaving me to make up my own mind.

'I'm pretty tempted,' I say with a grin. I'm rewarded with cheers.

That's when I see Tom's face. He's looking at me like I'm mental.

I get up and go over to him as everyone else finishes their drinks and gathers up their things. 'Honestly, it'll be fi—'

He cuts me off. 'Are you crazy? After what happened in England?'

'It's not like that over here!' I whisper, not wanting to draw attention to us. 'That was a one-off. Johnny's gone totally overboard on all of this security nonsense.'

'You're out of your mind,' he says. 'It's not worth it. Aren't you having enough fun here?'

'Yeah, but I want to dance. And everyone else wants to go, too.' In fact, Rafe, Sienna, Brandon, Lottie and Peter are already halfway across the room.

'Come on!' I urge.

'What's the problem?' Jack asks, as he joins us.

'Are you seriously letting her do this?' Tom asks Jack.

'Have you tried stopping her?' Jack replies, draping his arm round my shoulders.

'I have, as a matter of fact,' Tom tells him, his hackles rising.

'And where did that get you?' Jack challenges.

'Stop it,' I say, putting my hand on Jack's chest. It's hard as a rock, he's so rigid.

'Almost killed, if you want to know,' Tom states furiously, balling up his fists.

'Tom, please,' I beg, slipping out of Jack's grasp to stand between them. 'I'm sure it'll be OK.' But inside I'm wavering.

'Are you guys coming or what?' Margarita shouts from across the bar. Miles is standing beside her, frowning at us.

213

Oh, God, *I don't know!*

'We can stay here with you, Jessie,' Agnes offers. I glance from her to Drew. He's staring at Margarita, but Agnes, I can see, will do whatever I ask of her.

I look at Jack again. *What should I do?*

'Don't,' Tom warns me.

'Fine!' I snap, sitting down in a huff, my mind made up. Or at least Tom's mind made up for me.

He sighs and sits down next to me.

'But don't let me stop you,' I say to Drew. I can see him hesitating. 'Go, seriously, I really don't mind.'

'Are you sure?' he asks.

'Of course I am.' I'll only feel bad if he stays. I don't even know him that well.

'I'll let the others know,' Agnes says.

'Don't stay behind, Agnes,' I call after her reluctantly. 'Go have fun.'

She glances back at me and shakes her head. 'No way.'

I stare up at Jack miserably, but he doesn't look down at me because he's glaring at Tom. I glance at Tom to see them in an all-out staring match. They look like they're going to thump each other.

'Shouldn't you be going to the club with your friends?' Tom asks Jack sarcastically. 'After all, Jessie's not your girlfriend. Why would you stay here?'

'They know,' I tell Tom, as Jack slumps down on the bench seat next to me and slides his arm round my waist.

'Jack told them earlier,' I add. Tom looks shocked. I glance at Jack to see him raising a smug eyebrow at Tom.

'Stop it.' I whack Jack's stomach.

'I'm not doing anything,' he replies casually.

'Do you know what?' I say, sitting upright. 'If you two don't cut it out, I'm going upstairs to bed.'

'What have I missed?' Agnes asks, returning.

'Nothing.' I sigh. 'I'm sorry. Clubbing would've been fun.'

'I didn't feel like going, anyway,' Agnes says. 'My feet are killing me.'

I smile at her. She's such a good friend.

'Thank you,' I murmur. I feel a little stung that the others barely even looked back.

'And thank you, too,' I say to Tom. 'You're right. I would have only regretted it.' I sigh. 'Jeez, I've become a right bore.'

'I'm going for a smoke,' Jack interrupts, getting to his feet. 'Anyone for a drink on my way back?'

'I'll sort out the drinks,' Tom says, standing up.

Agnes and I watch as they walk away from us. Side by side, they're about the same height and build, one with black hair, the other with brown. Jack peels off to go outside while Tom heads to the bar. I turn to Agnes.

'So it's all out in the open now, is it?' she asks.

My eyes widen. 'I can't believe I didn't tell you! Jack came clean to Brandon and Miles before the show.'

'Were they angry?'

'Furious.'

I fill her in. Her phone beeps, distracting us. She yawns as she pulls it out of her bag.

'I'm so tired,' she says. 'I was up late, FaceTiming Brett.'

'What the hell do you talk about?' I ask with a grin. She's always FaceTiming him.

'Sometimes we don't talk at all,' she replies with a smirk.

215

I give her a perplexed look and then I realise what's she's saying. 'TMI alert!'

She laughs and blushes beetroot. 'Surely you and Jack—' Then she stops herself. 'No, actually, despite what I said earlier, I don't want to know what you and my brother get up to in the bedroom.'

'Good, because I wouldn't tell you, anyway,' I say primly. 'Not that we get up to much. Well, we don't get up to anything.'

'Really?' She seems surprised and a bit curious.

'I thought you didn't want to know.' Now I'm the one who's blushing. 'Who's your message from?' I nod at her phone.

'Nice change of subject, Jess,' she says with a grin, reading the message. Her face falls.

'What is it?'

'It's from Drew. He says that Dana's at the club. She's with Sienna.'

'You are kidding me!' I snatch the phone from her. 'Oh my God! Can you imagine if I'd gone? If Johnny had found out?' It would have been bad enough me disobeying him about leaving the hotel, but, if he'd heard that I'd been even in the same room as Dana, he would've hit the roof.

Over the next half an hour, Agnes's yawns become so violent that I can tell my friend is on the verge of falling asleep here in front of us.

'Sorry, Jess. I know it's only eleven thirty, but I really have to hit the sack,' she says.

'I'll walk you back to your hotel,' Jack offers, standing up.

I open up my arms and engulf her in a hug. 'I love you. Thank you for being here for me.'

216

'Always,' she replies, squeezing me in return.

'I'll be back in a bit,' Jack says, shooting Tom a dark look before returning his gaze to me.

I nod. 'OK.'

When they've gone, Tom and I sit back down.

He turns to face me, resting his elbow on the back of the seat.

'I like your T-shirt,' I tell him, nodding at the Arcade Fire one he's wearing.

He glances down at it and then smiles at me. 'I like what you're wearing, too.'

'Agnes got this for me.'

'How does that work? Do you pay her?'

'Of course.' I pick up my drink and take a sip before explaining. 'Unless she's made it herself, she tends to buy what she thinks will suit me and return what doesn't work. I pay her for what we keep. Well, my dad does. He gives me an allowance,' I say with an embarrassed shrug.

Tom shakes his head at me. 'It's mad how much your life has changed.'

'You're telling me,' I agree, putting my glass back on the table.

'But you like it, though? You seem happy.'

I nod. 'I am. Well, as much as I can be, considering.' I swallow, as my thoughts turn to Mum. 'Obviously I still miss—'

I don't finish my sentence. He reaches over and clasps my shoulder and I stare back into his sympathetic brown eyes. A moment later, I force myself to avert my gaze and he in turn lets his hand drop, shifting in his seat.

I swallow again, trying to get rid of the lump in my throat.

'Are you looking forward to going home?' I ask, seeking a lighter subject.

He shrugs and stares down at the table. 'Not especially.'

'Will you call Isla?' So much for a lighter subject.

He pauses. 'Yeah, I guess we need to talk, clear the air,' he says heavily.

'Are you sure it's over?'

'I thought I was sure before.' He looks at me. 'Seems I can't be sure about anything any more.'

We hold eye contact and this time I really don't *want* to look away.

'So it's official with you guys, then,' he murmurs. 'Does that mean you've—?' His voice trails off, but it's clear what he's asking.

'No, not yet.'

He looks surprised, but pleased. I could kick myself for being so open. Jack would have wanted me to tell him that it's none of his business. *I* should have wanted to tell him that, but my reply just came out.

'It won't be long though,' I say.

I don't know why I suddenly wanted to hurt Tom, but the reason is irrelevant because it worked.

'Sorry,' I mumble. 'I don't know why I just said that.'

'You wanted to punish me,' he states in a low voice.

I pull a face. 'Why would I want to punish you?'

'Because you hate that I had sex with Isla.'

'That's not true—'

'Don't lie.'

'OK!' I exclaim. Suddenly red mist clouds my vision. 'I do hate it! Why the hell did you do that? You told me that you were done!'

'Finally we've cut the bullshit,' he says firmly. 'I knew it bothered you. Why didn't you just say so?'

'Because it *shouldn't* bother me,' I reply, my eyes stinging. 'You're a free agent. I'm with Jack and I'm happy with him, but…'

I shake my head helplessly, hating that I'm rapidly getting upset.

'You still have feelings for me,' he finishes my sentence.

I cover my face with my hands and sit forward. I can't believe we're having this conversation.

He places his hand on my back and edges closer, resting his chin on my shoulder.

'I still have feelings for you, too,' he whispers.

'Tom, stop it.' I come to my senses and shrug off his contact. 'I don't want to do this. You and I are just friends.'

'We were never friends,' he spits. 'I always wanted you, way before you became Jessie fucking Jefferson. I had the hots for you in Year Ten, even before you started going out with that little twat Dean Smith.'

'But you were with Beatrice, then,' I round on him, stunned. 'And Maria before her and Isla more recently,' I add unhappily. He's always had girls after him.

'Doesn't mean I didn't fancy you, though. You weren't interested.'

'I *was*,' I correct him. 'I just didn't want you getting a big head. It was big enough already,' I add acerbically.

He gives me a wry grin. And then his gaze drops to my lips and all the hairs on the back of my neck stand up.

'I think I should probably go to bed,' I murmur.

'Isn't Jack coming back?' he asks.

I bite my lip. 'I'll text him and tell him not to bother.'

He watches while I locate my phone and type out a quick text, pressing Send. As I'm putting it back in my bag, Tom caresses my face and draws me towards him.

'No!' I jump to my feet, realising with horror that he was

about to kiss me. 'No,' I say again, backing away as he resignedly stands up. My legs hit the bench seat and there's nowhere else for me to go.

We lock eyes and my heart pounds against my ribcage. He's so close and so familiar. It would be easy to step into his arms. But I can't do that. I don't *want* to do that. I want Jack.

Tom's expression softens suddenly as all of these emotions battle it out on my features. He looks almost sorry for me. I freeze as he bends down to press a gentle kiss to my cheek.

'I'll go now,' he says, as my throat constricts. 'I'll call you when I'm home.'

I nod quickly, but I'm not sure that he will. I watch as he steps away and walks out of the bar, and then I leave myself, fighting back tears as I press the button for the lift.

Chapter 21

I've only been inside my room for a few minutes, first texting Stu to let him know I'm safe and then sitting on the end of my bed and taking a series of deep, shaky breaths, when there's a knock on the door. I open it reluctantly to find Jack standing there. He gives me a black look.

'What's this about?' He shows me his phone.

'How did you know which room I was in?' I ask with surprise, as he edges past me into the darkened room.

'Johnny told you to charge the drinks to it, remember?'

'Oh, yeah.' I've been batting around the number 1056 all night. I shut the door behind him.

'Seriously, though, why didn't you wait for me?' He's frowning. 'You knew I'd only be gone twenty minutes.'

I sigh. 'I was tired. Tom and I had an argument—'

'About what?' he asks immediately.

'I'm so tired, Jack. I'm sorry, but I want to just call it a night.'

'Did he try it on?'

'Yeah, as a matter of fact, he did,' I snap, sick of fending Jack off.

He looks like I've slapped him.

'I'm sorry,' I say.

'Did you—'

'No, I bloody didn't! OK? I didn't. I pushed him away and now here we are.'

'Christ,' he mutters, slumping onto the bed and clasping his head in his hands.

I go to sit beside him. After a while, he sighs and turns to look at me in the low-level light.

'You pushed him away?' His brow is furrowed.

I nod. 'Yeah.' I swallow. 'I want to be with you, not him.'

He sighs and presses a tentative kiss on my lips. I instantly melt into him and, after a moment, our tongues entwine and we fall back onto the bed. I rake my fingers through his black hair as his hands skim over the curves of my body and shivers roll uncontrollably up and down my spine. I'm tingling all over as we kiss passionately.

He breaks away, staring at me heatedly. 'Do you want me to go?'

'No, I want you to stay. Not to, you know,' I add quickly, my face burning. 'But I want you here.'

'Slow,' he whispers meaningfully and the desire in his eyes makes my heart feel like it's going to peter out.

I slip my hands inside his T-shirt and his taut stomach retracts as I run my palms across his chest. I want his T-shirt off. As though reading my mind, he drags it over his head and discards it before kissing me again.

'I want to see you, too,' he says against my mouth, his hands firm on my waist.

I hesitate only a second before nodding, and then he's pulling my chest flush to his so he can reach round and unzip my bodice.

No boy has ever seen me naked from the waist up and I shiver as he eases me up and away from him, slipping my arms out of the straps. I'm not wearing a bra underneath and I'm not sure he was expecting that because his eyes widen momentarily. He stares at me intently, and then his hands are on me. I kiss him hungrily, and he pulls me harder against him, attacking my mouth. He reaches round to the zip at the back of my skirt.

'Can I?' he murmurs.

I don't reply, just nod.

I slip out of my skirt and place my hand on his stomach, my thumb brushing the buttons of his jeans. He knows what I'm asking and I blush and shyly avert my gaze as he stands up to take them off. He tugs down the bedcovers and I climb under them gratefully.

The warmth of his body heat shocks me as he returns to the bed and pulls me against him. We're only wearing our underwear now and it feels crazily good having his skin next to mine.

'You said anywhere I want, right?' he reminds me teasingly, as his kisses begin to trail downwards.

'I didn't mean it.' I clasp his head in my hands as his mouth finds one of my nipples.

And then I'm lost in the sensation, my face burning and my body tingling all over.

'I want to touch you,' he says, returning his lips to my mouth.

'Where?' I ask breathlessly.

His eyes, dark in this light, stare back at me as his hand traces across my stomach and further down. I squeeze my legs shut, trying to control the sensations I'm feeling. He kisses me gently.

223

'Let me,' he urges.

I force myself to relax slightly and then I jolt violently as his hand moves. He smiles against my lips before kissing me again.

I feel like I'm a firework with a very long fuse. The fuse has already been lit and the thought of it fizzling out is unbearable. I think I want the firework to go off.

A surprisingly short while later, that's exactly what it does.

'God!' I pant against his mouth, completely overwhelmed. 'What the hell just happened?'

I stare at him, stunned. My body is still quaking with aftershocks.

'Haven't you had one before?' he asks, perplexed.

'No.'

'What, not even by yourself?'

My face heats up and I shake my head at him. He looks bemused.

'Have you?' I ask curiously.

'Of course,' he replies with a smirk and a shrug.

'Show me how to do it to you,' I whisper, and all of the amusement dies on his face. He kisses me urgently and takes my hand, guiding it downwards.

The next morning, the hotel phone wakes me up.

'Hello?' I answer groggily.

'Wakey-wakey,' Stu says chirpily. 'Are you coming downstairs? Breakfast will be over if you're not quick.'

'I'll throw on some clothes and will be with you in five,' I reply.

It's not until we've ended the call and I've placed the phone back in its cradle that I remember.

I look sharply to my left to see the empty space beside me. Jack was there when I fell asleep. Where is he now? I sit bolt upright in bed and listen for sounds coming from the bathroom.

'Jack?' I ask the room, but it doesn't reply.

I flop back onto the bed and hold my hand to my forehead.

Oh. My. God.

A hot flush comes over me and my face grows prickly with embarrassment as I remember what we did last night. What *he* did. What *I* did.

And now he's gone. Why? Did I do something wrong? Did I not do enough?

I check around me for signs of a note. But there's nothing, just the indentation of his head on the pillow. I reach for my phone to see if he's called, but, when I switch it on and type in the pin, the first thing I spot is a text:

Call me when you wake up – Jack x

I smile and type out a quick text:

Just going for breakfast with Stu x

My phone starts to ring.

'Hello,' I answer, my heart thumping.

'Hey,' Jack says.

'You OK?'

'Are you?' He turns the question around.

'Yeah.' I feel my face heat up again. 'I'm fine. What time did you leave?'

'About two thirty. I woke up and freaked about your stepdad finding me there in the morning.'

225

'Aah,' I reply. 'Not just ducking out on me, then?'

'Are you crazy? After last night?' He sounds disbelieving. 'I wanna do it again.'

A thrill rockets through me. 'Me too,' I admit.

Chapter 22

After that, everything is different.

'Jesus, Jack, can you stop kissing Jessie long enough to talk about business? I preferred it when you guys were being secretive.'

Jack rolls his eyes, but taps my thigh. I hop off his lap and, smiling to myself, go to sit on the beanbag next to him.

It's exactly one week after our gig in San Francisco and Jack and I are now officially a couple – a full-blown, out-in-the-open couple. And I love it.

I'm at his house for Saturday afternoon band practice. This week has been even more mental than usual. I did my written driving test – and passed! – so now I have a provisional driving licence. I still need to do fifty hours of supervised driving before I can take my road test, so it doesn't look like I'll be able to do that before the summer. But I'll still be able to drive before everyone else in my year back home.

Because I didn't do any of my homework at the weekend, I've had to play catch-up every night after school. I had to cancel another week of singing and keyboard lessons, and I haven't done anywhere near enough of my GCSE prep, but the one thing I've refused to sacrifice is band practice.

Not that Brandon and Miles appear to appreciate my dedication.

OK, so I might be snogging their bandmate at every opportunity, but come on, a girl's gotta have priorities. I've only been allowed one measly hour here on Tuesday and Thursday.

Today I'm on a high, though. It's Saturday and I get to spend all evening with Jack because his mum asked me to have dinner with the family.

Even Johnny seemed a little taken aback by the invitation.

'It's getting serious, then?'

I shrugged. 'I guess so. More serious than it was, in any case,' I added, not wanting him to jump to any conclusions, however correct they may be.

'Do I need to remind you to be careful?' he asked.

'No!' I squawked.

Luckily he didn't give me a lecture.

'What sort of business?' Jack asks, bringing my attention back to Brandon, who's just returned to the games room after taking a phone call.

He holds said phone aloft.

'That was the manager of Marlin's.' His eyes are bright with excitement. 'They want us to do a gig there next Saturday.'

Jack is on his feet in an instant.

'You are kidding me?' Miles gasps.

Marlin's is owned by two members of nineties rock supergroup Downtown Pigs and it opened last summer in town. So far, the club has made a bit of a name for itself by allowing unsigned bands to support headline artists on Saturday nights. Rumour has it that a couple of bands were recently offered record deals purely off the back of their Marlin's gig. A&R music talent scouts regularly hang out there.

I knew Brandon had been speaking to Marlin's about trying to line something up, but this has come much quicker than any of us expected.

'Who are we supporting?' I ask, sitting up in anticipation.

Brandon grins. 'Cool Kids.'

Did that squeal come from me? 'No way! I love their music!'

'How many songs do they want us to play?' Miles asks.

'Six,' Brandon replies. 'So we can keep the same set as San Francisco, but just add one more.'

'"Fan Club Riot?"' Jack suggests. It's a new song that I had a hand in writing so I love the idea.

Brandon nods thoughtfully. 'Sounds good, but we're still gonna need to practise, so no bunking off.'

I hold up my palms. 'I'm in. If you want more of me this week, I'll cancel some stuff.'

'Do it,' Brandon states. 'Let's get to work straight away,' he adds.

We don't need telling twice.

I was hoping to have a little downtime with Jack before dinner, but our rehearsals run into the evening. Eventually Agnes comes to find us.

'Mom wants to know how much longer you're gonna be?'

A flurry of nerves goes through me.

'Sorry, dudes, we'd better call it quits for the night,' Jack apologises, lifting his strap over his head and going to hang his guitar on the wall.

I rub the back of my neck. My feet are aching from standing so long. Miles reaches for a towel hanging over his drum kit and dries the sweat on his forehead. Even Brandon looks knackered.

'Monday after school?' he asks.

I nod. 'Yep, I'll tell Harry.' I don't really want to cancel my music teacher again – especially in the run-up to a gig. He's built up my confidence so much, and really helped my vocals, but it can't be avoided.

Agnes sidles up to me. 'You ready to meet Tim?'

I narrow my eyes at her. For me, this dinner was about impressing her mum, so the fact that she's mentioning her stepdad makes me nervous.

'I guess so.' It's a bit strange that I haven't met him already, but he always seems to be working. 'Should I be worried?' I ask.

Jack comes over and throws his arm round my shoulders. 'Don't freak her out,' he warns Agnes.

OK, now I'm freaked out.

'So, Jessie, what are your plans for the future?'

I stare across the table and into the steely blue eyes of Tim Walkington Junior – aka Stepdad Number Two. Jack's mum and Tim have been together for over four years. He 'looks after her', apparently. He's also extremely wealthy.

'Well, I… I'm hoping it takes off with the band,' I admit, already sensing this will be the wrong answer.

He snorts. Beside me, Jack stiffens. 'You kids,' he chides

patronisingly. 'You all want to be the next Johnny Jefferson – am I right?'

I open my mouth to speak, but he cuts me off, shaking his head as he speaks. 'Living in dreamland.'

'Tim,' Jack's mother says quietly, but her tone lacks conviction.

Tim sits back in his seat and eyeballs me. 'We're just having a conversation, Lucille.'

'Dinner will be served soon,' she says apologetically, flashing me a shaky smile before glancing towards the kitchen.

Agnes looks distinctly uncomfortable as she takes a sip of her water and, beside me, Jack is tense as his eyes fix on his stepdad. Tim ignores him.

He's probably in his late fifties and is tall and tanned with silver-grey hair. He's wearing a smart white shirt over grey trousers and looks like the sort of man who would rarely be seen out of a suit. He reminds me of Johnny's solicitor, Wendel Rosgrove. He was daunting as well.

'So...' His voice trails off and he raises one eyebrow at me. 'Music.'

I nod, trying to locate my confidence. I didn't let Wendel bully me when Stu first contacted him about Johnny being my dad, so I'm not going to let this guy get to me, either. 'It's what I'm passionate about,' I state.

'Hmm.' He sneers. 'If we *all* went around doing only what we were passionate about, we wouldn't be very successful.'

'We'd be a hell of a lot happier, though,' Jack butts in.

'Well said, darling,' Lucille murmurs, reaching across the table to pat her son's hand.

Tim glares at Jack. 'And *are* you happy? Working in a shop?'

Jack shrugs. 'Yeah, as a matter of fact, I am. It suits me for what I'm doing.'

'Which is what, exactly?'

'We've had this talk before,' Jack states. 'You can't bully me into going to college. It's not gonna happen.'

'Are you planning on going to college?' Tim asks me, barely batting an eyelid at Jack.

'I'm not sure yet. I'm trying to keep my options open,' I reply.

'It helps when your father is a multimillionaire,' he says sardonically. 'Doesn't it, Jack?'

'My dad's not a multimillionaire,' Jack replies.

'I wasn't talking about Billy,' Tim says with distaste.

'*You're* not my dad,' Jack says in a low voice.

Thankfully the kitchen doors swing open and the cook comes out with our meal.

'Why didn't you tell me what he was like?' I ask, as soon as we've managed to get out of there. We're in Jack's car and he's driving me home. I haven't told Johnny. If he has a problem with my boyfriend driving me home rather than Sam or Davey, I'll deal with it later. I need to be with Jack.

He shrugs. 'I didn't know he'd be like that with you. He's never met any of my girlfriends before.'

'I didn't know he was even like that with you,' I say quietly, reaching across to touch his knee. I feel so bad for him. 'Why haven't you or Agnes ever told me?' I ask.

He stares rigidly out of the front window, concentrating on navigating the winding hills of Bel Air. I'm not sure he's going to reply, but then he shrugs.

'I guess we prefer to pretend it's not a big deal.'

'But it *is* a big deal!' I erupt. 'He's a complete wanker!'

This makes him smirk. He shoots me a look and then opens

up. 'He's not always like that. Most of the time he doesn't give a shit what we do or who we're with, but then he'll make up for it by being a total dick for days on end. He's a contradictory ass. Anyway,' he says with a sigh. 'I won't be living there forever.'

'Why are you still living there now? You're eighteen. You could get your own place.'

He shakes his head. 'I wouldn't leave Agnes.'

My heart expands violently as I stare at him and I feel more for him in that moment than I ever have.

'Jack,' I say quietly.

'Mmm?'

'Pull over.'

He glances at me sideways and then does as I ask, flicking on his indicator and turning into a lay-by. The City of Angels spills out before us, the street lamps stretching for mile after sparkling mile.

I unclick my seatbelt and climb onto his lap, threading my hands behind his neck. I kiss him gently.

He kisses me back, but doesn't deepen it like he usually would. Instead he clasps my head in his hand and presses his face to my neck, breathing in and exhaling heavily.

'I love you,' I whisper.

He sleepily lifts his head. 'What?'

His blue-grey eyes study me in the darkness of the car, his eyebrows pulled together.

'You heard me,' I say, gazing back at him.

Now his lips are on mine, teasing my mouth apart. I kiss him back passionately, wanting more, always wanting more. A car screams round the corner, its headlights momentarily blinding us.

'Where can we go?' I ask him.

'Drew's?' he suggests.

'Wouldn't that be weird?'

He shakes his head.

'Have you been there before?' I ask warily.

He looks instantly uncomfortable.

'Screw that,' I say with annoyance. I'm not going anywhere he used to take girls back to.

'Hey,' he says quietly, drawing me close.

'Let's go out,' I say suddenly. 'Seriously, let's go out. I just want to go somewhere with you, a club or something. Let's just go and have an ordinary night together without all the shit.'

'What about Johnny? He'd want Sam with you.'

'Well, for once, my dad is not going to get what he wants. I'm serious!' I exclaim, as Jack stares at me warily. 'He'll get over it. Come on, let's live a little.'

He shrugs. 'OK. If that's what you wanna do.'

'It is,' I say adamantly. And, with that, I climb off his lap and put my seatbelt back on.

'He wasn't like that in the beginning,' Jack confides. We're in a booth at the back of a dark nightclub. Drew is DJ-ing here tonight and Jack knew the doorman so we got in with no trouble at all. He's bringing me up to date about his stepdad.

'He seemed like a good guy, someone who'd take care of my mom. But he's become bitter over the years, resenting Agnes and me. He makes us feel like we're not wanted.'

'What does your mum have to say about it?'

'Nothing. She's weak.'

I bite my lip and stare at him.

'It's not her fault,' he says disconsolately. 'Dad screwed her around

234

so much that she was pretty messed up when they got divorced. I didn't understand at the time, but it makes more sense now. Luckily Tim's not around a whole lot so we don't have to deal with him. And I can always go and stay with Drew if he's on my case too much.'

'Do you do that often?'

'A bit.'

And there I was, worrying about him staying overnight at his brother's. I didn't trust him, wondered what he was getting up to, but it appears Jack was just trying to put some distance between him and his stepdad.

'Is he like that with Agnes?'

He shakes his head. 'He's not nearly as bad with her. But she's still at school. So far, she's doing everything he wants. Hell knows what'll happen if she doesn't do well in her classes. Luckily she *wants* to go to college, but Tim would prefer her to major in business or law rather than fashion design. But he can't have everything.'

Suddenly Drew slides into the booth opposite us. 'Hi!' he says, grinning across the table.

'Hi!' I reply, smiling. 'How are you?'

'Good. Almost time for me.' He nods at the DJ decks.

He's even taller and broader than Jack with dark-blond hair like his dad and ink all up his arms.

'You want to jump on the decks later?' he asks Jack.

'I haven't got my records with me,' Jack replies.

'Use mine,' Drew offers.

Jack shrugs and glances at me.

'Go for it,' I tell him. 'I'll amuse myself.'

Jack raises his eyebrows at me and returns his gaze to his brother. 'Why? You don't usually give up your time slot.'

'There's a girl here I wanna hang out with.'

Jack tuts and leans back in his seat. 'Sure.'

'Cool, thanks, dude.' Drew grins. 'You guys need drinks? I'm going to the bar.'

'I'm driving,' Jack replies, 'but Jessie will.'

They both glance at me. I nod. 'Thanks. Maybe a beer?'

'Done.'

He gets up again and strides off in the direction of the bar. I smile at Jack. He sorted me out a fake ID last week, but I don't need to use it with Drew around. Jack glances past me, over my right shoulder.

'Is that Sienna?' he asks.

I follow the line of his sight and see my friend on the dance floor getting up close and personal with a very good-looking guy.

'Wow, yeah, it is.'

She called me on Sunday while I was still in San Francisco and vehemently stated that she only let Dana know which club she was in after she heard I wasn't going. I hadn't even asked her about it, but I guess she knew I'd find out.

I can't stop Sienna from being nice to her sister. Why would I want to? I just hope she's right about Dana having changed.

'You gonna go say hi?' Jack asks.

'I should,' I reply. 'Back in a sec.'

I slide out of the booth and make my way onto the dance floor. Sienna spies me almost immediately.

'Jessie!' she gasps with delight, shoving the guy she's dancing with out of the way and coming over to engulf me in her slightly sweaty arms. 'What are you doing here?'

'I came with Jack,' I respond. 'Who was that?' I ask, nodding at the guy.

'Just a model from my agency. Hot, isn't he? Oh my God, this is so cool,' she gushes, not waiting for an answer. Abruptly, her face shifts.

'What?' I ask.

'I'm here with Dana,' she admits, looking awkward.

I instantly come over in a cold flush. *Shit.*

'Please don't stress out,' she implores. 'Seriously, why don't you come meet her? I think you'd really like her!'

'No way,' I say. 'I don't even want to be within ten metres of her.'

Sienna's expression blackens and she shrugs, looking away from me. 'OK,' she says simply. 'See you at school, then.'

Now I feel bad. 'Sorry.' I grab her arm before she can walk off. 'I know it's not your fault; it's just complex, that's all.'

'I know it is.' She frowns. 'But it's ridiculous. I'm sorry, but it is. She's my sister; you're my friend; Dana and Johnny don't even speak to each other. She's trying really hard to make amends. If you could just meet her, you'd see that. She's not on drugs – she doesn't even drink, for Christ's sake. What's the worst that could happen?'

I take a deep breath. Maybe she's right. And I want to be a supportive friend. 'Fine,' I say. 'Introduce me.' I can make up my own mind whether I think she's a bitch from hell.

'Yay!' Sienna says, beaming as she leads me off the dance floor. I shoot a look in Jack's direction, but can't see him for all the people.

Dana is in a booth on the other side of the club, surrounded by a group of hipsters, all in their late twenties.

'Little sis!' she cries, as we approach. 'And—' Her eyes widen at the sight of me. 'And Jessie Jefferson,' she finishes, looking surprised. I manage not to flinch at the name she uses, but how the hell did she know who I was?

'She's seen photos of us together,' Sienna says hastily, as Dana stands up and edges out of the booth.

Nerves tangle in my stomach as she joins us.

'I'm Dana,' she says, holding her hand out.

'I know,' I reply, obligingly shaking it.

She's strikingly attractive, in skinny black jeans, stiletto heels and a sheer gold top. She's tiny and her cheekbones are prominent, but she's nowhere near as gaunt as she was in the pictures I saw of her after her infamous overdoses. Her long dark hair is tied up into a high, sleek ponytail and her eyeliner is even thicker and heavier than Agnes's. She's wearing a dark shade of lipstick that's almost black in colour.

She shakes her head at me, seemingly amazed. 'You look just like your daddy.' I tense, but she smiles brightly. 'It's great to finally meet you,' she adds. 'Sienna says you're cool.'

'Thanks,' I reply, not knowing what else to say.

'You want to sit down?' she offers. I look at the people she's with and decide that I couldn't want anything less. They seem pretty daunting.

'Thanks, but my boyfriend is here.'

'The elusive Jack Mitchell,' she declares, grinning, as I stare at her in alarm. 'Don't look so freaked out, baby girl. My little sis has told me a lot about you. Let's meet him.'

'OK, sure,' I say, trying to sound nonchalant and mature. My pulse races as I lead Dana and Sienna through the crowd to the booth on the other side of the dance floor. Drew is sitting opposite Jack, nursing a beer. They both look up as we approach. Jack freezes.

'Dana's here,' I explain nervously. 'She wanted to say hi.'

'Hi,' Jack and Drew say simultaneously, as Dana slides into the booth next to Drew. I guess we're sitting down, then.

'Hey, guys. You DJ-ing tonight?' she asks Drew amiably. I remember that they met last weekend at the club.

Sienna sits down next to her sister. She looks happy.

I really need to relax. My friend is just trying to show me that her sister is OK. And maybe she is. I pick up the beer Drew bought me and take a large gulp.

Half an hour later and Dana is still with us. We've heard all about the plans for her comeback tour, and she seems genuinely thrilled for us that we've got a gig at Marlin's.

'I like your ink, dude,' she says to Jack, reaching across to take his arm. She brings it closer to her face, studying his POW! tattoo. 'Is this your only one?'

She releases his arm and he fiddles with the leather straps around his wrist to reveal his tattooed bracelet.

'Nice,' she says, pulling the neckline of her sheer gold top down to reveal a tattoo of angel wings just below her collarbone. 'I got this done before Christmas.'

'Cool,' Drew says, leaning in to study it.

'Ironic,' she replies, smirking at him before studying his tattoos in turn. 'Where do you go?' she asks.

I give Jack a sideways look as they start talking tattoo parlours among themselves.

Eventually she returns her attention to Jack. 'What are you planning on getting done next?' she asks.

'Er, I'm thinking about getting some soundwaves done on the back of my neck,' he tells her, rubbing the spot accordingly.

'Really?' I ask him in surprise.

He looks at me from out of the corner of his eye.

'Have you got any ink?' Dana asks me suddenly.

I shake my head. 'Not yet.'

'Johnny won't let her,' Sienna reveals with a grin and I wince at the sound of my dad's name being brought into the conversation.

Dana laughs wryly. 'Really?' She raises one dark eyebrow. 'That's rich, coming from him.' She smirks at me and I stiffen at her overfamiliar comment, but try not to let it show.

I shrug and force a smile. 'Tell me about it.'

'What would you get done?' she asks.

I glance at Jack, remembering the time he drew a couple of tattoos on me. We ended up snogging each other senseless.

'I was thinking about noughts and crosses,' I reply eventually. 'My mum used to play it with me when I was a kid. She always let me win.'

I suddenly feel tainted. I didn't want to share something so personal with her, but my revelation came out without me thinking.

Dana nods. 'That sounds really cool.' She reaches across the table and gives my hand a quick squeeze. I look down in surprise. Her fingernails are short and blunt and painted blood-red. 'I'm sorry about your mom, chick. I just wanted to say that.'

I'm caught off guard as she lets me go. It occurs to me that she used the same term of affection that my dad uses. 'Well, guess I should get back to my friends,' she says, as I remember with unease how much else she and Johnny used to have in common. 'It was nice meeting you.' Sienna stands up to let her out. 'Maybe see you around.' She looks at each of us sitting at the table, but her eyes rest on me.

'Bye,' I say, trying to shake off my bad feeling as I wonder what's going through that mind of hers.

Chapter 23

'Dana's coming to your gig at Marlin's. I'm sorry!' Sienna cries before I can say anything. 'I didn't tell her to get tickets – she just got them after you guys told her about it on Saturday night. She's bringing a bunch of her muso friends.'

'It's OK,' I reply with a sigh. It's Wednesday afternoon and we're at school, on our way to first period. Sienna accosted me as I was slamming my locker. 'Johnny's not even going,' I tell her. 'I need to chill out about it, so honestly don't worry.'

I'd completely forgotten, but, when Brandon lined up the Marlin's gig, it was for the same weekend that Johnny is launching his new album in New York. I'm gutted to be missing such a momentous occasion, but there was no way I could let my bandmates down by backing out. Johnny understood. He, Meg and the boys are flying to New York on Friday, straight after Barney finishes school. Gramps is coming to look after me. *Yes!*

'Did you like her?' Sienna asks of her sister, her face contorting into a hopeful expression.

I nod. 'I did, actually.'

She beams at me and links her arm through mine. 'I told you! She's cool, isn't she? I can't believe how much we've been hanging out. She's so nice to me now!' she gushes.

'I'm really happy for you,' I say, trying to keep a straight face at her enthusiasm as we reach our classroom.

Brandon and Miles were disappointed that Johnny wouldn't be at our Marlin's gig, but Jack seemed disappointed only for me.

Butterflies fill my stomach at the memory of us in his car on the way home on Saturday night. We pulled up and climbed into the back seat. Things got pretty heated. The windows were still fogged up when Lewis buzzed us in through the gates. I hope he didn't notice.

I sigh again. I've got it so bad.

My dad wasn't thrilled when he found out that Jack had driven me home, but he let it go. Thankfully he didn't discover that we'd gone to a club – or that Dana had been there. I'm sure I would have been in for it if he had.

But I don't regret anything. I loved being able to act like an ordinary girl again. It's addictive.

On Friday afternoon, I stand and wave off my family with a lump in my throat. I'm gutted to miss my dad's launch party. It would've been fun, and I had a genuine reason to celebrate because I'm singing on one track on the album. But it can't be helped. I'll see them all on Sunday night. Right now, I need to focus on the band.

'Righto!' Gramps exclaims, clapping his hands together as we return inside. 'Let's get this party started!'

I laugh at him.

'Where's the vodka?' he asks. 'Got any ciggies?'

'I don't smoke any more,' I tell him.

'You don't smoke *any more*?' he asks, aghast. 'When did you smoke in the first place, you bleedin' idiot? Don't you know it's a filthy habit?'

I roll my eyes at his teasing. To my surprise, he pulls a packet of fags out of his back pocket. 'Gramps!' I berate.

'I'll be outside,' he says with a cheeky grin.

He's such a bad influence, I think with amusement. But hopefully, between the two of us, we'll be able to convince Johnny and Meg that he's capable of being my guardian while they're away on tour. He might not be the best of role models, but he's good company, and most of the staff will be here, too. Annie and Eddie are going on tour, though I heard Annie talking to Meg about bringing in a temporary cook while they're away. I know they're seriously considering letting me stay here with Gramps. Score!

Eddie has done tacos for dinner and, as we sit in the kitchen and tuck in, Gramps wants to know all about tomorrow's gig. I fill him in.

'It's going to be fab. I'm looking forward to it,' he says.

'Are you coming?' I ask with surprise.

'Of course I am!' He frowns at me. 'I can still rock a mosh pit.'

I try not to laugh.

'How are things going with Billy Mitchell's kid?' he asks, taking a sip of his whisky and Coke. I'm just drinking Coke, but I can smell the alcohol from here.

'Good,' I reply with a smile. 'Better than good.'

'Is it love?' he asks wryly, and I can't tell if he's taking the mickey or not.

'Might be,' I reply with a smirk.

'So what's going to happen if you screw it all up, hey?'

'Christ, Gramps, in with the direct question!'

He shrugs, shaking back his wispy greying hair. 'I'm curious.'

'Well, I'm hoping we won't split up. I really like him—'

'And the feeling's mutual, is it?'

'Yes,' I state, surer about this now than I've ever been.

'That's nice,' he says amiably, taking a bite of his taco and crunching away. 'You'll be OK in any case,' he declares, reaching for his drink and taking a large gulp.

'What do you mean by that?'

He shrugs again. 'When you split up,' he says.

'Well, yeah, sure, I mean, *if* we split up, I probably will be OK. People get over broken hearts all the time, don't they?'

'I'm not talking about your broken heart.' He waves that comment away dismissively. 'I'm talking about your music career. You'll be OK. You're Johnny Jefferson's daughter. You'll be able to go solo. You don't need a band.'

'But I like being in a band,' I say, my heart squeezing at the idea of standing up on a stage alone without Brandon, Jack and Miles around me.

'Your dad said that, too, but look at him now. He didn't want to split up with his band,' Gramps confides. 'He loved those guys, but it wasn't meant to be. When you're on your own, you get to call the shots. You don't have to bow down to anyone. I think he found that liberating.'

244

'Do you think he ever misses being in Fence, though?' I ask thoughtfully.

Gramps looks nonplussed. 'He had to make the best of what happened.'

That didn't exactly answer my question.

'Yeah, I think he misses those boys sometimes,' Gramps says when I prod him for a proper answer. 'I heard Finch and Lennie were talking about getting everyone back together for a reunion tour a couple of years ago. Johnny vetoed it.'

'Really?' I never knew that. Finch was Fence's bass guitarist and Lennie the drummer.

'Yeah. A decade is a lot of water under the bridge, but some things should be laid to rest.'

'Well, if All Hype get a record deal, we wouldn't have any choice but to stay together. We couldn't breach our contract.'

'True,' Gramps says. 'That's what happened with Johnny. Thoroughly fucked him up, it did. Whoops, shouldn't swear,' he says as an afterthought.

'Forget it.' I purse my lips. 'Go on,' I say encouragingly.

'He needed a break, but they had to keep going. Drove them apart, it did. Then Johnny went off the rails. Dark times.' He shakes his head, remembering. 'Dark times. Been through a lot, my boy. Glad to see him settled now.'

I smile. 'Me too.'

Jack and Agnes come over to hang out that night and I notice how much more relaxed Jack is in Gramps's company than he is with my dad. We sit in the living room, chatting and watching TV. When Gramps and Jack go outside to have a smoke, Agnes turns to me.

'I've booked my ticket,' she says, her eyes bright with excitement.

'To Australia?' I ask, sitting bolt upright. 'Was Tim OK with that?'

'Mum booked it for me! Tim wanted to take her away to the Caribbean, anyway, so he doesn't really care what I'll be getting up to. I leave in a week!'

'That's amazing! I bet you can't wait to see him.'

She flops back on her seat and fans her face. 'That is the understatement of the year.' She shakes her head. 'Oh, to be in his arms again,' she says melodramatically. She casts me a look. 'You and Jack seem to be—' Her voice trails off. 'Closer?'

She gives me a knowing look, but at that point Jack and Gramps come back inside. 'Who's for a drink?' Gramps asks, setting off in the direction of the kitchen.

'I can't, I'm driving,' Jack calls after him.

'What?' Gramps halts in his tracks and turns round to gape at him. 'What did you have to go and drive for? Doesn't the great Billy Mitchell have a Davey?'

'No, he doesn't, actually,' Jack replies. 'Anyway, we don't live with our dad.'

'Shame,' Gramps says, heading into the kitchen. 'He was a lot of fun, that one,' he calls over his shoulder.

I glance at Agnes, but she appears to be taking the comment in good humour. She certainly didn't find it funny when her 'fun' rock-star dad was cheating on her mum.

'Why don't you lot stay over?' Gramps suggests, returning to the coffee table with the bottle of whisky he bought at Duty Free. Johnny doesn't tend to keep alcohol in the house. 'We've got spare beds. Don't we, Jessie? Why would we want to end this party before it's even started?'

246

Jack and Agnes look at each other and then at me.

Jack staying overnight here? Johnny would *not* approve. But is anyone going to tell him?

An hour later, Gramps has crashed out on the sofa and is snoring heavily. Agnes giggles.

'I think he might've been a bigger party animal in his heyday,' she says. 'Do you really think it's OK for us to stay? We could call a taxi.'

'No, stay,' I urge, steadily avoiding Jack's eyes as I experience a pang of guilt.

'I'm gonna have to hit the sack soon,' she warns, yawning.

'Let me show you where your room is.'

Gramps is staying in one of the spare rooms and the other has a super-king-size bed in it, but neither Agnes nor Jack seem thrilled about the idea of sharing.

'One of you could always crash in Barney's room,' I say edgily.

'Who are you trying to kid?' Agnes says, shoving her brother's arm. 'You'll be in with Jessie as soon as the lights are off.'

Jack's cheeks redden, and mine do, too. I'm pretty sure the same thought had occurred to us both.

While Agnes gets ready for bed, Jack and I go downstairs to try to rouse Gramps from sleep. He grumbles and groans, but we manage to get him to stumble his way upstairs and into his bedroom. I remove his shoes and Jack turns down the covers, but we don't attempt to take off his T-shirt and jeans.

'He's a lotta fun,' Jack whispers, as we leave his room.

I grin. 'He is, isn't he? Night, Agnes!' I call, as we pass her room.

'Night!' she calls back. 'Don't let the bed bugs bite!'

I nervously lead the way to my bedroom. Jack follows me inside and I push the door shut.

'I'm going to get ready for bed,' I tell him, walking into the bathroom. He leans against the door frame, watching me as I brush my teeth.

'Can I borrow that after you?' he asks.

I rinse and spit before looking up at him. 'We've probably got a spare around here somewhere.'

'I don't mind if you don't,' he says, holding his hand out for the brush.

'I don't mind,' I say with a small smile, passing it over.

He stares at me with amusement in the reflection of the mirror as he brushes his own teeth.

It's so strange having him here in my bedroom, in my bathroom. I know I'd love it if I didn't feel quite so guilty. I force myself out of the room to go and find my PJs.

We've been so intimate already, but I feel bizarrely uncomfortable about getting undressed in front of him, so, when he's brushed his teeth, we exchange places and I shut the door to finish getting ready. I come out of the bathroom to find him already under the covers of my bed.

I feel skittish as I slide in beside him. He opens up his arms to me and I notice he's undressed to his boxers.

'This is weird,' I say in a low voice. 'I'm supposed to be proving to my dad that he can trust me while he's away on tour. I feel bad.'

Jack tenses. 'Do you want me to sleep in Barney's room?' he asks. 'I can.'

'I don't feel *that* bad,' I exclaim. 'Jesus.'

He laughs softly. I reach behind me and turn off the light, then snuggle up against him.

We lie there in the dark, neither of us making a move on the other. Maybe the guilt is getting to him, too.

'I bet your dad has security cameras hooked up somewhere,' he whispers.

'God, can you imagine?' I whisper back.

'What if Gramps wakes up in the morning and freaks out?' he asks. 'He was pretty drunk when he suggested we stay here.'

'He did suggest it, though,' I reason. 'He invited you to sleep over.'

'Yeah, in your spare room.'

'I don't think he thought that through. My dad and Meg used to have more guest rooms, but then they had Barney and Phoenix – and I came along. He probably forgot there are just two rooms now.'

'Mmm,' Jack replies.

'Maybe we should try to sleep,' I say reluctantly.

'Mmm,' he says again.

We fall silent.

My hand is resting on his chest and I stroke my thumb back and forth, wondering how I'll ever be able to nod off when I feel this jittery. I run my fingertips across his chest and up to his neck, tracing along his jaw.

'God,' he says in a strangled voice, his hands coming to life on my body. He draws me on top of him as his lips crash against my mouth. I can feel him beneath me and I know he's as turned on as I am.

'I want you so much,' he says in a low, urgent voice.

'I want you, too,' I reply, gasping as he rocks me against him. 'But we can't. Not here, tonight. It doesn't feel right.'

'I know,' he says dully, kissing me on my lips and then sighing against my mouth.

I turn my face away. 'I bet you wish I was more experienced.'

'Are you kidding me?' he asks with disbelief. 'Your lack of experience is one of the biggest turn-ons in the world to me.'

'It is?' I ask with surprise.

He nods his head in the darkness, pushing his hand through my hair. 'I'm so into you, Jessie. Can't you tell?' he asks quietly.

My stomach flutters. A moment later, I lean down to kiss him.

Chapter 24

Jack and Agnes leave the next morning before Gramps even rolls out of bed. Incredibly, the old codger doesn't mention my friends when he finally makes it downstairs for what we should probably call lunch, so it's just as well they made themselves scarce. Maybe he really did only ask them because alcohol had loosened his tongue. He seems to have forgotten all about the invitation now in any case. No harm done, I hope...

I didn't get much sleep, but I'm on a high despite my incessant yawning. I feel intensely jittery every time I think about Jack. We came so close to going the whole way last night. I wanted to. I would have – he was the one that was restrained.

I'm not seeing him until tonight at Marlin's, though Agnes drives over in the afternoon to help me get ready.

'So who's coming tonight? All the usual suspects?'

'I think so,' I reply. 'I know Sienna's definitely going to be there, and Margarita and Gina said they'd try to drop in.'

Agnes continues to apply greeny-gold eyeshadow to my lids.

'I know they'll never be real friends,' I say, sighing. 'But it's good of them to come, don't you think?'

'I suppose so,' she says blandly, pausing in what she's doing. 'It's a shame Johnny can't be there. He's the one the press really want to see.'

'I know,' I say sadly. 'Forget the press. *I* want him there. But Gramps is coming.'

This is both a blessing and a curse. I'm glad of his support, even if it's a *bit* embarrassing to have my grandfather at a gig.

'My dad'll be there, too,' Agnes says.

I perk up. 'Really? That's good. Gramps knows Billy so maybe they can hang out together at the bar.'

She casts her eyes to the ceiling. 'I'm sure they will.'

The green room at Marlin's is much quieter than the one backstage at San Francisco, but then the band that we're supporting – Cool Kids – hasn't arrived yet. In fact, Agnes and I appear to be early. I'm relieved when Jack, Brandon and Miles walk through the door.

Jack comes straight over to me.

'Hey,' he says, locking eyes with me as he leans down to give me a kiss.

'Hey,' I reply, my heart already jumping at his proximity.

'You OK?' he asks.

'A bit nervous,' I reply.

'You'll be fine,' he says reassuringly.

After a while, the room begins to fill up. The manager of Marlin's comes over to introduce herself, and then Ross Whitely, the lead singer of Downtown Pigs and co-owner of the club, walks in. The noise in the room dies abruptly, before gently starting back up again. I've seen that sort of thing happen countless times with Johnny.

'Where's Miss Jefferson?' he drawls.

Why can nobody seem to use the Pickerill bit?

His eyes show signs of recognition as he quickly locates me. 'I just wanted to say hi.' He comes over to shake my hand and I almost die on the spot. 'Your dad called me earlier, told me to treat you well.' He smiles with amusement as I splutter my apologies. 'Don't panic, honey, it's all good. Johnny and I go way back.' He claps me on my back. 'Good luck, you're gonna do great. A few important people here tonight.'

Does he mean people from record labels? *Oh my God!*

'Introduce me to your bandmates,' he says. I quickly come to my senses and do as he asks, but, as soon as he's left us to it, I pour myself a glass of champagne from the green room bar. I think I'm going to need Dutch courage tonight.

'You're really freaking out, aren't you?' Jack says later, eyeing me contemplatively. 'What's got into you?'

'I don't know,' I say uneasily. 'I wish my dad was here.'

'You don't need him. We've practised so much. Just do what you've been doing. You're gonna rock it.'

I flash him a grateful smile. 'Thanks.'

He grabs my face and kisses my forehead.

'Damn this red lipstick,' I mutter.

He grins at me. 'We'll make up for it later.' He leans in close. 'Anywhere I want, right?' he asks in a meaningful voice. I quiver, my nerves momentarily forgotten as he pulls back to stare down at me.

'God, I fancy you,' I state, looking up at him. He grins. A moment later, it's time to go on.

I don't know what I was worried about. The venue is packed to the rafters and the atmosphere is electric. I automatically assumed it was busy because Cool Kids are playing after us, but, to my amazement, a big chunk of the crowd is singing along to our songs. The buzz is *incredible*.

'Wow!' I erupt, as we go offstage. Jack throws his arms round me and Brandon comes and jumps on him from behind.

'*Woo!*' he yelps. 'Guys, that was awesome! Did you see that crowd?'

Miles joins us, shaking his head, his face split into the biggest grin I've ever seen him sporting.

'Jessie, you rocked it!' he says, grabbing me for a hug.

'Nicely done, kids!' Ross from Downtown Pigs booms, stepping out of the shadows. 'Come and have a glass of fizz in the green room. I'll introduce you to Cool Kids.'

After a while, we head back out of the green room into the main part of the club to watch the gig. I find Gramps at the bar.

'Kiddo!' he shouts merrily. He's had a few. More than a few, actually. 'That was fandabbydozy!'

I laugh as he engulfs me. 'You want a drink to celebrate?'

'I've already had one.' *Or two. Or three. Who's counting?*

'I won't tell if you don't,' he says in my ear, flagging down the barman.

I'm missing Johnny less by the minute.

I'm on the biggest high in the next couple of hours. Jack and I go right into the crowd when Cool Kids kick off and I'm so happy to be able to watch a gig without a bodyguard eyeballing me. I'm stunned when a few people ask for my autograph. I can't quite believe anyone wants it. But, on the whole, no one bothers us and I'm able to hang with Jack and dance to the music.

Gina and Margarita didn't stay long because they had another party to go to, and Lottie avoided coming at all when she heard Maisie would be here. Brandon and his girlfriend have gone for dinner with Miles and his friend Paul, and Agnes, who was starving, but Sienna and Dana are lurking somewhere. I'm trying to avoid them. I'm not sure if Dana and Gramps ever met, but I don't want to risk it.

I've drunk too much champagne and I need the bathroom, so, once Cool Kids go offstage, I make a dash for the toilets. There's still an annoyingly large queue and I'm gutted to miss the encore. By the time I return to the emptying dance floor, Cool Kids have well and truly finished their set. I look around for Jack and freeze. He's with Eve, my All Hype predecessor.

She's tall and slim with ebony skin and a cool, sleek and shiny boy-cut. I watch, feeling sick, as she hooks her hand round his neck and leans in close to speak in his ear. A moment later, she drops her arm and takes a step backwards, giving him a long, meaningful look before spinning on her heels and striding away. He stares after her, but I can't see his face from here. I feel sick as I approach him. He turns round and catches my eye, his mouth stretching into a thin line when he sees the bleakness of my expression.

'What was that about?' I demand to know.

'She apologised.'

'What?' I'm shocked.

'For saying what she said about you. She admits you can sing.'

255

'Really.' I'm not sure I believe she means it.

'Really.' He stares at me pointedly. He shakes his head and clasps my face, planting a kiss directly on my lips.

I smirk as he pulls away. I applied fresh lipstick in the bathroom.

'Fuck,' he mutters, wiping his mouth on the sleeve of his denim shirt and grinning at me. My heart flips.

'There you are!' Sienna interrupts us suddenly, throwing her arms round our neck.

'Hey,' I say, looking for Dana. Yep, she's here, alright.

'You guys were great,' Dana says, smiling at us as Jack pulls me close. 'Are you hanging here for a bit?'

'I think so.' A DJ has started playing and people are already moving back onto the dance floor.

'We've got a table in the VIP area. Come grab a drink if you like.'

I glance at Sienna to see her eyebrows raised hopefully.

What the hell, my feet are killing me.

I don't know where Gramps is. He was up at the bar the last time I looked, sinking shots with Billy Mitchell.

He's such a badass.

Dana tells her friends to make room for us so we can sit down. Someone passes us champagne and we chink glasses.

'To music,' Dana says.

'To music,' we all agree.

I'm feeling pretty light-headed, but I'm so content. I turn to Jack. He still has a smudge of red at the corner of his lip. I brush it away, smiling.

'Aw, you guys make such a cute couple,' Dana says, nudging her sister. 'Don't they, Sie?'

Sienna nods as Dana sits back in her seat, eyeing us. She

points at Jack. 'You're like a mini Johnny Jefferson. And you're a mini Meg,' she says to me with a smirk before Jack can comment.

'Meg?' I ask with a frown.

'All sweet and innocent,' she states with a nonchalant shrug.

'I'm not sweet and innocent.'

She looks entertained. 'Sure you are.'

'I'm not,' I reply, bristling.

'If you say so,' she says genially. 'Hey, let me introduce you to my friends.'

After a while, I turn to Jack. 'I should probably go and check on Gramps.'

He nods. 'I'll come with you.'

'Leaving so soon?' Dana asks, as we get up, abruptly cutting off the conversation she was having.

'I want to check on my granddad,' I tell her.

She grins. 'You are just as cute as pie.'

I grimace, but I don't respond. A couple of her friends snigger.

'What?' she rounds on them. 'She *is* cute! I'm not being a dick about it.'

I start to walk away.

'Come back soon!' she calls after us.

'I don't know what to make of that one,' I say to Jack.

'She's a bit weird,' he comments.

We find Gramps with Billy and Marlin's co-owner, Ross, at the bar. A cheer goes up as about ten people sink a shot of God knows what.

'Kiddo!' Gramps shouts, spying me. 'You want one?'

I glance at Jack. Gramps is such a far cry from my dad. Jack shrugs.

'Sure, why not?' I reply.

Ross pulls a face and pats me on the back. 'Sorry, kids, but you can't. You're underage.'

But we were drinking in the green room! Hmm, out of sight of the other punters, I presume.

'Oh, you're no fun at all,' Gramps complains. 'Where else can we go?' he asks buoyantly, looking around.

'Back to mine?' Billy suggests, swaying slightly.

'House party! Hell, yeah!' Gramps cries.

'Christ,' Jack mutters, regarding me with a mixture of alarm and amusement.

'Come on, it'll be fun,' I urge.

'I gotta pee. You OK here?'

I nod and turn back to Gramps, but, a moment later, a hand clamps round my wrist and pulls me backwards. I swing round and come face to face with Eve.

'Oh,' I say. 'Hello.'

'I just wanted to give you a warning,' she says, her dark eyes flashing as she glares at me from a height, being several inches taller. 'I see you looking at him with those puppy-dog eyes and I feel sick.'

I can almost hear my heart thumping.

'I feel sick for *you*,' she clarifies bluntly. '*I* looked at him like that. I loved him. Yeah, I did,' she says firmly when my mouth drops open. 'He's a bastard. A player. You should get away from him while you can.'

'I feel sorry for you,' I say, staring defiantly at her.

She snorts and shakes her head. 'I am *telling* you...' She points her finger right at my face, jabbing it at me. 'You have got it coming.'

'Back off, bitch.' Dana appears from out of nowhere and gets right up in Eve's face. Eve looks stunned as she takes a few steps backwards. 'I said back off!' Dana keeps walking towards her. She's tiny compared to Eve, but she's clearly a force to be reckoned with.

Eve rolls her eyes and casts me one last look over her shoulder before stalking off. I realise I'm shaking.

'You alright?' Dana looks grim. 'I could see her from across the bar.'

'I'm fine. Thanks,' I think to add.

'What was her problem?'

'She's Jack's ex.'

'Aah,' she says knowingly. Her face breaks out into a grin. 'Jealousy makes us crazy. I should know.' She laughs.

'Who's this, then?' Gramps asks, stumbling over. I tense up.

'Hey, I'm Dana,' Dana says, offering her hand.

Gramps's brow furrows as though he's trying to recall a long-lost memory. He *must've* seen pictures of Dana, even if they never met. But his face shows no signs of recognition and I relax slightly as he shakes her hand. 'Brian. Are you coming?'

'No, Gramps,' I interject.

'Where?' Dana asks.

'Back to Billy Mitchell's house.' Gramps roughly shakes Billy's shoulder.

'House party?' Dana's eyes light up. 'Damn, yeah, I'm up for that. I'll go get my friends.'

My heart sinks as I watch her departing back.

'All set?' Jack asks when he returns. I give him a black look. 'What? What have I missed?'

*

I have no idea how late it is, but I am having the Best Time Of My Life! This party is so much fun. *Sooooo* much fun. I'm completely blathered and nobody gives a shit. None of the adults bat an eyelid when I help myself to vodka. They're all completely irresponsible and I love it! Gramps has fallen asleep on the sofa and some girl has kissed him all over his face with bright pink lipstick. It is *so* funny. He's going to crack up later. Jack is off somewhere with his dad, I think, and I'm here with Sienna and she's laughing at her sister and Dana is so much fun and I really like her and I have no idea what the big deal was about me meeting her. She's really funny! And so cool and talented, and Johnny, you're such a lame-ass for getting so worked up about it. Yeah, I *do* want a drag of that guy's cigarette! I haven't smoked in ages. Wow, it goes straight to my head! I'd forgotten this feeling.

'Can I keep it?' I ask him.

He shrugs and nods.

'I got it wrong!' Dana shouts at me over the music.

'What did you get wrong?' I shout back.

She gets up and climbs over the table, edging in between me and the guy sitting next to me. She flops back against the sofa.

'You're not sweet and innocent,' she says in my ear.

'I told you!' I reply, giggling.

'I expected you to be so boring, but you're fun. You're a good-time girl,' she says teasingly. 'A real little party animal.'

'Yep. That's me.'

'Can I?' she asks. I hand over the cigarette and she takes a long drag, blowing out several smoke rings.

'That is so cool!' I effuse. 'Can you teach me how to do that?'

She shrugs. 'Sure.'

I'm laughing my head off so much after a minute. I'll never get it.

'You're hilarious,' Dana pronounces.

I'm still laughing as she takes my cigarette and leans forward to stub it out in an ashtray.

'Where's Sienna?' I ask.

'She and Abe have gone somewhere.'

'Who's Abe?' I ask.

'My friend. He really likes her.'

'Who? That singer-songwriter guy?' I ask with confusion. Dana introduced me to him earlier.

'That's the one.'

'Isn't he a bit old?'

She shrugs. 'Sie can handle herself.'

I have a funny feeling in the pit of my stomach, but it doesn't sit well with the rest of the buzz I'm experiencing so I try to ignore it.

'Where are you gonna get this tattoo of yours?' Dana asks with a grin, turning to face me.

'I don't know,' I say, lifting my arm up. It feels kind of floppy. 'I was thinking here.' I point to my bicep.

She wrinkles her nose.

'Why? Where would you get it done?' I ask her.

She scrutinises me for a moment and then drags one fingertip down the side of my body, skimming the skin south of my crop top. She does it so quickly I don't have time to squeal about being ticklish and then she's prodding my hipbone. 'I'd go here. You're young, you don't want anything too visible for your first.'

'I can't get a tattoo until I'm eighteen, anyway,' I say.

She grins at me. 'Is that what he told you?'

'Who? My dad?' I shake my head. 'He doesn't want me to get one at all.'

'Bullshit,' she says with a smirk, shaking her head. 'Johnny loves ink. He's just saying that because that's what he thinks he *should* say. He'd totally dig your noughts and crosses idea.'

'You reckon?' I ask her dubiously.

'Definitely. He got two tats when we were together. Oh my God!' She sits up suddenly. 'Rick! *Rick!*' she calls across the room, cupping her hands round her mouth. 'RICK!'

A big, heavily tattooed rocker dude in a grey vest with long, stringy brown hair looks over. Dana beckons to him enthusiastically.

'Rick did Johnny's bird, the one on his left shoulder,' she says in a hasty aside to me, grinning brightly as Rick joins us. 'How was Jamaica, dude?' she asks, getting to her feet and throwing her arms round his neck.

'Sick,' he replies, smiling down at her.

'When did you get back? Man, it's been killing me that you've been gone so long!'

'Last week.'

'Please tell me you've got your kit here,' she implores.

He nods. 'Always.'

'Can you do me those tiny butterflies that we talked about?' she asks eagerly.

'On your shoulder blade, right?' He raises one eyebrow.

'Exactly!' she says.

He nods once and she beams at me. 'You wanna come watch?'

I hesitate. *Where's Jack? Where's Sienna?* Gramps is right here, but he's snoring. I purse my lips and shrug. 'Sure. May as well see what I'm letting myself in for.'

Dana bites her lip and stretches out her hand to help me up.

Chapter 25

'Who's the kid?' Rick asks Dana.

'A friend. She's twenty-one.'

'You sure about that? She looks younger.'

'I swear to you she's legit.'

'I have ID,' I interrupt, looking around for my bag. 'Oh. It's on the sofa,' I say.

'Forget it, but, if anyone asks, you don't know me.' He looks at Dana as he says this.

'I never reveal my sources,' she replies with a charming smile. 'You should know that from experience.' They both look down at me.

'Why noughts and crosses?' Rick asks me.

'My mum used to play it with me. She died a year ago.'

'So it's a tribute to her?'

'Yes. I'll have to draw it for you, though. There was a sequence she played so that I'd always win.'

'You sound like you've given it some thought.'

'I have. I've wanted a tattoo for ages.'

He shrugs. 'OK. As long as you know what you're doing.'

'Totally.'

Dana's eyes shine with excitement…

I jerk awake. *What the—? Oh my God, my head! Ow! Why is it so bright in here? Didn't I put my bedroom blinds down?* I squint into the light as the blurriness recedes. I'm not at home.

Where am I?

Through the fog in my head, pain starts to register elsewhere and I realise there's a stinging, burning sensation coming from my right hipbone.

And then it all comes flooding back.

Holy, holy shit. Please tell me it was a dream! Did I get a tattoo last night?

I sit bolt upright and look down to see a white bandage attached with surgical tape to my skin. My jeans have been partly unbuttoned and are folded over at the top. My head pounds violently. We're still at Billy Mitchell's and the place looks like a bombsite. Early-morning sunlight is streaming in through the windows. Gramps is still asleep on the sofa beside me, his face plastered with lipstick kisses, and there are a few bodies scattered across the floor, all out cold and breathing heavily. I can hear voices coming from somewhere in the house and a loud thumping noise accompanying them, but I don't have it in me to go and investigate.

I'm desperate for water and thankfully I spy a half-empty glass on the table in front of me. I scramble forward and grab it, not caring about consuming someone else's germs, and take a large gulp. I spit it out, almost choking as it sears my throat. It's neat vodka. That gets me up and out of my seat. I stumble across the room, growing closer to the voices and the thumping sound. Where's the kitchen? Where's the bathroom? I come across two people and ask.

'Bathroom's right there. They're trying to get it unlocked.'

Suddenly the door bangs open and two very beautiful, but very wasted-looking girls stumble out.

'Hey!' a guy calls, as I push past him, desperate to get to the sink. 'Join the queue!'

'Sorry,' I mumble, turning on the tap and drinking straight from it.

'Jessie?'

'Jack?' I straighten up, startled, and look down to see him sitting in the bathtub, his head in his hands. 'What are you doing—?'

I remember the girls coming out and the blood drains from my face.

'No.' Jack shakes his head, getting up. 'No,' he repeats more vehemently, as I back away. 'They locked me in here!' he shouts after me.

I tear back down the corridor, but he's right behind me. He grabs my arm and spins me round. 'I did *not* cheat on you,' he states angrily. 'They tried to get me to. Fuck knows, they tried,' he adds sardonically. 'I've been stuck in there with them for hours. Why didn't you come find me?'

My chest is heaving as I stare back at him, not knowing what to believe. He's making a good job of convincing me, but what do I really know? His eyes drop to my right hipbone and widen with alarm. They dart back up to look at me. 'What have you done?' he whispers.

My eyes fill with tears and I run to the sliding glass door, yanking it open.

'Jessie!' Jack follows me outside. There's a swimming pool out here and, for a split second, I have an intense urge to throw myself into it and wash away last night's horror, but Jack's arms are around me and he's holding me to his chest and I'm crying so hard, my brain trying to make sense of what's happened. How could I have been so stupid?

'Let me see,' he says shakily, sounding close to tears himself.

I'm still crying, burying my face in my hands as he kneels at my feet and folds the top of my jeans further down, gently peeling back the bandage. He lets out a loud breath. 'You got the noughts and crosses,' he says. I peek through my fingers at him. 'Did I?'

He nods up at me, looking relieved.

'Did he do it right?' I bend over, trying to look.

'What's the sequence again?' Jack asks me.

'Cross in the top left.'

'Yes.'

'Nought underneath it.'

'Yes.'

We go on like this until finally Jack says, 'Yeah, he got it right.'

I burst into tears again, this time from relief.

'Fuck,' he mutters, reattaching the bandage and adjusting my jeans. He stands up and grips my upper arms. 'What were you thinking? That could've gone so wrong.'

'What were *you* thinking?' I shove his chest. 'Going into a bathroom with those girls!'

'They followed me in there!' he yells. 'I needed a pee and the next thing I knew they were all over me! Someone locked the door from the outside.'

I stare at him, shaking my head.

'I swear to you,' he says heatedly. 'I didn't do anything with them. I swear on Aggie's life and you know I wouldn't say that if I didn't mean it.'

My face crumples and he pulls me against his chest. 'What about you?' he murmurs. 'How did the ink happen?'

'It was Dana,' I say. 'She convinced me.'

I hear someone let out a nasty laugh from the open doorway and shoot a look over there to see the woman herself, standing and watching us. She nonchalantly steps over the threshold and comes outside.

'This is so entertaining,' she drawls. 'You guys should film this shit and turn it into a sitcom.'

'You made me do it!' I yell at her, as Jack holds me back. She saunters towards us.

'I didn't make you do it, you stupid, silly little girl. You did it all on your own. All I did was convince Rick you were older. Poor guy. He is *so* in for it with your dad.' She smiles evilly.

'Why?' I ask in a small voice.

The smile drops from her face. 'Because I can. Because your dad had it coming. Not you, *him*. This is gonna kill him.' She laughs a tinkling laugh, looking like all of her Christmases have come at once, and her birthdays, too.

'Oh my God, I wish I could see Meg's face when he opens these pictures.' She holds her phone up and turns it round to show me a series of shots she must've taken last night of me, the party, Gramps looking wasted and, finally, Rick tattooing my skin. I think I'm going to throw up.

'Don't you dare send him those,' I warn, but my voice lacks conviction.

'Oh, I already have,' she says flippantly. 'He's gonna wake up to these babies.' Dana laughs again and shakes her head. 'I am *so* bummed I'm not gonna be there.'

'You psycho bitch.' Jack can barely contain his rage.

She sticks her bottom lip out. 'That's not very nice,' she says in a little girl voice. 'I would've thought you'd be in a better mood this morning after your fun with Miley and Lacie in the bathroom.'

'You set me up?' he splutters.

'Of course I did. Did they look after you?'

'You're disgusting,' he says.

'Where's Sienna?' I demand to know. *Was she in on this?*

'Oh, she left in tears earlier after Abe tried to get into her pants. She's a stupid little girl as well. What did she expect?'

My mouth drops open.

'What, you think I actually *like* my sister?' she continues. 'Correction. She is *not* my sister,' she spits, all trace of amusement gone from her face. 'That bitch stole my father away and she had it coming, too.'

She smiles again, clearing enjoying herself. 'It was so easy, befriending her.' She pushes her bottom lip out again. 'She wanted so much to be loved. I saw the pictures of the two of you together and thought, *Ching-ching! Revenge.*' She throws her head back and laughs.

I see red. I run forward and give her a hard shove. Her eyes widen momentarily as she flies backwards, landing with a splash in the pool.

'Nicely done,' Jack says ruefully, as Dana comes up spluttering. He grabs my hand and yanks me inside to collect Gramps.

Chapter 26

I bury my head in my hands and try to shut out the noise. Meg is screaming, Johnny is yelling and Gramps actually looks like he's going to cry. Annie has taken the kids somewhere so they're out of the house and it's just as well because I've never seen Johnny and Meg like this.

Jack offered to stay with me, to try to explain, but Johnny threw him out and shouted at him never to come back. They returned from New York early this afternoon after cutting their trip short.

I feel like I'm in hell.

And it's all my fault.

'No, Johnny, please,' Meg begs, as Johnny strides across the living room towards the door. She's crying as she runs after him.

'I have to have it out with her,' Johnny states furiously.

'No, please. I don't want you seeing her!' Meg cries.

'I have to!' Johnny yells in her face.

'That's what she wants!' Meg implores. 'Please don't! She wants you to run to her!'

'Well, she's getting what she wants, then,' Johnny says flatly, shoving past her to the door.

'Johnny!' Meg screams after him, before bursting into tears.

'Oh, Christ,' Gramps says from beside me.

My bottom lip is trembling uncontrollably. I can't believe what's happening, that I've done this to my family. How could I have screwed up so badly?

Meg storms over to Gramps. 'You stupid, stupid old man!' She picks up a cushion and he brings his arms up to protect his face as she whacks him over the head with it.

'Meg!' I cry, jumping to my feet. 'I'm sorry! It was my fault! My fault! I should never have trusted Dana!'

She shakes her head at me, tears streaming down her face. I'll never forget the look in her eyes as she turns and walks away.

In the distance, we hear Johnny's motorcycle roar out of the garage.

Stu can barely look at me when I walk out through Customs at Heathrow. I should be grateful he's here at all. I thought they'd send a car.

'Hi.' I come to a stop in front of him, my eyes already brimming over with tears.

'Come on,' he says gruffly, taking my suitcase. 'Don't lose it here.'

The last week has been a living nightmare. Meg took the boys and went to stay with a friend for a couple of days and I could tell that Johnny was close to cracking. Meg was so angry with him. I don't know if she's forgiven him for seeing Dana, even now. When she came back, she confided in me that the worst thing was that he kept his knowledge about Dana and Sienna from her. She considered that the worst betrayal. In that way, I betrayed her, too.

I haven't been allowed to see Jack. Johnny found out that he stayed over on Friday night and confiscated my phone, laptop and iPad so I can't call or email him. I've barely been allowed to leave the house for school and I'm in even more trouble because my last lot of homework came back with D and E grades.

Sienna hasn't been at school and Agnes says that apparently she hasn't replied to anyone's text messages. She must be crushed.

Thankfully Agnes has been able to exchange messages between Jack and me.

It wasn't even his fault. It's so unfair.

When Meg returned after staying with her friend, I asked Johnny if I could go back to England for Spring Break. Stu had already asked me to come home for a visit, and Johnny agreed without hesitation.

'Yeah. I think it will do everyone good to have a week's breathing space,' he said.

I think they need some time alone as a family. I feel like I'm becoming more of an outsider by the second. I've never said sorry so much in my life. My apologies have almost become meaningless now. I need to find some other way to make it up to them. I hate that I've caused such a major rift between Meg and Johnny. The night before I left, I heard her crying in the office.

'*Of course* we couldn't trust Brian.' She was talking to someone on the phone. 'I'm such a stupid idiot to think that we could. I just wanted... *so much...*' she said between sobs, '...to go with

Johnny on tour. He needs me. I know he needs me. It's all so fucked up.'

It was the first time I'd heard her swear. I left before she caught me eavesdropping.

'Well, this probably trumps everything else you've ever done, doesn't it?' Stu says wryly, as we climb into the Audi Johnny bought him at the end of last year to replace his crummy Fiat.

'Yeah, it does.' I'm not even going to argue with him. I've got a lecture coming to me and I'm going to take it on the chin.

'How could you be so stupid?' he asks.

I shake my head. 'I don't know,' I mumble, tears stinging my eyes as I look out of the window at the brown, leafless trees and muddy fields. It's a murky grey day, which feels highly appropriate. The sunny skies of LA are a long, long way away. I swallow. 'I guess I just wanted to feel ordinary again.'

'By getting *a tattoo*?' Stu asks in disbelief. 'By allowing a boy to *sleep in your bed*?'

I've already had a major reprimand from my dad about that one. I think that Wyatt, the overnight security guard at the house, told him that Jack and Agnes had stayed overnight. The entire conversation was absolutely *mortifying*. I even ended up confessing that I'm still a virgin. Johnny broached the subject of safe sex, but luckily I could tell him that Mum had beaten him to it by several years. I said I'd never make the same mistake she did by not using condoms and falling pregnant. I wasn't being rude – just honest.

'No!' I shoot Stu a look. 'I wanted to feel ordinary by getting drunk! By going to a house party! By not having to look over my shoulder to find a bodyguard standing there! I was letting my hair down.'

He snorts with astonishment.

'I didn't mean to get a tattoo!' I cry. 'God, I wanted one. I've been wanting one for ages! But I would have waited until I was eighteen.'

'I can't believe you allowed that to happen, even drunk out of your brain! And what the hell was Brian doing when you were having some random man cutting up your skin?'

'He wasn't a random man. He was a proper tattoo artist,' I say wearily. 'He's inked Johnny in the past.'

'Oh, that makes it all OK,' Stu says sarcastically.

I swallow the lump in my throat and look away.

'What would your mother have said?' he mutters.

I bite my lip until I taste blood.

We're staying at Johnny's mansion in Henley because the sale of Stu's new house hasn't gone through yet. It won't be far off, he says.

A few days later, when everything has calmed down a bit, he takes me to check it out. It's in Marlow, right near the river and just off the high street. It has high red-brick walls around a deceptively big back garden. I notice that there are CCTV cameras hooked up everywhere. Stu tells me that the current owner is a famous actress, but he won't reveal her identity. Needless to say, he doesn't trust me any more.

I like the house – it has a nice feel to it – but I have the biggest lump in my throat every time I think about my home in Maidenhead. Stu asks me if I want to go and say bye, but I burst into tears at the thought of it. I decide that no, I don't. It's probably best that I stick with the memories that I have.

I feel too raw to see any of my friends at first, but, after a few days, Stu lets me use the phone to call them. He reluctantly agrees to drive me to a pub in Maidenhead to meet them. The press haven't cottoned on to the fact that I've left LA, so we agree that I can go incognito.

It's only after Stu's driven off that I realise he's probably heading straight to Caroline's house – she and Tom live nearby. Stu has fended off any questions I've asked about her and he hasn't let me out of his sight since I got here, so he's probably desperate to see her.

Libby, Lou, Chris and Natalie are there when I arrive, but everyone is far less enthusiastic to see me than the last time we were all together. Since they all came over for my birthday, we've barely spoken at all, and now they're quite cool with me as a result. I'm reserved with them, too – I'm still coming to terms with how badly I've messed everything up and I don't really want to talk about it. I've been on a very different path lately and I'm not entirely sure how to realign myself with my old life here.

But, when Tom turns up after about twenty minutes, I almost lose it.

'Hey,' he says, startled as I hug him a bit too hard. 'You OK?'

I pull away and nod, but my eyes fill with tears. 'What's wrong?' he asks with concern.

I realise that everyone is looking up at us and they all seem taken by surprise at my reaction. All we've done up to this point is make awkward small talk. My friends are all so normal, so far from what I am right now, that it's harder to identify with them. But Tom was in San Francisco with me. He's witnessed even more of my whirlwind life in America than they did, and he knows me and the upheaval I've been dealing with. I feel closer

275

to him than anyone else here, and that's crazy because he's my ex, but it doesn't stop it from being true.

My nose prickles and I crumble. I end up telling everyone everything.

The evening isn't so bad after that. In fact, it's pretty good. The bond that was breaking strengthens again after I come clean, and soon my friends are trying to reassure me that everything will work out in the end.

'I can't even speak to Jack,' I say in a shaky voice, wracked with emotion. 'Johnny confiscated my phone and Stu won't let me use the home phone. I just want to talk to him, to check he's OK. It wasn't his fault,' I say with a trembling lip.

'I'd let you use my phone, but it doesn't have international dialling,' Natalie says.

But it's Tom who places his phone in my hands. 'Use mine,' he says.

I stare at it with surprise, my eyes darting up to look at him.

'Are you sure?'

He nods. I can tell by his expression that the offer is genuine. He may not like Jack, but he knows that he's the one I've chosen. And Tom is nothing if not a good sport. I guess that's what makes him one of the most popular guys at school. He's going to make some girl very happy one of these days.

I hurry into the bathroom and lock myself inside a cubicle before dialling Jack's number. *Please answer, please answer...* I know he won't recognise the caller ID, but—

'Hello?' He interrupts my thought process.

'Jack!' I exclaim, my insides flooding with relief. 'It's me!'

'Jessie?' he asks with amazement. 'Where are you?'

'I'm in England.'

276

'Agnes told me you were going.'

'I'm here.' Tears trek down my cheeks as I cradle the phone to my ear.

'Are you OK?' he asks.

'No,' I reply in a tiny voice. 'It's been hell.'

'I know. For me, too.'

'Jack, I'm so sorry. This is all my fault—'

'Don't,' he interrupts me. 'Don't waste time by talking about it. I miss you so much,' he says urgently. 'I just want to hear how you are.'

'I miss you, too,' I whisper. The pain in my heart is hard to take. I take a deep breath, bracing myself and trying to be brave as I open my mouth to speak. I've said it before, but I want to say it again, even if he's not going to reply.

'I love you,' I say.

'I love you, too,' he replies in a choked voice.

My eyes spring open. I'd squeezed them shut. 'You do?' I ask with surprise.

'I do,' he replies sadly. 'I just wish I could have told you in person.'

I return to LA, after a seven-day break, feeling stronger, if not happier. Just before I left the UK, I came to a decision. I talked it through with Stu and he agrees. It's the right thing to do.

'I'm going to finish my school year in England,' I tell my dad and Meg, as we sit on the living-room sofas, straight after Davey has dropped me home from the airport.

Johnny leans forward and rests his elbows on his thighs, clasping his hands between his legs. He stares at me jadedly. Meg looks stunned.

277

'Stu wants me to do my GCSEs, anyway. It's too hard here. There are too many distractions.' I'm trying not to cry. I need to be convincing for this. I need to show them I can be mature. I look directly at Meg. 'And you'll be able to go with my dad on tour without worrying about him – or me.'

Nope, can't do it. My vision goes blurry.

Finishing school in Maidenhead will mean spending about four months away from America – and Jack... And All Hype... It's going to be so hard, but my family *has* to come first, and I've done enough damage. There's no way Gramps will ever be allowed to act as my guardian if I stay in America, and I couldn't bear it if Meg had to look after me instead of supporting my dad on his world tour. That would hurt too many of us – Johnny was *crushed* when she went away after the Dana argument. He *needs* her.

'Oh, Jess,' my dad says, getting to his feet and pulling me off the sofa and into his arms. He cradles my head to his chest as I cry.

'I'm so sorry I let you both down,' I sob against him.

'Hey,' Meg says sadly, coming to join the family hug.

'So sorry,' I say, opening my arm to her. 'I hope I can make it up to you by doing the right thing now.'

'It's OK, chick. It's OK,' my dad murmurs, holding me tightly. A memory of Dana calling me 'chick' pops into my head, but I do my best to push the thought away. There's no way I'm going to let her taint the term of affection my dad has for me. She's done enough damage.

There's little point in me going back to school now that I've decided to finish the year in England, so, the following day, my dad lets up on my punishment and says I can see my friends to say goodbye.

'It wasn't Jack's fault,' I tell him imploringly. 'Please don't blame him.'

He's not convinced, but he doesn't argue with me. I call Jack and he manages to get off work early so Davey drives me over to his house with instructions to wait on the drive for an hour. It's not long enough, but I'll take what I can get.

Jack answers the door to me and my heart threatens to burst through my ribcage as he crushes me in his embrace. Nothing prepares me for how good it feels to be with him again. His warmth, his smell, the strength of his arms around me. Now I know how Agnes felt.

It's not until we're in his bedroom, lying on his bed, that I tell him I'm leaving.

'No,' he says beseechingly, pulling us into an upright position. 'No! You can't.'

'I have to. I'm so sorry.'

He looks absolutely crushed. 'But what about us? What about the band? Christ, you don't even know, but we've had interest from record labels.'

My heart leaps. 'Have we?'

'I've got so much to tell you,' Jack says hopelessly. 'You can't go.'

'I don't have a choice. I'll put Meg and Johnny under pressure if I stay. I won't do it. You should've seen them after Dana. It was awful.'

'Oh, God,' he says, pulling me close. 'This is gonna kill me.'

'It won't be forever,' I say. 'Just a few months. I'll be back in the summer.'

'I love you,' he says, cupping my face and forcing me to stare straight into his eyes. 'I've never said that to anyone before.'

'I know.' I laugh and cry at the same time, and I realise that the pain of being away from him will be dulled slightly by the fact that I *do* trust him. I *do* believe he'll wait for me.

I lean forward to kiss him.

As I'm walking outside with Jack to get back into the car, Agnes comes home from school.

'How was Australia?' I ask her, as we stand on the cobbled courtyard inside her property's gates.

'Amazing.' She's glowing, but her smile turns into a frown. 'How about England?'

I quickly fill her in. She looks to and from Jack and me with distress.

'Will you look after him for me?' I ask dejectedly.

'I already do, every day,' she replies.

I don't get to see Sienna before I leave, but she does answer my call.

'I don't know what to say,' she says flatly.

'You don't have to say anything,' I respond. 'I know she hurt you as much as she hurt me.'

'More,' she corrects me.

My heart squeezes. 'I'm so sorry.'

'It was all to get to you,' she says in a monotone. 'I feel like such an idiot'

'You don't need her in your life. Sienna, you're incredible. You're going to be über-successful, much more successful than she is.'

'You've got that straight,' she says. 'Apparently, her tour has been cancelled. She's been dropped by her record label.'

280

'What?'

'Your dad likes to throw his weight around.'

I'm stunned. I had no idea. 'Are you sure it was Johnny?'

'I'm sure. My mom told me.'

'Oh my God.'

'Yeah. So much for her attempt at revenge,' she says dully. 'What goes around comes around.' She sighs. 'I'm just gonna focus on me, now. Rafe and I are doing our first CiaoCiao shoot this weekend. It should be pretty cool.'

'I can't wait to see it in magazine spreads all over the world,' I say.

She laughs half-heartedly. 'Yeah.'

'Can I email you?' I ask. I have a feeling from this conversation that Sienna would probably like to wipe her hands clean of our friendship, but we did have fun before her sister came on the scene.

She sighs, leaving a long pause before replying. Perhaps she's weighing up everything, too.

'Yeah,' she says. 'And give me a call when you're next in LA. Maybe we can go ice-skating or something.'

I giggle and, after a moment, she does, too.

The time has come for me to leave LA, and Jack, Agnes, Brandon and Miles are here to see me off. I keep trying to tell myself that I'm doing the right thing, but it's hard. Johnny is setting off on tour next week and he needs to focus. Luckily the opening night is in London so I'll be able to go and watch with Barney, Phee and Meg from backstage. It's a little ray of light in these dark days.

'Have you heard back from Wendel yet?' I hear Brandon asking Johnny.

'Not yet. Stay cool,' Johnny replies.

He asked his solicitor to look over the offers we've received from two smallish record labels. Johnny initially advised against accepting.

'It's too soon,' he told me earlier today. 'Hang on for the big guns. You've got time.'

'But I'm going back to England! I don't want to miss this opportunity.'

'Believe me, more offers will come. You guys should use this time to write some new material, collaborate with other artists, even. When you return in the summer, it will either work or it won't.'

'But I don't *want* it not to work!'

'Don't force it, chick,' he said. 'What will be will be.'

'Sometimes I think you don't want me to be in All Hype,' I said sulkily. 'You won't help us. You won't even watch our gigs from the front.'

He stared at me for a long moment and I felt my face heating up.

'Sorry,' I mumbled, knowing I had no right to give him crap about anything.

'I want what's best for you,' he said quietly. 'If I think there's an opportunity that fits the bill, I'll advise you to take it.'

We left it at that.

'I'll see you in a week,' he says to me now, giving me a hug.

I nod, fighting back tears. I hug Agnes, Brandon and Miles before coming to Meg.

'I'm sor—'

'Enough,' she says, squeezing me tightly. 'It's OK. All is forgiven, remember?'

We had a heart-to-heart last night when Johnny was doing bedtime for Barney and Phee. She confided in me that it's been a fear of hers for a long time that Dana would try to get her claws back into her husband.

'She never got over their break-up,' she said. 'I was just so upset with Johnny for not telling me she was back in our lives, even inadvertently. I would have warned you about her, told you what she was like. She's pure evil, she really is.'

'Johnny did try to warn me,' I defended him.

She sighed. 'I know. And as for Gramps…' She'd sent him home with his tail between his legs soon after the incident. 'He never should have taken you to that party, but it's me I'm mostly angry with. I wanted to go with Johnny, so I put you at risk. I should have known better. You can't teach an old dog new tricks. And Brian is certainly an old dog.' She smiled sadly.

'Please don't stay angry with him for long,' I implored.

She sighed. 'I'm sure we'll bounce back. It's just going to take a little time.'

I brush away my tears as I crouch down to say goodbye to Barney. 'I'll see you next week, OK? We're going to hang out backstage together, yeah?'

'How many sleeps?' he solemnly demands to know.

'Seven,' I say.

'One, two, three—'

'Bye, Phee,' I say with a smile, as Barney continues to count on his fingers.

'Bye, Dezzie,' he replies obligingly. My heart squeezes as I stroke his little blond head.

Finally I straighten up and turn to Jack.

He can barely meet my eyes, and then I realise they're tinged red. That sets me off.

He holds me tight, burying his face in my hair as my chest heaves against his.

'Come on, man,' Johnny says gruffly after a long while. 'She's going to miss her flight.'

I step away from Jack and dry my tears on my sleeve.

'You can come and visit, can't you?' Johnny pats Jack's back. He feels bad for us, despite everything.

Jack nods, biting his lip as he stares disconsolately at me. My heart is breaking, I swear.

'Christ,' Johnny mutters. 'You can all come, if you like.' He looks around at my friends. 'How about I fly you all out for the opening night?'

I stare at him, gobsmacked. 'Are you serious?'

He shrugs. 'Why the hell not?'

This time when I throw my arms round his neck, I'm laughing hysterically.

He's just made leaving bearable.

Chapter 27

A week later, I'm sitting on my bed in a five-star hotel room, scrolling through Samson Sarky's gossip site on my iPad. It's so bizarre looking at old pictures of me with Gina, Margarita, Lottie and co. I can't believe that girl there is me. But then it's not me. At least not all of me.

I glance up at my reflection in the mirror. *This* is the real me, the me I still identify most with. I'm wearing blue jeans and a grey hoodie and my blonde hair looks dishevelled and messy as it spills around my face. My green eyes are clear and my lids and lashes free from make-up. I look at my lips and think of Jack kissing them. I can't believe he's going to be here later today.

Tonight is the first night of Johnny's world tour and it kicks off at Wembley Stadium in front of a sold-out crowd. He has three dates here in London before he takes his tour around the country. I've realised I'm actually going to be closer to my family here in the UK than I would have been if I'd stayed in LA. I'll be able to go to some of my dad's dates – certainly the weekend ones – and, by the time he sets off for the European leg of his tour, I'll be gearing up for my exams and will have to focus on school, anyway. Then Johnny will be back in America for the summer, touring stateside. I'll be able to make a few of those dates, too – and maybe Stu will come back to LA as my guardian for the summer holidays. In some ways, I couldn't have planned it better if I'd tried.

There's a knock on my door. I get up to answer it and find Meg with Barney and Phee.

'Jessie, can you take the boys for a bit? I want to go with Johnny to a meeting downstairs.'

'Of course,' I reply, delighted she asked. She may not trust me to behave around evil bitches with tattoo fetishes, but at least she trusts me with her sons.

Johnny told me I had to get my tattoo laser-removed, but I'm trying to convince him to let me keep it. I really did want it, even if it is two years too soon, and at least it's out of sight most of the time.

Hopefully one day I'll be able to look at it without feeling sick with guilt.

I scoop Phee up in my arms and take Barney's hand, running to the bed for a bouncing session.

I hadn't known how I was going to get through the next few hours before I can realistically start to get ready – I'm wearing the black-and-gold skirt and bodice that Jack likes, and I'm so desperate to see him. At least my little brothers will distract me for a while. Jack, Agnes, Brandon and Miles are all flying in this afternoon and going straight to the concert venue. Agnes's stepdad wouldn't let her have even a single day off school and Jack thought it would be unkind to make her fly out alone, so this is the earliest they could come. Unfortunately Agnes has to leave again tomorrow, but Jack is staying in the UK for a week. It's the Easter holidays here, and I'm dying to show him the places I grew up. I just wish he could stay for longer.

Libby, Natalie, Lou and Em are also coming to the gig and Johnny has given them Access All Areas passes. Natalie told me she thought Em was going to spontaneously combust when I called them at Nat's house to tell them.

I'm backstage at Wembley – something I've only ever dreamed about being able to say. I've just heard that Johnny's driver has arrived back from the airport and security is bringing my friends up. I'm so nervous. It's only been a week since I've seen Jack, but there's something about tonight that makes me feel even more on edge. Maybe I'm just feeling nervy for Johnny. This is the first big tour he's done in years. I hope it goes well.

Earlier I'd asked him how he was feeling.

'Pretty good. This might be my last world tour,' he said, 'so I intend to enjoy it.'

'Don't say that!' I gasped.

'It's true, chick. I'm thirty-seven. I won't always be selling out stadiums and arenas. And anyway I don't want to do this shit forever. You saw how stressed Meg got about the tour.'

'But this is what you love!' I said. 'Meg wouldn't want you to stop doing what you love.'

He smiled at me. 'I *love* making music. I *love* writing and singing and playing my guitar, but I don't really love touring and being away from home for months on end. No, I'd be happy doing the odd gig here and there, just the ones I really want to do, you know? That would suit me just fine.'

I've already had a look at the stage. It's absolutely enormous, at least twenty times bigger than the two I've sung on. I watched my dad do a soundcheck and he looked pretty far away even from where I was standing in the wings. To the people at the back, he's going to look like not much more than a pinprick. But his voice filled the stadium effortlessly when they tested out the mics, and two huge screens at either side of the stage will be projecting his image to his faraway fans. I can't wait to see him in action.

The door to the green room opens and my heart leaps as Jack, Agnes, Brandon and Miles walk in.

I run over and throw myself into Jack's arms. He laughs and picks me up, swinging me around. I plant a kiss on his lips.

'I've missed you so much,' I whisper.

'Me too,' he replies, smiling down at me.

He lets me go so I can say hi to everyone else.

We're in the wings and it's almost time. Earlier Johnny introduced me to his band and backing singers and he even stood beside me while we watched the support acts, one of whom was Contour Lines, the band Jack and I saw in LA. Now the stage is dark, but the crowd is electric. I peek out of the wings to see big spotlights moving over the stadium. Tens of thousands of people start to chant as one.

Johnny turns to kiss Meg. She hugs him tight and I hear him tell her he loves her. Then he bends down to give Barney and Phoenix a kiss and a cuddle – they're wearing ear defenders to protect their little ears from the loud music, bless them. Johnny straightens up again and a roadie hooks him up to his guitar. He's wearing a simple white T-shirt and jeans and the brown leather guitar strap stretches across his chest. He rakes his hand through his blond hair and smiles at me.

288

'Good luck, Dad,' I say.

He raises an eyebrow and grins as he bends down to peck me on my cheek. 'Thanks,' he says. I have a feeling he won't need it.

His band walks on to a roar from the crowd and then Johnny gives Meg one last kiss and turns and strides out onstage. The noise from the crowd is deafening, like nothing I've ever heard. Of course, I've been in crowds like that, watching my favourite bands, but back here it seems amplified. We're outsiders, looking in. I glance at Meg to see her eyes shining with pride as Johnny launches into one of his biggest hits, and then I turn to watch my dad. I think I must have the same expression on my face as Meg has on hers.

After a couple of songs, Johnny says hello to the audience and he seems so comfortable, so at ease. His body language and the way he speaks is sort of intimate, like he's addressing each and every one of them in person. They lap it up.

By the fifth song, I'm completely relaxed and loving every minute. Lou, Libby, Nat, Em and I are dancing away, singing along to the songs like we're at just another gig. It's so much fun. When the song ends, we clap and cheer like everyone else in the stadium.

And then Johnny speaks to his fans again.

'Hey, you guys wanna meet my daughter?' he asks casually.

The roar that goes up from the crowd is crazy, but it takes me a moment to register what he's just said.

I freeze as he looks offstage at me.

'Come on, chick,' he says, beckoning me towards him as though he's about to introduce me to a mate of his, not 90,000 strangers.

Anxiety attacks my body and my feet glue themselves to the spot.

'Go on!' Em hisses, pushing me and bringing me to life. I glance hesitantly at Jack and he grins and nods, and then Em gives me a shove out onstage.

The crowd *ROARS*. The noise is mind-blowing.

'Come here,' Johnny says, his green eyes twinkling at me as I make my way across the absolutely mahoosive stage. He throws his arm round my shoulder and turns me to face the audience. 'What do you think?' he asks me, casting a cheeky look at his tens of thousands of fans. 'Pretty, aren't they?'

I can barely hear myself think from the screaming response he gets to this comment.

'Everyone, this is Jessie. I should probably introduce you to her band, too, shouldn't I? She wouldn't forgive me if I didn't introduce you to her band,' he adds nonchalantly, smiling. He looks past me and waves at Jack, Brandon and Miles. The cheering continues as they step, stunned, into the light.

'Meet All Hype,' Johnny says into his mic, as they walk towards us. 'You should check out their stuff on YouTube. They're really good,' he adds as an aside to his audience. His tone is mischievous and overfamiliar and I'd laugh if this didn't feel so surreal.

My bandmates reach us, their eyes wide as they look out at the packed stadium.

'This is Jack.' Johnny addresses his fans again with a cheeky grin. 'Jack plays lead guitar. And this is Brandon on bass.' Johnny reaches behind Jack to pat Brandon's back. 'And Miles here is on drums. What do you think, lads? Reckon you could rock Wembley one day?'

Brandon and Miles laugh with disbelief and Jack drags his hand over his mouth, shaking his head, awestruck, as he stands and stares at the sea of people. The crowd is going absolutely berserk. They're loving this side to Johnny.

'I don't know if any of you saw it, but I sang one of All Hype's songs a couple of months ago at my daughter's birthday party,' Johnny says. The corresponding screams confirm that most of the people here did.

Johnny grins and cocks his head to one side. 'I'm kind of tempted to ask these guys to return the favour and play one of *my* songs.' More cheering. 'But my band would get jealous, and anyway, they haven't practised so that would be mean,' he finishes with a playful grin. 'S'OK, lads. You can go. Get yourselves a drink.'

My heart is pounding so hard as I turn to follow Jack offstage.

'Oi, where do you think you're going?' Johnny asks, tugging me back.

I spin round and look up at him with alarm.

'You've got a song to sing.'

'What?!' I splutter. 'But *I* haven't practised!'

My voice fills the stadium and collective laughter rolls back at me. Johnny's mic is picking up every word I'm saying.

'You don't need to practise. You know it by heart,' he says tenderly, his green eyes filled with humour. He looks over his shoulder and nods at his drummer and suddenly the band starts to play 'Acorn', the track I recorded with my dad.

I can't believe this is happening. What if I choke? A roadie jogs onstage and hands me a microphone and Johnny turns to face me, his green eyes sparkling as he begins to sing. His voice fills the stadium and it's so beautiful, so soulful. He nods

291

encouragingly as he approaches the lyrics where I come in. I look straight back at him and open my mouth, and he smiles as our voices come together. In the end, it's as natural as breathing.

It's over all too quickly. The noise from the crowd is colossal, but I barely register their cheers. All I can hear is my dad saying he's proud of me, as he presses a kiss to my forehead and gently sends me offstage.

And then I'm back in the darkness of the wings and staring out at the light again and I wonder if I dreamed it. Did that really just happen?

'Amazing, isn't she?' Johnny says to his audience, and then he launches straight into one of my favourite songs.

'She sure is.' Jack materialises at my side, smiling down at me out of the corner of his eye before my friends pull me away and hysterically engulf me.

Chapter 28

It is the best night of my life without a shadow of a doubt and the after-party has barely got started. I haven't even had one drink, but I'm on the biggest high imaginable. I wish Stu had been here to see the concert, but he's coming to tomorrow night's show – with Caroline. I still don't know if they're more than friends, but I hope I'll be able to cope with it if or when they take their relationship to the next level. I want him to be happy. I don't want him to be alone.

Tom will also join us tomorrow night. I felt kind of bad that he couldn't come tonight, but Johnny had loads of people that needed to be here – friends, family, both his and Meg's, plus press and competition winners – so Access All Areas tickets were limited.

I think Gramps might be coming the day after tomorrow. I hope he's OK. I know he feels really bad about letting loose like that. But I think Meg's on her way to getting over it.

She certainly seems happy tonight. Annie has taken Barney and Phoenix back to the hotel so she's able to relax. I notice she's not drinking, though. She tries to avoid alcohol when she's with Johnny. I heard her say earlier that once the opening nights are over she wants the booze backstage to be limited. It must be hard when you're an addict, like Johnny, and everyone's drinking and smoking and doing God knows what else around you. I didn't really get it before, but I think now I understand why Meg wanted to be here. I'm glad she'll be able to help keep my dad on the straight and narrow. There's every chance he'd stay on the right path himself, but Meg's right: it's not worth the risk. She doesn't want to lose him again.

And I don't want to lose him at all.

I look through the crowd at my dad as he greets person after person. He looks happy, like he's in his element. He catches my eye and his face lights up. He excuses himself and then he's striding straight past everyone else in the green room and sweeping me up in a hug.

'You were outstanding,' he enthuses in my ear.

'I can't believe you did that!' I squeak. 'I was so scared!'

'I knew you would be,' he says with a grin. 'I didn't want to freak you out by telling you beforehand.' He studies my face. 'You did enjoy it, didn't you?'

'More than anything *ever*,' I declare.

He chuckles and squeezes me.

Everyone is still in high spirits as we set off to the hotel in the tour bus. We're planning on continuing the party downstairs in the bar, but I'm having an attack of the jitters as I sit next to Jack. He's staying on the floor below mine and I've just whispered that I want us to sneak up to his room for a bit. His corresponding look was intense.

I think this could be it.

When we arrive at the hotel, we find even more people in the bar than there were backstage. Contour Lines and the other support acts have come back with us, along with their posses of friends and family, so it's easy to slip away unnoticed amid the mayhem.

My hand is clammy inside Jack's as we wait for the lift. A middle-aged couple join us as it pings and the doors open. I shoot Jack a sideways glance, but he's staring straight ahead once we're inside. We step out onto his landing.

'I'm along here,' he murmurs.

Is he nervous, too?

He pushes his key card in and unlocks the door, leading me inside. Once the door is shut behind us, the butterflies go into overdrive.

He stands in front of me, caressing my face with his hand as he gazes down at me.

'I love you,' he reminds me.

'I love you, too.' My mouth is dry as I look up into his gorgeous eyes. 'I want to,' I whisper. 'Have you got protection?'

He nods once, knowing I mean contraception.

'Are you sure about this?' he asks, his expression serious. 'Because I do want to be responsible. I'd hate to be the douchebag you tell your mates about in a few years' time.'

'Are you planning on being a douchebag?' I ask, my eyes widening.

His eyebrows jump up. 'Of course not!' he exclaims. 'I just want it to be perfect, that's all. For you. I want it to be perfect for you.'

'You love me. I love you. That makes it perfect,' I say.

He locks eyes with me for a long few seconds and then bends down to kiss me.

It does hurt. The pain is searing and intense, but sort of exquisite in its own way, sort of beautiful. I guess that's because I'm doing this with someone I really love.

When it's over and we're both lying in a heap, I feel overcome with emotion. It's done now. I've given myself away. Whatever I do, wherever I go, Jack will always be imprinted on me, like a tattoo I can't see, only feel. He was my first, a part of my history, and, I hope, a big part of my future. But in a week he's leaving, and I'm staying. The thought overwhelms me and I let go, bursting into tears.

Startled, he props himself up on his elbows and stares down at me.

'Are you OK? Did I hurt you?'

'It's not that, I just feel a little overwhelmed.'

'Baby,' he says, carefully rolling off me and gathering me in his arms. He strokes my hair as I cry, his fingertips running across my temples. His hands are warm, but I think of Mum, anyway, wondering what she'd make of Jack, if she'd like him. Would I have confided in her about tonight if she were still alive?

I guess I'll never know.

After a while, we get dressed and go back downstairs to the party, but for me, this time, everything is different. *I'm* different. I don't know what the next few months have in store, whether All Hype will make it, whether Jack and I will, but I have a funny feeling about him, about us. I'm pretty sure we've got some distance left to run.

And I am more than ready for that journey.

Epilogue

The lights are bright and so very warm, and on the dance floor, dozens of beautiful people are throwing their arms over their heads as they move to music that none of us can hear.

I feel like I'm in a very surreal dream, but actually I'm on the set of *Little Miss Mulholland*. Yes, Lottie actually did it! She got All Hype a slot on her TV show!

It's been four and a half months since I went to England to see out the school year, and despite my initial concerns, the time has flown by. I spent a blissful week with Jack in the Easter holidays, and I was in floods of tears when I had to say goodbye to him at the airport. But he flew over twice to see me, and we talked every day on the phone – and yes, FaceTimed, too, something which Agnes loves teasing us about. We are still going strong – stronger than ever – and, if anything, our time apart strengthened our relationship.

In fact, the distance did all of my bandmates good. Miles had initially been a little off about the publicity surrounding my dad and me, but in our months of breathing space, all of us have had time to think about what we really want. Both Brandon and Miles tried collaborating with other artists, but nothing really came of their efforts. Jack, meanwhile, used all of his spare time to write songs for All Hype. My sexy boyfriend was confident that his mates would come to appreciate what good a thing we had, and he was right.

As soon as I saw Miles again a couple of weeks ago, he gave me the biggest hug and told me how much he'd missed me and that he honestly couldn't imagine being in a band with a different frontperson. We are all completely committed to making this work.

This new determination must've been apparent to Lottie. She's talked for ages about getting All Hype on her show, but she's only just made it happen. I can see her, right now, on the other side of the set, acting out a crazy shouting match with Peter, who plays her brother, Zachary. It's so much fun to watch them in action.

'CUT!' The director shouts, making me jump. He turns and points his finger straight at us, standing in the wings. 'Right, All Hype – you're next! Take to the stage!'

I feel a flurry of nerves as the set becomes a hive of activity around us, with huge cameras being wheeled our way and film crew buzzing round.

We're in a big studio in Hollywood, and the set that we're currently standing in is a pretend nightclub called The Looking Glass where Lottie's character, Macy, and her friends hang out. On TV, the club looks so real, but one glance upwards shows cables and wires dangling from the ceiling, and the walls are so flimsy, I could probably push them over. Brandon told me earlier that the bottles behind the bar contain water, dyed with food colouring. I guess the crew aren't taking any risks with their underage cast…

The extras are having a breather and chatting amongst themselves, but soon they'll be dancing to one of our songs. At least they'll be able to move to real music next time, even if it will only be coming from a recording we did a few days ago. I hope to God I can lip sync, because we have to mime.

Jack reaches across and squeezes my hip. 'You OK?' he asks in a low voice, his eyes steady on mine.

I nod, wondering how long it will be before we can escape to his place. His stepdad, Tim, and his mum are currently in the Bahamas, so we've been making the most of our privacy.

'Don't be nervous,' he whispers, stepping closer to give me a kiss on my forehead.

I grab his wrist to stop him from moving away again and he pauses, before enfolding me in his arms. He holds me there for a moment and I begin to feel calmer, but I still want to kiss him. I tilt my face up to do just that.

'NO!' I hear someone yell, and we break away from each other to see the make-up artist hurrying towards us, wielding her make-up bag like a weapon.

'Sorry!' I exclaim. *Whoops.*

'At least it's not red,' she mutters under her breath as she reapplies my lipstick. Jack and I grin at each other, but I'm the one who gets told off for not managing to keep a straight face.

'Stay still!' she warns as she puts the finishing touches to my lips.

'*I love you,*' Jack mouths at me, his face growing serious. It's everything I can do not to mouth the same thing back.

'Your turn,' the make-up artist says to Jack. 'And then no more kissing!'

Jack solemnly flashes her the Scout promise as she cleans him up.

Lots of upcoming bands have stood on this exact same stage, and many have been propelled to stardom after their episode has aired. We still haven't signed a record deal – Dad urged us to wait for the big guns and we're taking his advice. Who knows what the future has in store? I still have two more years of school here in LA, but I'm relieved that my GCSEs are out of the way.

Oh! I passed! Not with flying colours – come on, this is me we're talking about – but I was beside myself to get an 'A' in English, and Stu was proud of my efforts, especially considering what I've been through in the last year and a half.

'OK, everyone, take your places!' the director shouts.

More butterflies cram into my stomach as the extras return to the dance floor, and then the crowd parts and Lottie – Little Miss Mulholland herself – waltzes towards the front, flanked by the two actresses who play her onscreen besties. She catches my eye and gives me the thumbs up, but then she's looking past me and it doesn't take a genius to work out that she's smiling at Brandon. I glance over my shoulder in time to see him look away, and when I return my gaze to Lottie, her smile has slipped, the light diminished slightly from her eyes.

My heart hurts on her behalf. Brandon is still very much devoted to his girlfriend, but I have a feeling he and Lottie will have their own story to tell one day.

At least Agnes has been lucky in love. Brett is moving to America permanently next week after getting a job here, and Agnes has been practically bouncing off the walls in her excitement. I am so, so happy for her. I like Brett, and it's going to be fun hanging out as a foursome this summer.

Sienna and I have stayed in touch by email and we're catching up for a coffee when she returns from Italy where she's shooting the next CiaoCiao campaign. She seems to be in a good place. We haven't really talked about Dana or what happened, but I think her wounds are beginning to heal.

As for Margarita, Gina and co, I haven't heard a peep from them for months. Maybe our teen girl squad will reform once I'm back at school, but I'll be taking it all with an enormous pinch of salt. I still like them – they were nice to me, after all – but I'm not confusing what we had for genuine friendship. Agnes, on the other hand, I love to bits.

'Hey,' I hear a deep voice say, turning to see my dad hop up onto the stage to join me. A frisson of excitement passes over the extras and, out of the corner of my eye, I see the director do a double take. Johnny has stayed out of sight until now.

'Good luck, chick. You look the part.'

'Thanks, Dad,' I say warmly.

He flew over from Stockholm to be with me for this – he's right in the middle of his European dates, but he had a few days off, and I'm so grateful he used them to catch up with me.

Meg told me on the phone a couple of days ago that she's had it up to her ears with touring. She and the boys are coming back at the end of the summer for Barney to start the next school year, and Johnny is going to carry on with his US dates alone. Meg is hiring a nanny to take care of the boys – and me, I guess – so she can fly out to support her husband whenever she wants to. She must be feeling more secure; that he's not going to spiral downhill without her around to take care of him. I'm so glad they're back to their best after what I put them through.

'Any tips about miming?' I ask my dad.

'Nope.' He smirks. 'I've always played live.'

'Damn,' I mutter.

He chuckles and squeezes my shoulder. 'You know this song like the back of your hand, Jess. Just sing it like you've been doing and you'll be fine.'

I take a deep breath and exhale in a rush of air. I notice we still have the director's attention.

'Do you fancy doing a cameo?' I ask with a cheeky grin. The director's ears prick up. He is *so* eavesdropping on our conversation.

Johnny chuckles and shrugs, but he doesn't say an outright no.

Wait, *is he considering it?*

'Oh my God, go on, that would be so cool!' I erupt. I would *love* to see him out the front!

'Shhh!' he warns, frowning at me in alarm before looking round to clock the director. The man's jaw has just hit the floor. He hurries over to us.

'Kevin Mansini,' he introduces himself, shaking Johnny's hand. 'I couldn't help overhearing. Are you serious?' he asks eagerly.

Johnny gazes at him calmly, then at me, before looking back at him. 'Yeah, what the hell,' he says finally with a shrug.

I actually squeal.

'But you're not putting that shit on me!' Johnny warns, stopping the make-up artist in her tracks.

She gives him a puppy dog look. 'Just a little powder, I promise. You don't wanna look shiny under the lights,' she beseeches.

302

Johnny sighs. 'Go on, then.'

I try to stifle my giggles as she gets to work.

Stu didn't come to the studio today, but he's looking forward to hearing all about the filming tonight. He's in LA for the summer, acting as my chaperone. I know he's missing Caroline – they're well and truly an item now and I'm at peace with it. I've always liked her and I want Stu to be happy – Caroline, too. I feel guilty that I'm the reason they're currently apart, but Caroline is coming to California on holiday soon, so they'll be spending lots of time together then.

Tom is also coming, and his sister Becky, but they're staying with their dad. It'll be Becky's first time meeting Riley, and Tom tells me they're both nervous. Fingers crossed it will go well. Apparently Becky's really missed having a relationship with her dad. I can relate.

And yes, it has occurred to Tom and I that, if Caroline and Stu get married, we'll be stepsiblings. That would be so weird… He and I are good friends now – and it's completely platonic. He was my rock when I went back to school. I found it hard at first, being ogled like I was some sort of celebrity, but after a while, everything settled down and people got over it. Everyone except Nina. For some reason – jealousy, probably – she really had it in for me, but when Tom overheard her telling me that I thought I was 'it', he gave her hell. She's had a crush on him for ages, so his rant must've stung, but it did the trick: she was saccharine-sweet to me after that.

Not that her good behaviour got her anywhere with the object of her affection. Tom now has a new girlfriend – a lovely girl called Ava who, funnily enough, was in his class all along. Together with Libby, Lou, Chris and me, we had a great little gang when I was back at school in the UK. We hung out most lunchtimes and some evenings, when Nat and our college pals would join us. I'm going to miss everyone now that I'm back in LA, but no doubt we'll see each other again soon. I guess I'll always be jumping back and forth between two different countries and two sets of friends, but that's OK. I've learnt that I'm pretty adaptable. And of course, I also have two dads, now, too.

I've promised Stu that I won't give him any trouble this summer – not with him forgoing his Caroline-time to be with me. I will *absolutely* one hundred per cent behave myself.

Well, maybe one hundred per cent is pushing it. Let's say ninety per cent. Or eighty… On second thoughts, perhaps I shouldn't make promises I can't keep. This is Jessie Jefferson we're talking about, after all.

Yes, Jessie Jefferson. I've come round to it, to the idea of who I am, who I want to be, and I believe in my heart of hearts that if Mum could see the journey I've been on, she'd understand me taking my dad's name at last. This is the way it *should* be, and Johnny *is* my dad – the best dad I could hope for. It only took him sixteen years to get there…

'OK, everyone into position!' Kevin, the director, shouts.

A powerful thrum of nerves pulses through me as I step up to the microphone, trying not to be fazed by the enormous camera pointed at my bandmates and me. My dad is standing front and centre of all the extras on the dance floor, looking up at the stage. From what I overheard being discussed, he's playing himself, here to watch his daughter – *that's me, folks* – and her band. Lottie, to his left, is going to spot him and have a fangirl moment, and later, she and her friends will ask for his autograph. *Oh God, this is going to be so brilliant!*

Little Miss Mulholland has had celebrity cameos before, but I don't recall any at the level of Johnny's fame. A sudden surge of exhilaration replaces my nerves – when it airs, this episode will be a really big deal.

The press attention surrounding me went completely crazy after I sang with my dad at Wembley – he called me back onstage over the next two nights, too, and at all of the weekend gigs I was able to attend: Manchester, Glasgow and Dublin, to name but a few.

But that press was about Johnny and me, not All Hype. This exposure is going to send us rocketing into the stratosphere...

I flash Jack a sideways grin, excitement bubbling through me. He blows me a cool, sweet kiss and my heart melts.

'Let's go!' Kevin shouts. 'Take one and cue the music! One, two, three, and...'

Miles syncs in with the opening drum beats of 'Blue Tuesday' and suddenly it's happening, we're doing this. It's *as easy as breathing*, I remind myself. *As easy as breathing...*

The song is over before I know it, but our work has only just begun. We're going to have to film more takes and capture different camera angles. Johnny grins up at me as the crew get the next shot ready.

'OK?' I mouth.

'*Brilliant,*' he mouths back, his eyes shining with pride.

Not only do I have a dad now, but I'm making him proud...

The thought makes me feel suddenly emotional. I really need to get my act together before I incur the make-up artist's wrath again. Mascara running down my cheeks would so not be a good look...

I can't believe it's only been just over a year since I first set foot in LA, beginning my journey from ordinary girl to rock star's daughter. I still think of my mum every day and I know I'll miss her for the rest of my life, but I like to think of her up in heaven, smiling down at me with a big, cheesy grin on her face. I hope I've made her proud, too.

No, I *know* I have. *I love you, Mum…*

I blink back tears and take a deep, shaky breath. It's almost time for our next take.

I feel like I've come full circle, but now I'm back in the glittering City of Angels, and this time, I'm hoping – just hoping – that I'm here to stay.

But anything could happen.

And I'm starting to realise that that's just the way I like it.

'Take two!'

Acknowledgements

Thank you, above all, to my readers. I love hearing from everyone who messages me on twitter @PaigeToonAuthor and Facebook.com/PaigeToonAuthor, so please say hi if you haven't already! This may be the third and final book in the Jessie Jefferson series, but I'm sure you will hear from Jessie and co again, so please sign up (for free!) to my book club, *The Hidden Paige*, at www.paigetoon.com to receive my emails, which sometimes include mini sequels about your favourite characters...

Thank you to the whole team at Simon & Schuster – my brilliant publisher for a whopping ten years now – but in particular, thanks to my lovely editor, Rachel Mann; my editor on the adult team, Suzanne Baboneau; my young adult agent, Veronique Baxter, and everyone else at David Higham – it is such a pleasure to work with you all and I'm truly grateful for everything that you do.

Thank you to the following people, who helped me suss out the ways in which America does things differently, not least with their school system: Kendall Reid, Kimberly Floyd, Susan

Rains, Jen Hayes and Michelle McGill. Thank you also to my old English teacher, Chris England, for his help with the British side of school life.

Huge thanks to all of my friends who so sweetly continue to let me natter on about my characters and book ideas, especially my fellow author, Ali Harris, whose suggestions and advice without a doubt made this book better.

Finally, thank you to my family: my parents, Jen and Vern Schuppan; my husband, Greg, who helps me in so many ways, and my gorgeous little children, Indy and Idha. I love you all very, very much indeed.

Read the first two books
in Paige Toon's addictive
Jessie Jefferson series!

Sunshine, rock gods and
Hollywood heart-throbs!

#HASHTAGREADS

Bringing the best YA your way

TOMMY WALLACH
MORGAN MATSON
ROBYN
SCHNEIDER CASSANDRA CLARE
CLARE FURNISS
DARREN
SHAN #R
HONOR
& PERDITA
CARGILL
SOPHIE
MCKENZIE
C.J. FLOOD
STEPHEN
CHBOSKY
AMY ALWARD
JENN
BENNETT
PAIGE TOON GAYLE FORMAN
BECCA FITZPATRICK
SCOTT WESTERFELD
S.J. KINCAID

Join us at **HashtagReads**,
home to your favourite YA authors

Follow us on Twitter
@HashtagReads

ind us on Facebook
HashtagReads

Join us on Tumblr
HashtagReads.tumblr.com